I0685514

Published in 2025 by Provoco Publishing who own the publishing rights.

PUBLISHING

ISBN: 978-1-0686412-5-1

Cover Design and Artwork - © Provoco Publishing
Logo Design - © MJC at Martyn Carson Creative
Photographs reproduced under license
Edited by Jane Murray

KEY TO DECEPTION

KE JENNINGS

CHAPTER ONE

Drip.
  Drip.
  Drip.

Stagnant water softly falls in the dark.

The pungent odor of mold permeates my nose as I crouch against a rusty stove. Fear has a distinct flavor, and I can taste it. The stillness of the cabin is offset by sounds of the water. Shivering in the brisk early morning air that is seeping through the drafty windows, I adjust my stance. My legs are slowly going numb.

Creek…creek.

The sound again. Someone is outside in the fog. Heart thumping wildly, I squeeze my eyes shut and try to make out what I had just seen, less than a half hour ago. Having just taken a walk after drying off from my swim, I felt something watching me. A feeling that you get when you know a person is nearby. I dried off hastily on the beach, my toes numb from the cold. Slipping on the rocks that lined the shore instead of sand, a crackling from the wood line could be heard.

Squeezing harder, I frown deeply. I need to remember. It had just happened.

Then something flashes in my mind. I had seen a man, and he was tall. Just a glimpse of a figure, but it was a man. And now he is waiting for me, outside of the cabin I took refuge in about fifty yards into the wood line.

I need to do something. I can't stay here.

Thoughts jumbling, I hear a branch snap outside. Something big is there. The man must be as tall as I thought. Even through the rudimentary mortar that plugs the holes between the massive logs in the wall, I can hear the sounds outside. Or it's an animal. Which is also possible. Just a week ago, a black bear was in the area.

It's not a bear. Someone is stalking me.

Heart beating faster, I can feel each thump in my chest cavity. Wildly, it pounds like a drum; one that is out of control. Blood rushing to my head, I drop to my knees, to get the pressure off my feet. Lightheadedness overtakes my senses, but I pull myself out of it. I have to focus. Staying in this cabin indefinitely is not an option.

Kate, Brian and Peter will be looking for me. But not for hours.

By then, it might be too late.

The rumors might be true.

Whidbey Island has lore and rumors, most of which I thought were false. But now, now something is telling me they aren't. What monster lurks outside the cabin? Which one of them could it be, if not the man I saw?

Crack.

Another twig snaps. It resounds in the chilly air and might as well be in the cabin with me; the sounds are that close. Tendrils of water weave in through the cracks once more, caressing my skin in its grasp. Goosebumps form on my arms and legs.

Snap.

More sounds.

I struggle with my breathing, fear palpable in the air. I move across the dirty floor, slowly, on my knees, until I am near one of the windows. Holding my breath and with a shaky countenance, I move my head towards the distorted glass. One can barely see out of it with the amount of caked on grime and filth from years of unuse. But I need to see what I am up against.

With one short exhale, I glance out. Branches twist along in the sudden burst of wind. I hear the howl resounding from the weather that seemed to have moved in. Rain was surely soon to follow. The dark flashes move violently as the wind carries through. My eyes dart to each side of the forest that I can see. Barely see. No figure. No person at all.

It's there, though.

Heart racing, I continue to look. Then I see something pitch black dart by. Stifling a yelp, my eyes wildly search for what moved. As if on cue, rain begins to pelt the window. Now I can't hear anything at all, except for the water. Whidbey Island has storms like this often in the fall. Nothing much you can do but wait for the weather to clear.

What was that?

Something else dark flew by the window. I blinked and then it was gone. My heart hammers in my chest as thoughts race. I never thought a swim would bring me a stalker, or a person wishing me harm. I hope that I can get out of the cabin before too long. My coworkers will know where I am at, though. I come for a swim every morning prior to work. Eventually, they'd come looking.

Being trapped feels like a hamster stuck on a wheel or a goldfish in a bowl. It's stifling, and the reality of it slams into me.

I'm not going to die like this or be attacked here.

Resolution kicking in, I stand slowly, careful to keep my body away from the window. Cold begins to wrack every nerve and cell as a shiver washes over me, like one of the waves outside I was just battling with. Goosebumps form on the skin under my wetsuit. I cannot stay here. I have to make a run for it. Whether I get caught by whoever is outside or not, I am a fighter. Not a person who cowers. The rain is still pelting the side of the cabin, I think of the path a mere few steps away. All I need to do is get to it, then I can run like hell. The trees are thick for about half a mile, then I will hit the road and be where my rental Jeep is parked. Before my swim, I ditched my dry bag right outside the cabin door and will grab it. I need the car keys at the very least. This will work. It has to.

Working up courage, I decide it's now or never. I walk briskly to the half rotted and heavy door. It's the only way in and the only way out.

Now or never. Just GO.

Sucking in a breath, images flash in my mind of what could possibly happen to me. Shoving them aside as quickly as they come, I pull the door open and run.

Crack. Snap.

Loud sounds resound from the wood line. I can hear whatever is there and it is close. Snatching up the rubber bag, I grip the handle and take off, barefoot. The ground is wet and squishy as I run. I stumble through the muddy parts, slipping in the muck. The rain pelts my skin. Wind howls above and makes the trees shake violently. I can hear nothing behind me, but fear grips my psyche. It is still there, following, chasing, I know it is.

Barely able to make out what is I front of me, I grunt.

Why is there a storm NOW?

Thunder booms and shakes the ground. Or it might be my imagination. I'm not sure. Then a loud crack fills the dense forest space. Lightning. It was close too. Pounding onwards, I grip the bag tighter. The rubber is cold, and I can barely hang onto it as my hands are already numb. Just a little further and I will be out of the woods.

"Ouch!" I yelp.

Something sharp stabs the bottom of my foot. Hobbling now, I see the bend in the trail. Just beyond I will hit pavement. Only I can hear loud footsteps behind me. And someone breathing. Terror rushes within as I turn my head around to see who is chasing me. Only when I do, I see nothing. Just an empty trail. It might have ducked into the woods on either side. I run faster, ending up on concrete just as fast.

My foot throbs as I fumble with the bag, until I can open the waterproof zipper wide enough to get the Jeep key out.

Wildly glancing around me, I see nothing, I am alone. Or am I?

Get in the Jeep!

I know I need to hurry and waste no time unlocking the door then fling myself inside. Pushing the lock button, I start the engine. My eyes scan for anything around the vehicle or coming from the dark path in the woods. But there is still nothing. Nothing but dark shadows that seem to jump out towards me. My eyes are playing tricks, and I know it.

I quickly back out of the parking spot and throw the shifter into 'drive'. As I leave the tiny parking lot, I turn towards the woods one last time. A silhouette appears briefly through a set of trees but then vanishes just as quickly. Blinking, I pull out onto the main road and drive away. Levi was right. It was stupid of me to swim here every day, alone. His warning echoes in my head.

Lily, you need to be careful on the island. Swimming alone is reckless and one day, you might disappear and not come back.

Today could have been that day.

CHAPTER TWO

"Lily. *Lily.*"

The corner fan clicks every few seconds, metal on metal.

"Earth to Lily!"

"What?" I ask, coming out of the haze that had descended on my brain over the last hours of work.

"Are you done with those? I want to get this corner cleared by the end of the week, if we can."

Glancing down at what I am holding, I notice the words.

Top Secret, Department of the Navy.

"Well?" Kate asks briskly.

She is agitated at my hesitation but also, she is hungry. We had decided to work through lunch and eat later, in order to get more headway with this room.

"I found Top Secret documents. This makes zero sense; they wouldn't be lying around like this. Classified at this level..."

"Wouldn't be here. Yeah, I know. The Navy really fucked up letting whatever idiot they assigned to clear this room."

Kate, who is quite a bit older than me, saunters over to see what documents I am holding. Even though she is cranky, she still maintains a modicum of decorum and doesn't hover.

"May I?"

"Sure," I reply, handing her the offending papers, which were stapled in such a way that I imagined a commander holding it, reading in a meeting behind closed doors. Probably in this very building.

"Shit, Lily. This is about medical testing."

I turn at her words, looking up into the dark brown eyes of my coworker. Her usually only lightly wrinkled face is now scrunched, making her appear much older.

"Medical testing?"

"Yes! I've heard of there being tests like that here...but now we stumbled upon evidence of it!"

If we ever were to encounter Secret or even Top-Secret documents, we were instructed to contact our supervisor on Naval Air Station Whidbey Island, CDR Lessing. Commander Lessing was then supposed to sound the alarms up his chain. Only this find, it felt different.

"Call this in?" I ask.

Kate's face relaxes as she sits back in her metal, folding chair, the packet still in her hands. I know her by now, well enough to discern that she is thinking otherwise.

"No. Let's read it first. Lily, things like this don't just happen. I have been alive long enough to know that. And it's not like we are going to make a copy of it or take it out of this room. It stays between just the two of us. Are you okay, though?"

Her hesitation isn't reckless, although if anyone else were in the room, they might think so.

"I am fine, Kate. This morning was just a figment of my imagination."

"No, it wasn't. There was someone chasing you, Lil! You know I don't believe in coincidences. Finding this is a clear sign."

She settles into her chair and begins to slowly read the forbidden documents. I shrug and stretch my arms. If she wants to dig, I am not going to stop her. What happened this morning still has me in a brain fog, and I can't focus very well. But Kate is right, the room needs to get done. This was one of dozens filled to the brim with documents. Documents that we have to sort through. One at a painstaking time.

"You ladies still at it? Sure you won't join us for burgers? The ferry is almost here."

Brian opens the front door and calls in to the empty spaces, his voice carrying with baritone. He often acts as a father figure, even if we don't ask for it.

"We are good. Need to keep working," Kate calls out.

"Oh, well, okay," Brian yells back.

We continue our work in silence as the front door shuts, clicking into place. Old buildings such as these are full of odd noises, noises that can carry.

"He drives me nuts sometimes. We will catch the two o'clock ferry and get lunch then."

I know Kate was talking to reassure herself more than me, so I don't reply.

Picking up another stack of documents, I settle into my metal chair and carefully read the first page. The Navy wasted an enormous amount of paper on printing things that probably could have been relayed in person, not immortalized for the entire fleet or gaggle of sailors to see. But apparently the Army and Marines do the exact same thing, according to Kate. This is her twelfth job like this, being a 'documents cleaner' after a base has closed.

Life on the road like we live is stressful. We are not only temporarily calling a new state home, but we are put in the weirdest accommodations. Not to mention working in the oldest of the old buildings. Fort Waren had its start in the late nineteenth century and the current room we were in was erected in mid-1910. Then there was the crazy history of the area. Human trafficking was quite common in the early 1900's, mainly Chinese that were used for illegal labor. I had done some research before coming, as I usually do before beginning work at a new post. Fascinating but also haunting, I hope to learn more while here.

"I knew it!" Kate exclaims, shifting in her chair.

"What?"

"They *did* carry out experiments on people. This is proof of it. A Navy doctor was in charge of the program. It references a 'Dr. Katz, Chief of Internal Medicine.' They had kept a whole slew of chemicals to use on the naval personnel. These documents confirm the area was used for human trafficking in the early nineteen hundreds! Lil! They trafficked people in here to disperse them through the US for cheap labor, but by the time the poor souls got here, half of them were sick because of the journey and the conditions they were kept in. They were the people used for the Navy experiments! God, this is HUGE, Lil! What the hell was this sort of sensitive document doing here, with all the rest?" She shakes her head at the abysmal security, the carelessness.

"Already sick? Like whom were already hospitalized?"

Kate clucked her tongue.

"No. Worse. The poor people who were trafficked and who got here sick." Kate scans the document again. "It says here the people were brought here from China. That's a helluva journey, and the conditions must have been real bad. I guess these people got sick on the journey here. They used these people, Lil. That's awful!"

I got up and walked over to inspect the document further.

"Use them, how?"

"It doesn't specify. This appears to just detail the overview of the program. It would take me all day to read it, though, so I'm gonna have to take my time with this."

"We really can't take documents home..."

"Oh, I'm not taking it back to the cabins with me. I'll read it on my lunch breaks, here."

Shrugging, I go back to my place to sift through the remaining pile I had started. More boring clerical documents. Leaves, shore leaves, change of transfer. It was all the same at this point. Except for what Kate found. How such a high-level document could be randomly placed amongst the rest of this stuff was beyond me.

"Lily, has Levi ever told you about secret societies in the Navy?"

"Secret societies?"

To an outsider this would be a very weird question. But to me, this was our normal daily chatter.

"Yeah, you know, like the freemasons but for the military, and the secret society groups like what fraternities have in colleges. Only for enlisted and officers."

I sigh, trying to recall anything.

"No. To be honest, Levi barely tells me anything about his joining and then what he does for work. I mean, I get the gist of it. It's secret."

"He wouldn't probably tell you anyway, that was a dumb question," she says.

"It's all probably there, though, those kinds of groups."

"Oh, indeed," Kate agrees. The idea seems to excite her, as though she had stumbled on something big.

We go back to our comfortable silence, each sifting through piles of documents that need our attention, lost in thoughts. The work on this base is different than anything I have ever done. For Kate, too. There is *something* about it. The entire island chain seems to harbor its own secrets.

After a half hour passes, I feel the urge to pee.

"I need to use the restroom, I'll be right back," I tell Kate.

Kate grunts, struggling to open a filing cabinet. I help her quickly, giving the door a swift elbow to the old metal frame. It pops open.

"Thanks. I am kind of getting sick of these. We should destroy one just for fun before we leave this job for good."

Chuckling, I wave her off and head out of the room and into a dark hallway. The paint smells like a sour drug store, chemical laden. I cough, wondering how much of the particles I am ingesting as I walk. Light doesn't reach this far into the building, so I stop at a room that has a door and open it, hoping to get some much-needed light to see the rest of the way to the Ladies' bathroom.

Instead, I gasp. The large window is busted open, and rain

has gotten in.

"Shit," I mutter.

Water begins to run along the baseboards, and I can tell this has been this way for at least a day or so. We are required to check the perimeter of the buildings each night before leaving the base. At least the buildings we are working in at the time. My coworkers hadn't mentioned this one yesterday, though.

"Well, there isn't anything we can do about it now..."

Leaving the door wide open, I keep walking so I can offload my now hurting bladder. I feel as though I could pee myself at any moment. Finally reaching the door, I push hard. It's also heavy and old, and the frame doesn't quite fit the door itself. It would be easy to get locked in. I flick on the lights as I keep moving. Opening a metal stall door, I hurry and get to business. Relief washes over me, and I close my eyes.

Then, the bathroom goes dark.

CHAPTER THREE

When I was a small child, I always hated the dark. Darkness made me feel unsafe. My parents would insist I sleep without a nightlight, so that I could 'toughen up'. They were both in the Marines, and were good parents, but often their parenting was blurred between reality and how they acted at work. Their 'work personas'. Carrying over to my adulthood, darkness still bothers me.

"Now Lily, I am only going to tell you once. Don't scream for us in the middle of the night. We have to get up at four in the morning. And you have school."

I still remember that night when we had a wicked bad storm outside. The sounds of branches cracking and rain pelting the side of our house on the Marine Corp base will forever be etched into my mind. I resisted the urge to yell for my parents, too, just as my mom ordered. It was the longest night of my life. And now, I find myself in another such scenario. Can twenty-seven-year-olds be traumatized still?

Breathing elevated, I reach my arms out to touch the stall. Cool metal greets me as anxiety rushes through my system. Listening to any sounds, I hear absolutely nothing. No footsteps, no external noises whatsoever. Only the frantic beat of my heart. Bile rises in my throat. I swallow it back and picture my mom's steely face. She was a blonde with blue eyes and could give anyone a huge ego boost with one look or shoot you down in flames with another. She had been a drill instructor at Marine Corps Recruit Depot, Parris Island, in South Carolina.

Drawing from my mom's strength, my fingers fumble for the stall lock. Clicking it open, I push the door and stumble out into the communal area of the bathroom. Not knowing who or what is in here with me, I feel like I have to get out.

"The best thing you can do is run."

Levi's voice is in my head. That is what my boyfriend always tells me when we talk about me working alone. He taught me what to do, over and over again. How to avoid getting shot, to run from guys that might try to harm me. Even teaching me basic hand to hand maneuvers. But right now, all I can do is find the door out. As I reach, I picture a large man grasping at me. Anticipation claws in my psyche. Then my fingers touch the heavy wood, and I shove hard.

Flying into the hallway, I see light again, coming from the room where I left the door open. My heart thumping hard, I can't breathe well. I jog to the light before turning around. Catching my breath, I scan the darkness. Nothing is there. No one is there.

Thump.

The sound came from the bathroom.

"Shit!" I shriek.

I picture a man. The man from the woods who chased me into the cabin.

"When you get paralyzed by fear Lily, you have to force yourself out of it. And run."

Levi's voice rings out in my head.

He was right. I have to move.

Thump, thump.

More loud sounds emit from the Ladies' bathroom. Not thinking twice, I turn and finally run. Feet nimble from being sedentary for so long, I fly back into the room where Kate is working. A look of sheer terror on her face, Kate yelps as I come to a stop in the middle of the room.

"The hell, Lily?!"

Clutching her chest, she stands raggedly, fear on her face.

"The … the lights went out in the bathroom!" I breathe out, gasping. Standing with hands on my hips, I'm shocked at how fast I made it back into here.

Kate's brows furrow in contemplation.

"Let me go check."

"No!" I whine. "Don't, not yet!"

"Why?" Kate asks, puzzled. "Didn't you say the lights went out? I should check the fuse box. I might want to use the bathroom too, you know. And not in the dark."

Nodding, I drop my hands and follow her out of the room we have been working in and into the dreaded hallway. I am acting like a huge baby. Which is totally out of character for me. Things never scare me this much. Maybe what happened after my swim really got to me more than I thought. Kate knew, though. Which is why she isn't questioning my reaction at the moment.

She leads us to the metal box on the wall by the huge front doors to the building. The doors themselves probably weigh upwards of a thousand pounds; frame included. Back then, they would fashion such things for the most important buildings on bases. Grandeur at its finest.

"Damn. The fuse looks fried! This could've started a fire. Well, we have to take flashlights with us from now on to use the bathroom. Unless we go next door and use the one there."

Kate turns to look at me, her words slowly registering as a question and not just chatter.

"Oh, yeah, let's just go next door. I don't want to use this one, even with flashlights. It's got no windows in it. Too dark." I'm gibbering.

"Right. Let's walk over and see where the other one is, then, before we take a break for lunch."

Nodding, I follow her outside after we pull the heavy doors open. Chilly air slams right into my chest. Fall is temperate in the Pacific Northwest, but still cold. At least compared to Southern California where I last worked. Goosebumps form on my arms, underneath my clothing. I picture Levi, at work, probably out training in this weather right now.

His dreamy brown eyes smile at me in my head.

"Want to talk about anything?" Kate asks.

Leaves crunch underfoot as we walk the few hundred yards to the next abandoned building. This one is much smaller, clad in peeling, white lead paint over its wooden frame. Asbestos is one hundred percent in there. Really, we would be safer squatting behind a tree.

"No. I'm okay."

"Missing Levi?"

"How did you know?" I smile.

"I was younger once too, and in love," she retorts, coming to the side door and giving it a good yank, "believe it or not."

This time I laugh.

"Of course you were."

"Crap, this one is in even worse shape," she says, alluding to the building.

Both of our mouths drop as we step into the musty space. In fact, dusty and musty doesn't even do it justice. Mold must be growing between the walls and in the ceiling.

"This one will be a mask only space. Great."

Kate grumbles about various things as she looks around at the building where we have yet to begin working in. She is right. No one wants to possibly get sick from toil eight plus hours a day in those kinds of conditions.

"Well, hopefully, it's not got much in it. I doubt any documents would have survived here. Not in this type of interior conditions."

"You want to know something else interesting that I read in those documents?" Kate asks.

"Yeah, what?" For some reason, my heart starts to thump wildly again.

"There might be a correlation to tunnels in nearby mountains and this base. I can't be for sure..."

"Tunnels? It said that?"

"Well, no. Not directly but I'm skilled at reading the codes they have for places. I'll have to show you later. Right now," she said, "we need to get into this rickety ass bathroom."

Huffing and puffing, Kate throws her weight into the wooden door that appears to be stuck. Or possibly locked. It isn't budging, though. I begin to help as well, tired of having to deal with these stuck doors. Time and weather hadn't been kind to this base, that is for sure. Just as we think we are never going to get in, the door gives, sending us flying on the floor beyond. I hit my head hard on the stall doors. Stars form in my peripheral vision. I didn't black out but that was a hard hit, nonetheless.

"Shit! Lily! Are you okay?" Kate asks, tugging on my arm.

She had barely missed the same fate, by mere inches.

"Ouch...." I moan.

Creak…

We both stop and turn, looking towards the sound emitting from the corner of the bathroom. Darkness shrouds the area with only soft light coming from a tiny, frosted glass window on the far end of the room. Something skitters along the floor.

"What is that?" Kate breathes.

"I don't..." Before I can finish my sentence, I hear it; feel it.

Bang!

The sound shakes the ground. I whimper with fear as a huge, dark shadow emerges and comes towards us.

Kate screams.

Then, as quickly as the shadow appears, it drops off, disappearing as quickly as it came. Trying to adjust my eyes, I squint. How hard had I hit my head? Kate tugs on my jeans urgently.

"There!! Do you see it?" she hisses.

Squinting into the blackness I search for whatever she is talking about but see nothing.

"We need to get up, we need to leave!"

Tugging me up, Kate shoves me back out of the bathroom doorway and into the musty dankness of the bright hall. Suddenly confused at what is actually going on, I stumble as she pushes me towards the entrance door.

"Keep going, Lily!" Kate says with exasperation in her voice.

"Why?"

"There was a bloodied man in the corner!"

Eyes wide, I run and so does Kate. As we pass the parking lot, we keep going until we reach the wood line. Then, just as I did this morning, we take off into the dark forest.

CHAPTER FOUR

Running for one's life shouldn't be a commonplace occurrence. Definitely not more than once in a day. If I told myself this was to be my fate a week ago, I wouldn't believe it. Sweat pours down my face from my forehead as we run. Kate, being significantly older than me, shows her agility by leading in the front. I had no idea she was this in shape.

"Come on Lily!! Keep running!" she shouts.

Glancing behind me, I catch sight of the bloodied man, shrouded as if he were clothed in darkness. He is still chasing us. My mind reels and spins like tumbling water in rapids. Who is he? What does he want? How did he get into the building and why?

"My leg!" I cry out.

A sharp pain shoots up the side of my leg at an alarming rate. I keep running but something has happened. Letting my eyes drift downwards as we get closer to a clearing, I see red pouring out of a wound on my thigh. Searing pain radiates again from my leg.

"I am hurt!"

"What did you say, Lily?" Kate shouts.

Her voice becomes loud then trails off. Too quiet to hear.

Suddenly the woods resemble a painting, one that melts when water is poured on it. Similar to Monet or one of the other Impressionists. Green branches turn into watercolor works of art, as does the brown of the dirt path we are running on. I turn my head and see the man is gone, no longer following us. Turning back, I see Kate is gone also. Confusion taking hold, I open my mouth to scream.

"Lily? Lily, what did you say?"

I open my eyes, and a sharp pain radiates from my head. It's dark. I am back in the bathroom. The one we just left and ran from. I have no idea how I got here. Trying to remember to no avail, I let a whimper escape my lips.

"I... how did I?" I say, incoherently.

"You hit your head, Lily. When we finally got this damn door to open up. I didn't think we'd go flying inside. Can you see clearly?"

Slowly, I nod.

"We left, though. We saw a bloodied man in the corner…"

"We saw a what?" she asks, worry in her voice.

"We didn't leave this bathroom?" I ask, rubbing my eyes.

"No…we literally *just* landed in this bathroom."

Voices resound from the hallway. Male voices. I tense up and Kate notices.

"It's only Brian and Peter. Lunch is over and the ferry brought them back."

"Kate!! Lily!!"

My brain slowly comes to, and I know whose voice I hear. It's Brian.

"Yeah, hang on!" Kate yells.

She helps me slowly stand and turns the flashlight on her phone to bright mode, illuminating the space.

"There isn't anyone in here, Lily. See?"

Waving the phone around, light hits all the angles of the old bathroom. She is right, no one is in here except us. My mind races with thoughts of what to do with this information. I had *seen* someone in here, in the shadows.

"You hit your head so hard. Shit. We are probably going to need to report it to Commander Lessing."

"What? No, no. I am fine. Just a bit out of it, but I think I am fine."

"Alright…" she says, carefully.

We leave the bathroom and enter back into the bright lights of the hallway. Brian and Peter are waiting patiently for us, a look of excitement on their faces.

"So, the fleet at Whidbey are wanting to extend us. But move us, to the nicer cabins in a week."

The nicer cabins.

This was big news indeed and I can see now why the shouting and excitement. We have been in limbo with the Navy for weeks on how long our contract would run. They only initially agreed to six weeks, but we are rapidly approaching that date with no real end in sight given the amount of buildings and paperwork we have left to go through. Short of working almost twenty-hour days, there was no way to finish in time. Hence, the Navy decided to extend.

"It means more money! I can finally take that vacation to Costa Rica that I wanted. To suss out my final home. Retirement is calling my name," Brian quips.

He is always going on about retiring but never dropping the paperwork to do so. Kate glances at me and subtly rolls her eyes. We are both thinking the same thing. The day Brain retires is the day Kate owes me forty dollars. We made the bet back at the beginning of the assignment here. Living so close to each other can take its toll!

Peter chimes in, "Actually that's right. We get the bonus, too. The one that guarantees my wife will get the France vacation she wants."

Peter is only a year older than me at twenty-eight and he is already married. He will not shut up about his wife, either. Literally, he talks about her all day. Sometimes I envy them. Levi isn't that way with me.

"France is going to be so lovely for you guys," Kate says. "Especially if you go in the fall."

"You both should get lunch. The ferry comes again in roughly ten minutes. If you hurry, you might make it. We're gonna get back to it," Brian says.

"Shit! Come on Lily, let's go."

I follow Kate back to the room we were working in and grab

my purse as she does the same. Then we take off on a jog out of the building and into the sunlight. Crisp air hits my face. Fall is here in full swing. I can see the small dock at the end of the grassy area to the left. We run now as the small ferry approaches. Waving her arms, Kate picks up speed. The ferry captain spots us and waves back. The Navy arranged this transportation for us and a few various workers each day like clockwork.

Reaching the dock, our feet clack on the wooden planks. A gust of wind rustles my hair as I scramble on the walkway to the awaiting deck. There are a few extra passengers today, workers from the other side of the base that are most likely done for the day as they are covered in sweat. They nod at us as they continue to chat among themselves. Kate takes her usual place at the bow of the boat, choosing a plastic seat to sit on. I join her.

"Let's go to the sandwich shop. We can get something light and easy and get back quicker. I want this day to be over with already."

I nudge her elbow and grin.

"You just want to sit on your cabin porch and read the secret documents, admit it."

"Oh, that I do."

A comfortable silence settles over us as we take in the view. The water parts as the bow cuts through the gentle waves of Puget Sound. I breathe in the salty air and close my eyes for a brief moment. Levi's face pops up in my mind. If he would only take a day off, we could come out here and enjoy the water.

I miss his arms and his lips….

Being the girlfriend of a Navy SEAL is not easy. Operator, SEAL, they go by many different names. All of them basically mean 'we do things you have no idea about and never will'. It was that, if I am honest, that drew me to him in the first place and made me accept his advances. Opening my eyes, I see a whale breach in the distance.

"A whale!" I exclaim.

Kate murmurs and looks, pointing.

"There, oh, I see it!"

Water splashes up from the depths as another whale breaches the water, only to disappear below. I imagine where they are going and why. Do whales have families and a hierarchy? I pretend they do, but who knows.

Boom!

A loud sound resonates from where the ferry engine compartment is located. Both Kate and I jump, not expecting to hear what we did. The captain and crew begin to shout as thick white, almost grey smoke, begins to billow from below. Suddenly transported from tranquil to emergency, we spring up and run over, as do the men from the base.

"We can't stop the flooding! It looks like someone cut the fuel lines!"

Shouts echo in the air as we wait to see if they need any help.

"Call it in! We need the Coast Guard!"

The Coast Guard??

Thinking about sinking in the middle of a channel in Puget Sound is definitely not how I saw this day ending. And it's not even the end of the day.

"Lily, I'm calling Commander Lessing..."

Kate's words don't quite register. The boat begins to lower in the water more noticeably. I absentmindedly look out over the dark waters and spot the whales again, their heads popping up as they watch our peril.

"Lily, they are sending a team out. Right now. Lily..."

Turning to look at Kate, something on the shoreline stands out. Something dark.

A man.

CHAPTER FIVE

"Holy shit, Lily! Water is coming up!!"

The Titanic sunk in a matter of a few hours, and it was a gigantic ship. The ferry that I am currently on holds only passengers and zero vehicles. And it is holding its own, but not for long. It won't take hours to sink. Water laps at my shoes, only a few inches, but rapidly growing.

"Put on this life vest!" a crew member shouts, tossing us yellow floatation devices with dangling straps.

Fumbling to put on the life vest, I begin to sweat. Fear starts creeping in. We are *actually going into the water*. This isn't a joke and it's serious.

"Fuck, the water has to be like forty something degrees! You swim in it daily so it can't be too bad, right?" Kate asks loudly.

She is thinking out loud, and her thoughts merge with mine. The waters out here are cold as fuck. I swim in a dry suit, or a wetsuit. I have to, or I'd get hypothermia. And we are in normal clothing. Plus, we are way out in the straight, the deep channel of the Sound. No, this is not good at all.

"Everyone go to the back! The stern!" A voice shouts.

I think it is the captain, but I am not sure. Clutching my purse, and Kate hers, we quickly cinch up our vests and move to where the crew and other passengers are gathered. The wind whips hard, gusting as the waters begin to get choppier.

"Great, the waves!" Kate laments.

The boat begins to sink now, noticeably and rapidly. Water covers our ankles, then our calves, then our knees. We are about to be *in* Puget Sound. My pulse pounds and I pray silently that God would bring a rescue boat soon. The captain no doubt alerted the Coast Guard. Their response time would be pretty fast. Just not fast enough to save us from going in. "Kate, we have to tread water softly. Not thrash too much.

Conserve energy. That will help with hypothermia," I say.

She nods, eyes wide, searching mine. She trusts me and she knows I know the water. But my knowledge can't stop creatures from investigating. Like killer whales and sharks.

"It will be okay. Just try to stay calm, and by me."

The captain shouts at us, directions on what to do. He is keeping as collected as he can. For that I am thankful.

"We are about to go in, jump off the back, tread water and stay calm!"

Just like I had said, he knew the dangers of the water here.

"Stay by me, Lily!" Kate cries, in terror, as we jump into the water. Cold shocks every fiber of my being as we become enveloped in the waves. I reach with one arm and grasp Kate's life jacket strap that floats near me. Tugging lightly, she floats to me, our bodies bumping upon impact.

"It's so cold! Shit!" Kate chatters.

She is correct, it's freezing. Glancing down, I look for anything below, but I can't see through the darkness. The water is an abyss. And we are just specs in the middle now. Thoughts flash of what could happen next. We might drown, we might begin shaking and succumb to the effects of hypothermia or ocean creatures could come up and investigate. The latter being my biggest fear. The ferry splutters and sinks deeper, the top of the cabin disappearing under the water.

"My shoes are gone, Lily!"

I look into Kate's eyes as we bob in the water, the floatation vests keeping us afloat, but just so. She is terrified, and I know she wants to rely on me. Hopefully, I can stay calm enough.

"It's okay. So are mine. Try to keep your breathing slow," I reply loudly.

The waves pick up as the wind whistles. It's louder now than I would have imagined. The rest of the ferry bubbles in the water as the hull goes under. Now it's completely gone. The captain is treading water wearing a very large professional-grade life vest. So are his crew. They look at each of us with somber gazes, making sure we are okay. No-one makes a sound. An eerie silence settles over the group.

We are alone in the water. Time ticks by and I lose track of the minutes.

Until…a low sound emits from somewhere far away. I can hear it but not pinpoint where it is coming from. We turn our heads in the water, waves lapping at our necks and splashing on our faces. Swallowing a bit of water, I cough.

"It sounds like a boat…" Kate says, tugging on my life vest.

It does. The Coast Guard should have gotten a crew sent out by now surely. Then we see it. A giant amphibious black boat. *The SEALs.*

It wasn't the Coast Guard at all, but my boyfriend's team. Or one of the teams. I've seen these boats when visiting him at work. Still too far away to make out any men on board, we move our arms in the frigid water.

"'Bout fucking time! We have hypothermia already!" One of the workers shouts.

Closer and closer, the black boat speeds. Until we *can* see who is on board. I see the face I had wanted to see. *Levi.*

He directs the team to stop as close as can be to us, pulling the men out first as they were floating on the edges from us. But I swear he never takes his eyes off of me. Concern, and something else, radiates off of him. It makes me shiver.

"Lil, grab my hand."

I stare up at his handsome, tanned face. His brown eyes glint in the surreal light.

"Lil."

Shaking myself out of it, I lift my hand. Fingers tugging, in a swift motion, he pulls me out of the water. Kate is already being huddled with a black towel by a team member. Levi wraps me in his arms, and I exhale as tears fall from my eyes.

He smells of aftershave and woodsy cologne. Muscles cradling me, I finally feel safe. Sensing my relief, my usually distant boyfriend leans his head down to whisper to me above the rescue noise.

"I'm here, baby. I'm here."

My heart beating out of control and water drops dripping down my face, I shiver. Levi's warmth radiates through the fabric of his tactical clothing and begins to penetrate my chilled state. He feels like *home*, never before as much as he does right now. I have missed him a lot more than I thought.

He is here.

"Get the blankets on them, all of them!" He barks orders.

There is no doubt that he is in charge of the group. He usually is, from what I understand. It's his team to run. Moving from the east coast to Washington was all Levi ever wanted, in order to take this coveted position. I gladly followed, too. This job was not the highest pay for me, but it brought me to where he was.

"Going back to base, baby. Don't worry, you'll be warmed up soon enough."

His words comfort and I let my body settle and let myself melt against him. Closing my eyes, I listen to the sounds of the working vessel we were all now, and most importantly, safely, aboard. Buzzers dinged and a low rumble was felt as we took off, speeding across the Sound. This boat is much quieter than anything I have ever been on before. It is one of their combat response vessels.

Levi keeps me from swaying in his firm grip. His arms cradle me as a prized possession. The chilly wind whips my hair as it begins to dry. Levi gently smooths the free strands and pulls the wool blanket around my back up over the top of my head, so I won't feel cold. Every single tiny thing he is doing feels so much more in the confused mental state that I am in.

Hypothermia had indeed begun to set in. The rescue was timed perfectly.

He is here.

"Take it back to the beach. Skip the dock, it's closer."

Opening my eyes, I see the black fabric and the tanned hands of my boyfriend. He holds me close as the boat approaches the beach. Then a big bump is felt as we come ashore.

"Lily, we're here. I want to check you out instead of the medics, is that okay?"

Of course, I nod. I only want him at the moment. And to make sure that Kate is okay. We begin to disembark, and I unwrap myself from Leiv, turning to look at the others. The workers are red-faced still and Kate looks shell shocked. She doesn't even notice me, looking instead towards the beach and the Naval team personnel that have come out to help us. I know she is in good hands, but I can't help but worry. She is like a second mom, even if just a 'work mom.'

We are the last to get off the vessel. Levi guides me with a hand on the small of my back. I clutch the wool blanket like the safety vest that had saved my life in the water. Cold still permeates my body as my clothes are still wet. We pass the others and go into a large white building by the water.

"My office, baby..." Levi says softly.

I've never been here before and have no idea where it is, but he continues to lead, until we hit a hallway that looks abandoned. Stopping at a large wooden door, Levi flashes a grin.

"In here."

CHAPTER SIX

"Baby."

One word has the ability to ignite every cell in my body.

"I've missed you."

Levi runs his finger tenderly across my cheek and tucks a few strands of hair behind my ear. I shiver again but for a very different reason. The power he holds over me in the bedroom is undeniable. I can never say no to him.

"Let's warm you..." he begins, sliding my wet top off slowly. "...up."

His mouth finds my neck and I feel his hot tongue run along the artery, stopping at my earlobe. Taking it into his mouth he gently sucks. Electricity shoots through my veins, along with a heady desire. Letting out a slight moan, I begin to melt under his touch. Warmth floods my legs and then my torso. Pulling me gently with him, he pops my earlobe free only to capture my lips next. I let him in, fully. Tongues colliding, we make it over to his desk.

He shoves the papers off it along with his nameplate and a few various items that crash onto the ground. We have never had sex in an office before. I have never been allowed into his work domain. Thanking God for this twist of fate, I feel his hands lift me swiftly under my ass, plunking me onto the desk's surface.

"When I heard you were on the ferry, I got the team ready," he breathes.

Kissing me deeper, he slides my jeans off with a few hard tugs. Goosebumps pepper the exposed skin. His eyes are a darker shade of brown now, as he breaks our kiss to look deeply at me.

"I love you, Lily Morgan."

My heart catching in my throat, I reply with a shaky voice.

"I love you, too, Levi."

He's only said my full name a handful of times, and never during sex, so my mind wonders if it's playing tricks on me. Desire can cloud one's sense of reality. But so can hypothermia.

"Am I….am I hypothermic?" I ask softly.

A grin breaking out over his handsome face, he laughs.

"You are in the first stages, yes. But I am getting you warm again!. Don't. Worry."

When he finishes telling me I am going to be okay, he pulls me to the edge of the desk. His hands now doing other things, I throw my head back and sigh. Levi is right, all worry is long gone.

After an eternity of bliss, we collapse on the leather couch by the window. Levi breathes normally while I can barely catch my breath. I swim and hike almost daily but am still not in as good shape as my hot boyfriend. It's simply not fair.

"Lil…my God."

"Yes?" I ask, still trying to get my brain to work properly.

"You are everything to me."

More words that he hardly ever says. Now my curiosity is piqued. I sit up and cover my bare breasts, there's a sheen of sweat coating them. Levi's eyes follow my hands as he licks his lips.

"What's going on, babe? You usually aren't so…"

"Vocal?" he laughs.

"Yeah. Vocal. About your feelings."

He wrinkles an eyebrow upwards and studies my face. Now *this* is the boyfriend I am used to. The one who studies me. Analyzing. Levi is nothing but special operations through and through.

"I can't tell my gorgeous girlfriend how much I love her?"

Scoffing, I tighten my grip on my ample breasts.

"Of course you can. You just don't. Not very often."

Grunting, he pulls my hands, setting my breasts free. His eyes trained on them; he licks his lips again.

"You know we have been together for going on four years. It's long enough for me to open up, don't you think?"

Suddenly, I am hoisted onto his lap, straddling him. In true Levi fashion, before I can answer, his lips crash into mine. Everything about the day, from the swim to being chased to seeing things after hitting my head to nearly drowning in the water fades as he works his magic. Making love for a second time, we pour all of the unsaid words into each other's bodies.

"Were you scared, in the water?" he asks as we lay on the couch, my head on his chest. It's an innocent question and I don't know how to answer it. Closing my eyes, I can see the water moving all around me. I bob in the waves as fear grips my mind.

"Lily…" Levi says, gently shaking my back with his hand.

He strokes my hair with the other. Reopening my eyes, I exhale and whisper a reply.

"I was. How could I not be? It was terrifying."

"I'm sure it was. But you were calm, right? You looked absolutely calm when we got there. I noticed your coworker was, too; Kate is her name? She must have listened to you."

Kate.

I need to check on her. I try to move but Levi tightens his arms so I can't.

"You need to rest. Don't worry, Kate is fine. She and everyone else will already have been taken to the medics, and then back home. You don't have to go back to your cabin tonight though, you're staying with me, and I'll take you to work tomorrow. My team has training anyways on a nearby island."

"I… I guess that's fine. But my phone, my purse…"

"They are fine, except your phone doesn't work. I have a spare you can have. Don't worry, baby. I have you."

34

He lightly rubs my arms as goosebumps form.

"Did you see any animals in the water when you were near the sinking?" I absentmindedly ask.

"Animals, babe?"

"Yeah, any whales or anything?"

Levi hesitates to answer, and I can feel his body tense up.

"Did you see anything in the water?" I press.

He sighs, making the tension palpable. A familiar feeling creeps into my gut. I felt this way earlier when the figure chased me after my swim, and I felt this way in the bathroom when I saw the second dark figure. It can't all be connected, can it?

"My team saw a few whales. And a shark, but not exactly right where you were. So don't worry, baby."

Shark…

I hadn't actually thought a shark was near us. I had wondered, but I'd pushed the thought out of my crowded head. I hadn't wanted to think about sharks.

"Did you see it? The shark?"

"Yes. But we had weapons trained, it would've been killed if it got to close to your group."

His hands graze my neck as he turns my face upwards, to face him.

"What else happened today?" he asks, and I suddenly wonder if his question is entirely innocent. Why?

"What do you mean?"

Levi frowned.

"Your day, Lil, what happened? Tell me about it."

I should tell him what happened, all of it, but that would probably unleash a long lecture. One I am not in the mood for.

"Come on. Something happened I can tell, besides the ferry sinking. I know you."

If I don't spill something he won't stop, he is in one of those moods. I can tell.

"Well, this morning, after my swim, I thought I saw someone

in the woods, watching me. I ran to my rental Jeep and took off. But nothing happened. It was just scary is all."

Suddenly sitting up, Levi took hold of my forearms.

"Someone *was watching you*? What do you mean, Lily?"

His eyes dart over my face in fear.

"Yeah, but I couldn't tell who it was. A man, or woman. I don't know."

"So, you were swimming and then you saw someone on the shore? Explain..."

I shift my weight and sigh. How much should I tell?

"It began normally, I got up at four thirty, took the early ferry to the island by myself and then got dressed in my wetsuit on the shore. Like I always do. No one was there. The ferry captain even said I was the first one of the day. He always tells me that."

Levi's jaw muscle flexes as he nods, waiting for me to continue the story.

"Then I went out into the water for my swim. I went out to the point then turned around. On the swim back, I saw a dark figure in the wood line. I thought so anyways, it was hard to see as I make strokes. Only when I got out did I look harder and noticed the shape more."

"Was it tall? How tall?" he asks.

"I don't know, I guessed around six foot five. But probably taller."

"That is a massive human, Lily…."

"I know, I know. I mean, it was cold and then it started to rain. I tried to get a better look, but I was scared. I knew I needed to get to my Jeep."

"This pisses me off, babe, you should've called me! Right away!"

"I couldn't, my phone was in my dry bag, and I didn't have time…I just ran." He didn't need to know that my bag was thrown when I ran into the cabin, or that my mind was terrified

36

and not working correctly as I hid. The tall man *was* real. I heard him, and I was chased.

"It's okay, Lil. Don't cry."

His hand swipes at my cheek, capturing tears I hadn't realized I had cried. Today has been too much. Pulling me to his side, he swings my legs over his lap.

"Let's go to my place and get some rest."

I close my eyes as he kisses my forehead. Images of the tall man are all I can see and strange as it seems, the only thing I can think of is why he is so interested in my day. I get the feeling my safety is not what he is concerned about.

CHAPTER SEVEN

"Lily, what the hell happened yesterday? Kate is taking the day off and sleeping in at the cabins."

Peter looks at me with concern, coming into the room from where he and Brian are working. I set my purse down on the table where Kate had been yesterday, next to the thick folder she had intended to take back to the cabins and read in private.

"We capsized. There's not much to tell."

"Yeah, but how? We've been on those ferries daily for months! I just can't fathom one sinking! Spill the details, how did it happen?"

"Peter. Let's leave Lily be for a while. I'm sure it was awfully traumatic. You saw how upset Kate was."

Brian, the older voice of reason, comes to my rescue. He enters the room and stands awkwardly by the doorway, hand on hip. Dark circles are under his eyes. He looks like shit. But no wonder, he probably stayed up most of the night near Kate, if not in her cabin, with a book and thermos of coffee in hand. Being the group 'dad' is a job he takes seriously.

"Do you need anything, Lil?" he asks.

I shake my head. I need to sleep more but I told Levi I was fine to come back to work. I Insisted he take me actually. I didn't want to be alone. I can't be, not right now.

"I'm okay. I don't think I want to leave for lunch, though. One ferry ride back is enough for today."

"Of course. Say no more, I'll bring you back a nice sandwich, how does that sound? Turkey and mustard with only lettuce. Just like you take it."

"Thanks Brian, I appreciate it."

He nods in acknowledgement and leaves the room, ushering Peter out, much to his annoyance. Peter is probably a bigger gossip than most women are, which makes me wonder how he attracted his wife. She is the polar opposite to him. Once the door shuts, I glance back at the thick folder. It is beckoning me, calling me over. Something is in there that I need to read, I can feel it. Kate often spoke of ghosts and paranormal when we were on the job. What if the Navy had knowledge of that, too?

The dark figures in the bathrooms might be ghosts.

As the thought pops up, goosebumps do as well, on my arms.

There is something here, I can feel it.

Taking a seat, I hold the folder and start to skim the pages one by one. One thing I know about documents, anything of importance will have highlights at the beginning, and it will be obvious what is in it. Unless it's a Top-Secret document. Then it will be buried deep within. I am hoping for the former.

"For the Undersecretary of the Criminal Division, for the Undersecretary of the Navy, for the Undersecretary of the Medical Corps…"

Medical Corps.

There is the mention again, of medical. Kate had brought it up earlier when she was reading through it. But she didn't get too far. I read until I get to page four and then I spot it. A small detail, but one, nonetheless.

Gold mountain.

The words pop off the page. They are nestled in ever so slightly, next to 'locations' of the document. I have heard of that place before, I just can't quite remember where. The rest of the first one hundred pages are all a jumble of military jargon. The classified nature makes it Top-Secret and not written or structured to the point, instead it rambles on. Realizing I can't read through this and also get this room sorted fast enough, I close the folder and set it down on the table, under my new purse that Levi gave me early this morning.

Thankfully, my IDs and bank cards were all good, even after being submerged in Puget Sound for a long time. Plastic can handle water. My photos and other various assorted paper cards though, those didn't make it. Not even the vintage picture of my grandparents when they were young. That tore my heart to see it a mushed mess on Levi's kitchen counter. I cried a bit even.

"Gold mountain is on the mainland, by Bremerton," I say, absentmindedly.

There are some rumors surrounding it, making it a place that gets attention online from the conspiracy theory mill and people who make videos on YouTube. In fact, I had watched a video late one night, that detailed a firsthand account of a man venturing into the mountain. He said he saw cages with people in them...and a lab. Of course this can easily be dismissed as crazy, but the man telling the story was a respected member of the neighboring community. So, it did make me take a pause. You just never know.

Picking up another stack from Kate's area, I randomly shuffle the documents, checking for the classification markings. So far, everything is basically declassified. Still though, it amazes me that a unit could leave so much behind. Whoever worked in this particular PSD or Personnel Support Detachment, was terrible at bookkeeping. To not shred a single thing...

Then I spot something.

"Does that say Deception Pass?" I mutter, as I spot the corner of a document sticking out. It's dog-eared. Deception Pass is a hugely popular canyon of sorts over the water of the Pacific Ocean that is winding through island chains. There are a *lot* of rumors about that area.

Why is this here, in a defunct Naval Base?

Hairs stand on the back of my neck as I reach for the paper. A sensation that I am viewing something I shouldn't washes over me. Before I can read it, though, an incredibly loud bang resounds through the building.

"Shit!"

I drop the paper and immediately jump up off my seat.

"What do we do?!" Peter shouts.

"Don't. Fucking. Move."

Brian speaks in the loudest tone of voice I have ever heard him use. Running to the door, I peer out down the opposite hallway. Standing down by the far entrance is a huge bear.

A BEAR!

A ginormous black bear is on its hind legs, chuffing low and loud at us. Fear courses through my veins. Now I am frozen, paralyzed to my spot. I can't think, I can't process anything. Emotions raw, a rumble grows from the beast of an animal. It shakes the floorboards in the old building.

Brain and Peter stand alongside the wall, seemingly as paralyzed as I am. The bear's eyes are black and beady, and its mouth opens and shuts over rapidly as it begins to chuff louder. Then, it lets out a roar. My bladder suddenly feels full, as terror takes over. I hope to God that I don't pee myself.

This cannot be real. This cannot be real.

The words flow over and over, like a gushing waterfall in my mind. How can this be happening? Was the door left open? By accident? Or deliberately? How in the hell did it get in?

The bear roars again, its gums flapping with spit as its teeth are on full display. But it doesn't advance, not yet.

"Inside!! It's inside!!"

A voice shouts as men fly into the building from the opposite direction. All I see is black clothing and long guns. Performing tactical walking, the group of men descend into the hallway and then I hear a loud shot.

"Lil, are you okay?"

Levi.

He sounds underwater. Muffled. But it's him. A firm hand on my lower back, he gently squeezes me, then moves on with his team. The bear is now on the worn hardwood flooring, it's body slack. I can't see much but I know it's now dead.

"Holy fuck!! How did they know that thing was in here?"

Peter immediately begins to chatter, nervously, as he usually does. Brian holds up his hand and glances back at me, catching my eyes. Concern fills them and I know he is worried about my mental state. It's been one helluva twenty-four hours.

"Call in animal control. At Whidbey. They can get the state involved; we need to get back to training."

One of Levi's men chats with Brian.

"We were training nearby and spotted the bear running towards the buildings. It was chasing a worker. Halting, we tracked it to *your guys'* location. Thankfully too, it had already killed a few deer on the other side of the island."

"Deer? I didn't think bear ate deer!"

"Oh, shit, yeah, they do, especially bigger males like this one," he says, patting Brian's shoulder.

"We will carry it outside and we've let Whidbey know. They are sending a team over to take it from here."

I watch as the men drag the hulking bear out the doorway where it had presumably entered from. A pool of blood smears along the floor as they do. The dark maroon is a sharp contrast to the honey-colored wood. It's odd and scary at the same time. Just a moment ago, nothing was there but some dust and beams of light from the dingy windows.

Levi approaches me again, this time with his rifle slung on his back. He pulls me in for a tight hug.

"My God, Lil. I think we need to rethink your job here. You are having the worst luck lately," he whispers into my ear.

The heat from his breath sends a shiver up my spine and heat through my veins.

How am I turned on right now?

"Tonight. You, me, and a bottle of wine with pasta. Yes?"

I nod into his chest as I feel his muscles move beneath me.

"Okay, then. I've got to go, baby. Back to work."

Pulling back, he tilts my head up for a kiss.

42

Passion ignites like a pilot light being lit on the stove. But before I can adjust the temperature, he is gone. Nothing but silence fills the now empty building as Brian and Peter stare at me.

"I am beginning to think this place is haunted," Peter mutters.

"Let's finish up so we can take lunch when that team gets here," Brian says, in a voice of command.

The men retreat back to the room they are working in, and I do the same, slowly sitting down on the chair I had leapt from barely moments ago. My mind is a jumble. Thoughts float slowly. A fucking *bear* was just in the building. How rare is that? Then, as if in a flash, something moves by the window next to me. Turning quickly, I see it.

A man in a dark hoodie.

CHAPTER EIGHT

I run.

For what seems to be the hundredth time in the last few weeks.

"Everything okay?" Brian shouts.

There is no time to reply. Jumping over the still wet blood that is pooled and streaked along the wooden floor, I shove the giant doors open as my feet contact the wet dirt outside. It's soft from rain, squishing softly. The adrenaline is flowing freely again, coursing harshly through my body. I have to find the man.

He was following me earlier, I know it.

Aware that this might not be the smartest thing to do, I keep running. Something is compelling me to chase, and I have to follow the urge. Plus, I want to catch whoever it is and get them to *stop*. This assignment was supposed to be easy, in a pretty location, and refreshing, not terrifying.

I round the building and see a black hoodie lying on the ground. Beads of sweat fall from my brow as I approach. Glancing to the left then the right, I tentatively scan around me. I haven't imagined it. The guy outside the window was real and he left evidence of himself. Sunbeams begin to peek through the dense cloud cover above me. A tendril of light hits my hand as I bend down to pick up the hoodie. It's warm. If it's warm, is he real? Do ghosts have a body temperature?

"Lily!"

Brian jogs over to me, huffing and puffing. I drop the hoodie and turn.

"Crap! What happened? Whose sweatshirt is that?" he asks.

"I don't know. I saw a man go by the window outside and I had to check. I wanted to see.,"

"… If it was the man who watched you in the woods?" Brian

interrupts. "The one you told Kate about?"

I nod absentmindedly. Dawning on me that this sounds crazy, I look around once more for anyone lurking. *Someone* left this hoodie. And recently too, because of the heat coming off it, body heat from just being worn.

"Are the other workers here today?" I ask.

"Yes, but over by the old post headquarters building. They are taking out the bigger furniture. And there isn't anyone else out here."

We both stare at the dark garment on the ground. Neither of us speak for a few minutes.

"Hey guys! The group from Whidbey are here to deal with the bear!" Peter shouts.

Brian and I turn around to see a group of, maybe six, Navy uniformed personnel walking up to the building. They have duffle bags in tow. Must be the cleanup team.

"Oh Lord, the circus begins. Let's take an extended break, say an hour? Relax your mind, okay? Then we can finish up and see if the ferry will take us home early."

I nod as we make our way back to the building. I need to grab my purse then I'll go sit by the water in the reluctant sunshine, only partly obscured by dull, white clouds. The bear smells horrid as we pass it on the way indoors. Already, flies swarm around its carcass and buzz in the chilly air. Goosebumps form at the thought of that thing actually charging at us. Or worse. The face sags lifelessly. What once was a formidable creature is now dead.

"They say they saw it on the shore running up to the buildings…"

"The team was awful close. Don't they train elsewhere?"

"SEALs do whatever they want, you know that."

Listening to the conversations that fill the hallway I meander back to my workspace and grab my bag. Deciding it's best to hide the folder Kate found, I tuck it under a large filing cabinet in the corner. There are huge repercussions for hiding Top-Secret documents or for taking them away from the areas we found them in without letting Commander Lessing know. Things like jail and being fired. I have to be careful.

"See you in an hour," Brian says, as I leave the building.

He already has his sunglasses on, ready to relax. The Navy personnel are too engrossed in their work to notice me again, which is fine by me. I want to get away from the carnage. Moving past them, I take the worn dirt path towards where the ferry picks us up and drops us off. The air feels somehow damp, and the sun has retreated into the cloud cover. It might rain soon. Washington is an intensely moody state. More so than any of the others I have worked at.

Buzzing from my pocket interrupts my train of thought. Pulling my cell phone out, I see Kate is calling me. Levi must have made sure Kate had my new number.

"Hey..." I answer.

"Hey girl. How is it going there?" she asks, worry in her voice.

"Okay. Other than a fucking black bear getting into the building..."

"Woah, wait. *Black bear?*"

"Yeah. One minute I am working and then next, Brian and Peter shout and I run to the door only to see this massive black bear! And by massive, I mean it looked easily as big as a grizzly."

"How did such a thing get into the building?? Didn't you guys shut the doors?"

"I did when we came in. I don't have a clue."

"Well, what happened?!"

"It stood on his hind legs and roared…. then Levi and his team came and rescued us."

"Wait, back up, you said Levi. *Your* Levi? How did he know it was there?"

"Yes, my Levi. And he said they were in the water passing by the island when they saw it on shore running towards the buildings. Apparently, it had killed a deer by the water, and they could see the carcass."

Silence fills the line.

"What's wrong?" I ask Kate.

"What a stroke of luck that was! Levi being right nearby. I suppose they do train right by us, so..."

"Yes. But what's wrong? You only call me when something has gone to shit at work."

Kate laughs softly, then clears her throat. I can sense her apprehension, and it gives me pause. She is quite a bit older than I am and usually serious as the day is long. Whatever it is, she feels the urgency to call instead of waiting until I get back to the cabins this evening.

"This morning, I saw a man outside the cabins here."

Pausing, she doesn't continue on. I know that Kate isn't one to get scared so this must have rattled her. Plus, why was *anyone* by our cabins?

"A man? Where and what did he look like?"

"He was wearing a black hoodie, and it was drawn pretty far out so it hid his face."

Blood drains from *my* face as I feel my hand go numb while holding the phone.

A man in a black hoodie.

I had just seen a man in a hoodie running by the window outside the buildings here. Now Kate sees one where she is. It couldn't be the same man, could it?

"What was he doing?" I ask, my voice laced with fear.

"I got up to pee and I usually glance at the front door when I come out into the hallway. Habit. You know, check to see if the deadbolt is still locked. I did that and out the front window, facing the porch, I saw the man walk by. Real quick like, too. My heart raced because I am here alone."

You all left this morning, and no cleaners are scheduled to be

Here, or anyone this else. Right?"

Her question throws me off as I struggle to remember the cleaning schedule.

"No, I don't think so. I thought they come on Sundays?"

"Yes, that's right, just like I thought. He wasn't a maintenance worker, Lily. I don't know who he was, but I put on my boots and ran outside to see. Which in hindsight, I would never do something so dumb. Not without my *Smith & Wesson*."

"You ran out after him?"

"Sure as shit did. I wish I hadn't because all I found was his black hoodie, lying in the mud around the side of your cabin. Then the footprints led into the wood line, and I didn't go further."

She saw the same thing I did!

My hand begins to shake I move it to cradle the phone to my ear. All of my senses are working in overdrive. What Kate is saying is exactly what I experienced not more than thirty minutes ago. In fact, the similarity makes me think it has to be the same man, and we reacted in the exact way as well. Feeling compelled to follow him.

"Kate, what if we are being haunted?"

"Lily, I've seen a lot of things over the years. I mean a lot. I had a pretty scary ghost experience in Virginia on an old Army bunker. And Germany. But I have never felt that I needed to follow one of them. I can't figure it out."

"Was it like you had to follow, you needed to catch him?"

She coughs.

"Yes. That's how it felt. Impulsive. Which I am *not*."

I don't want to scare her further, but I should tell her so we can figure this out.

"Kate, I saw a man less than an hour ago outside the window here. And I chased him too."

"Are you joking?" she asks tentatively.

"No. And Kate," I say, quickly.

"Yeah?"

"He also dropped a black hoodie."

CHAPTER NINE

Some things you feel with all your senses.

Like fall in the Pacific Northwest, with its wet, earthly afterglow when rain has just passed or the scent of the coastal waters and all the various creatures that float within. Magic in its purest form.

A Man in a black hoodie.

Kate needed to rest, so we hung up. Still sitting on the bench by the water, the sun disappears behind a set of darker clouds. Storms might be blowing in. Glancing up, I see the anger in the black and grey swirls. They look like huge clumps of cotton, stuck together and back lit by a huge dark flashlight. The opposite of happiness. In fact, staring at the sky is making me feel depressed.

I check the time on my phone. I have about thirty minutes left before Brian said we needed to be back at work. The group with the black bear has already loaded it onto the ferry and are now milling around taking pictures and copious amounts of notes that will probably, one day, fill a cabinet like the one I have been meticulously going through. Just more garbage for someone to deal with. The irony is not lost on me.

Sighing, I stand and stretch.

"I'll take a walk," I mutter to myself.

Resolve filling my mind, I begin to follow the shore until I reach a small pathway where the sand turns to rocks. It leads to a section of the base I haven't yet explored but always wanted to. Our days here are just too busy and then we leave on the ferry. Maybe Brian needs to give us more mental health breaks, more often.

"He *definitely* needs to do that,"

My tennis shoes slip on the wet rocks. I slow down and gather my thoughts. I need to let my mind calm down. It's too muddled and clouded by all the things happening here. It all began with my swim.

"I like to swim, though." I whisper, rounding a bend only to come face to face with a concrete bunker.

The sheer size of it stuns me. I didn't know such a thing was here. Walking slowly, I hear water dripping from inside and also by the crumbled entrance. Smells of dampness hit my olfactory system as I step slowly into the cavernous opening. There are leftover remnants of a war station inside. A cannon mount with old parts attached stands between two affixed areas. Water and mold cover the barrel of what I assume was a cannon to my right. To the left, it is missing.

Assuming this comes from the Second World War era, I stare in awe, picturing the scene that must have taken place here on any given day back in time. The men that manned the place, overlooking the ocean waters, had to have been different to the men that serve today. Perhaps back then they were more – I don't know – vigilant, maybe. Everything was manual back then, there was no sophisticated equipment. Perhaps they took more risks because of this. Plus, the uniforms in that era would have been so uncomfortable and not at all warm enough. Yeah, that generation of sailors and soldiers were built differently. There is no barrier to the weather. None whatsoever.

My eyes catch a door to the very back, almost visible through the darkness. I feel compelled to check it out and absently walk into the darkness. By now I am in the back of the bunker, and I can't see a thing. Something wet drops on my forehead, dripping down my nose. I brush the water off. I should feel scared but oddly enough, I am not. Nothing will happen to me here. I'm sure of it.

"Where is it?" I mumble, feeling along the wall for the door handle.

Finally, my fingers contact the cold bumpy metal. It's old; it feels as if the paint is peeling off. No doubt my hand will have rust stains to prove it, once I get back into the light. Gripping the handle, I pull the door open, hard. As if opening a vacuum seal, the door whooshes and cold air hits my face. No light emits though. I have found an inner room.

"Too dark!" I cry, pulling out my cell phone from my jeans pocket. I turn on the flashlight mode. Suddenly a bright beacon of light fills the room, and I slowly walk in. I make sure the door stays open, so I don't get stuck, I turn and examine the area. It's quite large and mold coats the inner walls. Probably, I shouldn't be breathing it in, but here I am. As I sweep the space with my phone light, something big looms in the far left corner. Walking closer, I see what it is.

You have to be kidding me, a filing cabinet.

Of all the things to find and the only piece of furniture, it would have to be a filing cabinet. One of the things I work with for hours on a daily basis. Curiosity is tugging at every fiber of my being, so I walk closer to inspect. It's completely rusted but I reach out to jiggle the top drawer. Nothing happens. It's locked. Pulling hard on the second drawer down, I find it also locked. I do the same to every drawer until I realize I can't get a peek. I would need tools to pop the lock. Which is surprisingly easy to do, but not at the moment.

"Well, that's disappointing," I vocalize into the void.

I want to see what's in there but begin to move away and shine my light in a defeated manner, quite lazily, along the wall. Instead of hidden documents, I spot something etched into the plaster.

"The hell…"

I stop and shine the light directly on the section in question. Rudimentary words are carved into a lower section. I imagine the long dead person, scoring them into the wall for posterity, using their pocketknife. I shiver, thinking of the dead. Squinting, I try to make out the words etched underneath all the grime and mold. My heart drops as I sound it out. There is a hard, loud thumping in my chest until I swear, I can *hear* my heart beating.

DECEPTION PASS

The words are all upper case, on purpose no doubt. But why? Why have I seen this place mentioned again in one day? I need to research more and figure out if any Naval operations were conducted there. Kate might know. She is the queen of research.

Research...

My brain suddenly jogged out of its fog; I glance at the time. "Fuck, I'm late."

Brian is no doubt looking for me. He is our unofficial supervisor next to Kate. Shaking my head, I turn away from the words on the wall. Intending to leave through the door I came into, a strong wind gusts through the bunker suddenly. To my horror, the door slams shut with a loud clink. I run to the door and try to pull it open. It won't budge.

"Shit! Shit!" I curse.

Pulling as hard as I can, it still won't budge. This isn't good. "I'm trapped!" I yell, in desperation.

My voice echoes in the large space with an otherworldly tone. As if I have never heard myself before.

"Brian won't know where I am. Kate isn't here, and Peter will have no clue what to do…."

My lamenting is not going to get me out fast enough. Then it hits me. I am holding a phone. Fingers shaking, I turn off the flashlight mode so I can go to calls. Hitting Brians name, I wait for the dial tone. Only, I hear two beeps then the call is lost. Confused, I look at the screen.

No signal.

Of course I won't have signal in here! I am in a concrete bunker, for God's sake! Nothing electronic will work in here unless designed to do so. Even now, decades later, technology isn't made for every place. The little green battery light in the upper right hand corner blares out at me. My phone is now on low battery as well.

"Great…" I said, loudly.

I need to conserve what is left. So at least my phone still works for tracking. Well, I hope it does, at least. Flicking the flashlight off, the room goes dark.

"Think….. think."

Racking my brain, I can't figure out what to do without cell service. With the door jammed, I am literally stuck. And it is darker than dark, here. Remembering what Levi would say in this situation, I focus on my breathing. "*If you can steady that Lil, you can focus on staying alive.*" To which, he isn't wrong. It is good advice.

Water continues to drip from various cracks in the concrete bowels, sending echoes in my ears. The sound of rain always calmed me as a child, so I try to pretend I am in my bed at home, and it is beating down on the rooftop above me. Somehow it is comforting. My heart rate begins to slow and sort of return to a normal beat. After an hour or so passes, I know that someone will come looking for me.

"It's possible that one of the Navy personnel saw at least the direction I went in…" I whisper.

By no means am I fan of the dark, so I take a seat on the cold, most likely filthy ground, and close my eyes. I can't panic. No matter what, I have to keep calm. I picture who used to work here and why. The officers and enlisted who must have manned this area fill my mind. Were any women in here? I wonder about this and many other things. Before I know it, my head finds my arms as I sit with my knees under my chin. And I begin to drift off.

Then, out of nowhere, a loud sound wakes me.

CHAPTER TEN

Now I'm afraid. What the hell just touched me?

My eyes scanning the darkness, a dizzy sensation takes hold. I can't tell what is up or down, only that I can hear something nearby. There's another loud, indescribable noise, like a moan of pain or terror; this time much closer. I gasp as I hear footsteps treading along the concrete floor. I stare into the darkness wildly. Do I stay put? Do I move and try to foil whoever or whatever is here with me, in my makeshift, unintentional prison. Suddenly, another thought enters my brain.

How did they get in here; the door was shut tight? I'm pretty certain that no-one followed me inside, *so how did they get in here?*

Terror elevates my breathing until I'm panting in fear.

Touching my phone screen, I see it light up and look for the bars of service. I still have none.

"Shit, shit. . .. *shit.*"

It moves closer. Long, loud sounds resound in my ears. It's unlike anything I have ever heard.

Scrape, scrape!!

It's walking back and forth. The breathing gets louder then farther away. Standing now, I grip my phone hard, as I feel goosebumps form on my skin. Cold begins to creep through my body. I wasn't aware of the temperature until now. Fear has a way of doing that to you.

Groan!

There is another unnatural sound. It's very close by. Yelping, I move away in terror. I can't think straight or form a coherent thought. My brain is frozen. Unsure of what to do, I listen as the groaning continues. Footsteps begin to resound in the silence again. It's only a matter of time before it gets me. Then I am screwed. I'll be – shit! What will happen to me? What does it want? Will I be killed and become another person trapped inside the bunker, groaning into eternity and terrifying anyone who comes in? Is that what happened to them? This is not the way I thought I would die, not at all.

The filing cabinet.

I hear Levi's voice in my mind, urging me.

"Filing cabinet..." I say loudly.

There is a mighty roar of anger, and the footsteps quicken. Scrambling towards the corner of the room, I flick my cellphone light back on. If my battery dies, so be it. I need to see. Rusty metal greets me as I heft the corner of the large cabinet to the side. It slides but barely. I need to move it all the way to the door. To try and jam the handle so it won't get in.

Shoving the phone into my front jeans pocket, the flashlight still glows bright enough to light my path. Digging deep, I use all my strength and get the filing cabinet to move away from the wall. Pulling then pushing, I alternate between sides as I move it very noisily along the concrete. Metal bites at my fingers, rust now coating them with a red pallor. This thing has to weigh a hundred pounds. They don't make filing cabinets like they used to. Not this solid anyways.

Thump. Thump. Thump.

It's nearer! It's here! Oh, God!

"Come on!!" I yell with terrible desperation.

I shove and push, pull and curse. The cabinet moves inch by painstaking inch, towards the door. Finally, I am a few feet away. Rattling violently, the door is still somehow holding. Budged firm. Thankful for that, I use the last of my strength to get it to where I can tip it. Pushing with force I don't know I even had, I get it to fall forward and then wedge it under the door handle. Now the thing can't get in.

Collapsing on the ground I can feel the sweat rolling off of my body. I am soaked. My stomach aches and I have no idea why. Probably because I haven't eaten today.

How much time has passed?

I don't know how long I've been here though it feels like an hour, maybe more. Surely my coworkers will be looking for me. My thoughts snap away from my coworkers to the sound I am now hearing.

The filing cabinet! Whatever it is that is out there is pushing the filing cabinet away from the door. The handle, being old and worn with age snaps easily under the force being exerted upon it. It's going to give! Then, it can get in; it can get me!

Forgetting everything that Levi ever told me about how to save my life, I am breathing fast and sweating profusely. I run into the farthest corner and turn off my phone light to resume my dark vigil, tucking knees back under my chin. Maybe it won't see me in the dark.

My thoughts drift off to Levi. How he will react once he hears that I trapped myself and an unknown entity is stalking me. Does he believe in ghosts? The talks of me quitting will come up again, I think this time I will have very few reasons to defend my position. Work is how I live but if he moves me in with him...

I won't do that unless he asks me to marry him.

Surprised at myself, I know deep down that is really how I've always felt. I have loved Levi for years and he has never wanted to commit that deeply. Not yet anyways. Funny how it takes a life-threatening event to give one resolve. But excellent sex alone isn't going to make me move with him. Not anymore.

Now I just have to remind myself of this when I am in throes of passion with little to no clothing on. *That* will be the hard part.

THUD!

A very loud sound shakes the ground, and a high-pitched whine pierces the air, hurting my ears. I grasp them and squish my eyes shut. Not that I need to, it's dark as death in the room. Something is happening but I don't know what. Then I hear the distinct sound of shots being fired, in the distance. And muffled shouts.

People.

I let out a huge sigh of relief and hope seeps into my body like sunshine when suddenly, I feel it. Cold breath on my cowering face and as I begin to scream, a cold hand grabs at my forearm and begins to pull me out of my corner of safety. The hand is slimy and frozen. My arm is hurting; such is the strength of whoever or whatever has hold of me. I am trying to resist but I can feel myself being dragged along the floor, my feet having no grip on the ground. I am still screaming. Tears of fear and pain course down my face. We are near the door. What will happen to me if it gets me outside?

Suddenly, I feel myself being pushed. The hand frees my arm, and I stumble, my back hitting something cold and solid. It's the filing cabinet! The thing begins to make a high-pitched sound, a bit like white noise. What is it trying to say?

Deception Pass.

The words fill my addled brain as clearly as if they have been spoken.

The distant shouting is become clearer, more discernible. I am being rescued. They finally came for me! I shiver in the cold and suddenly I am aware that I cannot hear the thing that grabbed me. My terror and confusion make me break out in a cold sweat, and I can't warm up. Shaking takes over as adrenaline dumps from my body. The high-pitched sound has dissipated but the voices are so far away. They are saying my name.

"Lily! Lily!"

I scramble to stand, arms out in front of me so I don't run into the filing cabinet. It's still dark.

"I'm in here!!! IN HERE!!!" I hoarsely shout back.

The voices are far though, too far. They can't hear me.

"Help! Help me!" I plead.

My throat sore and my body racking with waves of cold, I shout a few more times into the void of the bunker. Only silence answers back.

"They don't think I am in here…"

Suddenly, I lurch backwards onto the filing cabinet and brace myself. Ouch! My back radiates pain as well as my arm. I feel sick now, like I am going to vomit. The rusted metal is cold as well, but I can't move. I need to calm down. Realizing I am beginning to have a panic attack, I put a hand on the cabinet and close my eyes again.

Think of something happy. Think of Levi.

Immediately I picture him in the kitchen of his place. He is shirtless and holds onto a knife as he gingerly cuts a lemon on a black cutting board. My eyes take in his form, glazing over every single muscle and dipping in his physique. He doesn't see me yet and I want to wait to alert him to my presence. There are two fillets of salmon on the stove, waiting to be cooked. He takes the lemon slices and begins to squeeze them softly over the fish, the juice splashing over the meat.

Wearing only one of his tee shirts, I walk silently to where he is, stopping directly behind him. I reach out with both hands and trace down the center of his back. Instantly reacting, Levi groans.

"There you are. Awake already?"

"Uh huh, sort of…" I respond.

Taking me by surprise, he flicks off the stove and in one motion, picks me up under my butt, and plunks me onto the cold quartz countertop. I exhale in anticipation, wanting him badly.

"You drive me crazy, Lil. You know that, right?" he says, huskily.

Fingers latching onto my shirt, he slides it off and throws it over his shoulder. I am left naked before him.

"Levi…"

Taking a fresh lemon slice, he gently squeezes it over my bare breasts. His fingers rubbing the juice in as he grazes them.

"Yes, my love?"

He dips his head down before I can respond and takes my breasts into his mouth, one at a time. I throw my head back, unable to think. Passion with Levi is out of this world. He knows exactly what to do, at exactly the right moment. And this is one of the best memories I have of us at home. It's the night he told me he loved me for the first time.

A ding from my pocket interrupts my mental escape. Cold floods my senses as I pull my phone and look at the screen. It shakes in my hand. I have a text message somehow. Staring at the words I feel confusion. How did I get this with no signal?

Stay in the room, I am coming, baby.

CHAPTER ELEVEN

Hands shaking, I drop my phone. Wind begins to howl through the bunker. The weather has turned outside. It is probably starting to rain as well. Levi's words stare back at me from the ground. Blue light glows eerily towards me. Fear pulses as I try to comprehend how he knows I am in here, and how the phone received a text when service is nonexistent.

Levi.

Maybe I am hallucinating. But no, I can't be, I think to myself as I realize that my back and my arm are aching badly.

"This can't be real..."

No sooner have I said the words than my phone shuts itself off. The battery died. I try to turn it back on to no avail.

"Crap, crap."

Now my only light source is off. I am in the dark until someone comes for me. The text wasn't real.

It wasn't real, Lily. You imagined that, because you were just fantasizing about that day with Levi.

In times of stress or danger or both, the mind can become skewed. Exactly the situation I find myself in now. This is the classic scenario that you might see in a scary movie, or a thriller. I've watched things like that with Levi. And the outcome is never good. Biting cold stinging my skin, I know that my time is limited before I become hypothermic. Just like in the water.

Only this time no one knows where I am.

As my thoughts race and I struggle to get control over them, my eyes become heavy. Bowing my head down onto my knees, I succumb to the feeling and drift off. Outside the bunker, the group of Navy personnel continue searching for me, though I don't know it, long into the afternoon. I hear voices but I'm not sure if they are real, or imaginary. Thoughts induced by hypothermia.

"Here....in here!"

"Where?"

"The corner, the door."

Footsteps echo softly as men descend into the bunker.

"Got it. Try it."

"It's stuck. Jammed."

"Here try this, In the corner. Stand back."

"Wait, is she *against* the door?"

"No, about a foot away to the right..."

"Her heat signature, see?"

"Yep. Okay. Hang on."

A loud sound awakens me from my slumber. Eyes flying open, I look around in the darkness, confused. I don't know what is happening, but something is. Then I hear them. *People.*

"Almost done..."

"There. Ready to go off its hinges."

"One, two, three, *pull.*"

Metal scrapes on the concrete as the door next to me slowly moves. Whipping my head to the left, light streams in, forcing me to squint. Sharp pain fills my face as I struggle to look.

"Lil. I'm here."

Levi! Levi's voice soothes my mind as he bends near me, his hands roaming my body. I think how strange it is that he is trying to undress me *now* of all times. He is usually horny, but this seems inappropriate.

"She's hypothermic. No cuts. No breaks."

He is checking you for injury...

Slowly I begin to come round fully. Levi's text was real, and he is here again, saving me.

"Let's stand, Lil, we have to get you out of here. Our boat is outside."

Without another word, he helps me up and takes my cell phone, slipping it into his pocket. I hadn't realized I was holding it still; my hands numb from the cold. The rest of his team follows us out as we leave the dark room and into the larger main area.

"This was one bad ass assignment back in the day." They joke behind us.

"Of course it was. Nothing to do but man the guns day and night. No action like the poor fucks in Europe."

I see a curtain of rain falling just outside of the bunker. Storms *had* rolled in. But the thing, the man who grabbed me...

"Where is the man?" I ask, weakly, my voice almost a whisper.

"What, baby?"

Levi bends his head down so he can hear over the sounds echoing through the concrete.

"There was a man..."

"There was no man, baby. No-one is here except for you and us and the bear from the building is dead, baby. We shot it. It's gone now, loaded up onto the Navy vessel. Not ours, but the other one from Whidbey."

I start to protest, tell him about the monster that had come into the bunker, but Levi leads me directly out into the rain. Without a jacket to shield me, I get hit soaked by the deluge immediately. The men also. They train with minimal gear which shouldn't surprise me. It's cold but I can't do anything about it.

Leading onto their amphibious craft, Levi tucks me into his side as one of the other men takes charge and motors us off the beach. For the second time in a few days, I am being rescued by my boyfriend. I know I will never hear the end of it. Thoughts of Brian and Peter fill my mind. Do they know I am found? Do they know I am okay? Too tired to ask, I close my eyes and brace my legs against Levi as we bounce around in the water. It feels like the boat is flying, and it probably is.

"Back to base, our entrance," he barks.

I am getting treated to off limits areas this time it seems.

Something Levi has never done before. Or couldn't.

"We're done with our mission, baby. I'll check you out then we can go home."

"I have work..."

"Not for the rest of the day you don't," he counters gruffly.

Just like the boyfriend I know who wants me to stop working.

"Levi..."

"Lily, I already told Brian. You have another day off. Commander what's his name knows too. So, stop worrying."

He took it upon himself to talk to my work. I shouldn't have expected less. But I have to admit, I am somewhat relieved. Wet and tired, I just want to be warm and fall asleep.

We reach the secret Navy SEALs area of the waterfront and pull into a shed of sorts, which consists of a floating dock and a covered area leading into a building. Nondescript, though, and dark. No markings or signs. Just what I imagined special ops areas to be like. Why do they need to have all sorts of signs when they are all used to covert operations?

"Come on, babe," Levi says, tugging me along as he steps off onto the wooded dock.

Our feet clunk on the planks with each footstep. I want to take it all in, to pay attention more, but I'm finding it very hard to concentrate. Levi squeezes my hand as we come to the glass doors leading inside. Without a word, we enter as heat hits my face from the ceiling vents. It feels heavenly. I must have audibly sighed because Levi glances back and grins.

We move down a few hallways, void of anything on the walls, until we reach a set of doors labeled 'Team 6'. Levi's team. He pushes the door open, and I follow. It smells instantly of shoe oil and gun powder. Distinct, and pungent.

"Over here," he commands softly, showing me a bench in front of lockers.

Senior Chief O'Neill.

Levi's rank and name adorn the worn black locker faces.

64

It surprises me for some reason. I thought he had a separate office here in this building instead of being right next to the guys.

"This is the actual team compound, Lil. I only took you to the main offices the other day. No one and I mean *no one* comes to this area."

He pulls out a first aid kit and slips a blood pressure cuff on me, as well as sliding an oximeter on my index finger. Playing field medic is second nature to him.

"You probably won't remember it, either, once you get to my house and actually sleep."

Beeping, the machine on my arm decompresses.

"Low, Lil. You need water and salt."

He puts the gear away and takes my temperature next, the old school way, under my tongue. I want to gag but I don't. It's been all day since I've eaten, and I feel nauseous. I know he can sense my thoughts, too. Suddenly, I wonder how he can do that.

"Let's go, babe."

Pulling out a hoodie from his locker, he slides it over my head. His cologne lingers in its fabric, causing my insides to knot with happiness. He tugs my hand slightly and I follow him again, out of the building. This time we leave from a different hallway, exiting out under a covered parking area, which, thankfully, shelters us from the rain.

Levi's sports car beeps as he opens my door, helping me in. I love it when he drives this one. His truck is higher up. Jogging around to the driver's seat, he slides in and starts up the engine. Heat hits my back and legs through the heated seats. I lean back fully and close my eyes, relishing the feeling. Putting the car in drive, he pulls out and rockets down the road. Drifting further into a trance, I hear the phone ring through the car speakers.

"O'Neill," Levi answers.

"You done for the day with your girl?"

Levi clears his throat.

"I am. Taking her home to get rest."

"Understood."

"What's up?"

"We need to get a brief name for tomorrow…"

Lulled by the voices, I allow myself to spiral into sleep but not before I hear one last name.

"Deception Pass."

CHAPTER TWELVE

Levi wakes early, while it's still dark out.

"No, not today. Tomorrow. Bring the gear."

He talks so softly; I can barely hear him. I know he is being polite and doesn't want to wake me up.

"She is still here. Naw, man, I need to take her to work. Yeah, her boss is an asshole, they wouldn't authorize her sick days for it."

My boss is an asshole?

He already talked to Commander Lessing, my 'official' boss. I bet that conversation was interesting. Levi can be, well, abrasive when he is trying to get things done. And most officers I have found do not appreciate anyone coming at them in such a manner.

"I need to go. Lil is waking up. Yep."

Ending his phone call, I hear him hum as he pads to the kitchen. Then the faucet turns on and plates are being brought down.

How does he always know when I am waking up?

SEAL training seems to have given him magical powers. He is the most in tune with everything that a person could be, no doubt how they stay alive during missions. As he begins to make us breakfast, he clicks on the TV in the living room. The local news echoes off the concrete walls. Levi lives in a fancy loft apartment. The kind with concrete walls, cedar beams and industrial metal accents. Not my style, but it suits him perfectly.

I stretch and inhale his side of the bed. It smells like cologne which I am in love with. A memory floats to the top of my brain, though, interrupting the moment. Levi had said 'Deception Pass' before I drifted off in the car. I know he did.

What is going on at Deception Pass?

Whatever it was inside that bunker with me said those very

Deception Pass.

Although I get the distinct impression from Levi that there was nothing in the bunker with me, that the door slammed, I got locked in, I passed out and he rescued me. There was no ghost, no bear, no terror.

I stare down at my forearm. If what Levi says is true, how come I have a bruise on my arm where the ghost, or the thing, grabbed me.

It happened. I know it did. It was not my imagination.

Bothered by it all, I glance at the nightstand beside me where my purse was neatly placed last night. And it contains my cell phone.

"Baby, do you want turkey bacon?" Levi calls out.

I smile as I pick up the small leather bag that is now my replacement purse since my original was too waterlogged from being immersed in Puget Sound for so long.

"Yes please!" I call back.

He has excellent taste, I muse, setting my purse back down. And he spent far too much money on it, too. Something I would never do for myself. I tap my phone on and see Levi had also charged it, the battery is now at one hundred percent.

"How in the world did he talk to my boss, charge my phone and obviously get me showered without me knowing?"

My cleanliness isn't going unnoticed. I had been filthy and wet from being in the bunker. Was I also hypothermic and that's why I can't remember?

"I have the worst luck in the entire world," I mutter.

Pulling up a search engine on my phone screen, I settle back onto my pillow and type in 'Deception Pass'. Pictures of the bridge over the water pop up. It is undoubtedly the most gorgeous place. Especially for this part of western Washington. Nothing of any importance jumps out at me, though. I need to broaden my search. Thinking harder, I type something new in. It nets me nothing, though.

"I'm gonna take you in to work after we eat, Lil. You might want to shower," Levi calls out.

"Okay!" I shout back.

Distracted by my search, I type faster, needing to find something, *anything*, that can give a glimmer of an answer to why Levi was talking about Deception Pass. Remembering that pertinent info is usually buried in plain sight, I scroll through the resulting pages that are now on display.

"Hmmm..."

I see park service pages, personal blogs, even travel sights. But then, at the very, very bottom of the search page, I spot something. An obscure article in a medical journal, of all things. And not a common one, either. Goosebumps forming up my arms, I open the page link. It sends me to a lengthy article that has a strange title.

Effects of Deception on the quadrants of the amygdala as seen by nature.

"Lil, are you gonna shower before we eat?"

Jarred out of the trance my mind is in; I hear Levi's voice. I don't want him to know I am looking up this stuff.

"Yes! Getting in now!"

For one, he is smart and will quickly put things together, which could lead him to the documents that Kate and I found. Then two, he would most likely dissuade us from reading it as it's classified above what we are supposed to read. We *have* Secret Clearances, but not Top-Secret. And Levi is by the freaking book with OPSEC, or operational security.

A groan is all I can muster and groan loudly I do. Then I roll out of bed. My body is sore and achy and screaming, "Get a massage." Feeling this way without having worked out is an odd sensation. One I am not used to. I just want to get back to normal. Swimming before work, doing my job and enjoying my evenings in the cozy cabins that the Navy allocated to us. It was easy and predictable. The past few days have been a veritable nightmare.

The luxuries of this loft are appreciated, though. I smile as the rain shower shoots out the most heavenly tumble of water onto me as I step in to get cleaned up for a second time. Aches become soothed as I soap up. Kate should be back today, which is good. I have so much to talk about with her. The man that we both saw, the bear, the bunker, the business with Deception Pass. This assignment has proven to be the most mysterious yet.

"Finally, lazy bones," a low voice rumbles.

It's Levi, coming in to check on me.

"I'm not lazy, just tired. What time is it anyways?"

Opening the shower door, he steps in, sans clothing. I admire his physique as he does mine; our minds are in sync, each magnetized by the other.

"It's barely six, baby..." he says.

Licking his upper lip, he moves closer and reaches out for me. Letting him, I feel pinpricks of desire shooting through my body. Why is sex with Levi so good? And why do I feel that he is holding back at the same time?

"You're overthinking, aren't you, Lily?" He breathes the words into my hair, and I have to laugh softly.

"You are psychic, aren't you?" I ask.

"What if I am?" he asks, enigmatically and pulling me into his arms, I have to giggle.

"If you found out tomorrow that life was simple. Lil, would you move in with me?"

He begins to kiss my neck as I mull over the question. I knew this was going to come up.

"Levi, I like my job. I really do. I can't move in because then I would have to quit."

Tipping my chin up, he narrows his eyes at me.

"And why is quitting off the table?"

"It just is for now..." I protest.

Leaning down to kiss me, I can tell this is not over.

He intends to press for an answer. And Levi can be quite convincing. The kiss deepens as I groan. I feel him in all the right ways. But finally, I break our embrace.

"I'm serious, babe. I love my job. And we aren't married. I can't stop working all together and just be a live-in girlfriend. That is not smart *at all.*"

He touches my cheek gently and looks into my eyes, creating a vacuum in time as we both search without words. I love the way his gaze scrambles my brain.

"I don't expect you to give it all up just to stay my girlfriend, Lil. But you don't have to decide right now. I just want you to think about it."

Gingerly reaching behind me, he grabs the shampoo bottle and begins to wash his hair, what little he has. I sigh and begin to do the same with mine, my thoughts drifting elsewhere. I want to think about what Levi said, but I can't get Deception Pass out of my mind. I might need to sneak off with Kate and take a drive. Once we get to Sunday, we could do it on our day off. And luckily, today is Friday.

We can plan to leave on the early ferry Sunday; tell Brian we are going exploring Whidbey.

Kate will most definitely be down for that. In fact, she will bring snacks.

"I know you're worried, Lil, but you don't need to be. We did a sweep of the island. Every inch of it. There aren't any more bears. The big mother fucker who came into your building was alone. I think hypothermia had set in badly in the bunker and you hallucinated the guy you thought you heard..."

"You guys cleared the island?" I interrupted.

"Of course we did. *You* are there. I had to make sure you were safe and that you would be safe moving forward."

"I didn't think you would have time to do that."

"I didn't do it personally, but the team did. And they were thorough. Trust me."

71

"I do babe..." I say, my head under the rain shower, eyes closed.

I gasp as a pair of lips touch mine. He can be sweet and caring in his own way. And I appreciate it very much. As he works magic on my mood, I see a flash of something dark in my mind. The figure of the man who watched me as I swam from the wood line.

He had a dark hoodie. Levi has a dark hoodie.

CHAPTER THIRTEEN

"Lily, it feels like weeks since we've seen each other. Good grief!"

Kate hugs me, her perfume lingering in the air. Somehow, she brings peace to the situation on the island.

"I know. It's been two days." I grin.

"So," she begins, pulling back to look at me. "Tell me how the hell you got trapped in a bunker?" I laugh as we both sit on our folding chairs in the room we've been working in for weeks.

"Oh, hang on, before I forget!"

Getting up, I look for the folder that Kate and I were looking at, the Top-Secret one. Only now, it's not there. Pulse quickening, I search harder.

"What are you looking for?" Kate asks.

She tries to help me as I rummage through stacks of folders.

"It's ... it's not here! Where did it go?"

Panic sets in as I become frantic.

"Lily, what are we looking for?"

"It's not… it's not..."

Knocking things over onto the floor, I sift rapidly until I feel a hand on my shoulder. Kate's hand.

"Lily Morgan. Calm down!"

Her words are firm, and they snap me out of the desperate state of my mind. Looking over my shoulder, I know exactly what happened. Or at least I think I do.

"I bet the man took the folder."

"What folder?"

"The Top-Secret one we found, and you were reading. I hid it and now I can't find it. But that man, the one that I saw outside the window, and you saw earlier on the island, I bet it was him."

Kate softly gasps.

"I thought you brought it with you..."

"To Levi's? There is no way. *He* of all people, would have taken it immediately and then he would have called Commander Lessing."

"He would *not*, Lily!"

"Oh yes, he would! He is such a stickler for that sort of thing. He cares about OPSEC more than he does our relationship."

"Well, he is a SEAL. I can see that. But what did you do with the folder, then, if you didn't take it home to Levi's?"

"I hid it, tucked away in here. But now it's missing."

Kate nods in acknowledgement and continues helping me. It is clearly important to her, almost as equally as it is to me. I bet she wishes she had just taken it home the day she found it, instead of leaving it and reading it here.

"Well, we technically were supposed to turn it in right away. So, we can't get too upset. Wait, weren't there a crap ton of Navy personnel here yesterday when the bear was here?"

"Yeah, they sent a recovery team to take the carcass away. They were in the building for hours."

Kate stopped searching and looked at me.

"Then they probably came in here. That is the most logical explanation."

"Or..." I begin, "the man we both saw, outside the windows, he snuck in the building."

Walking around the stacks of documents towards the filing cabinets, Kate bends down to pick something up.

"Or..." she counters, "someone *was* in here. But not who we think."

Holding up a small metal object, we both softly gasp. It's a pocketknife. One that we have seen before.

"Fucking Peter," I mutter.

"Did he come in here to help you at all?" she asks.

"No. No. He stayed with Brian in their area, but obviously he *did* come in here, after I left. Maybe when Brian gave us the hour-long break after the bear incident. That's when I left to take a walk outside and found the bunker along the south side of the shoreline."

"This is definitely his, the turd. Look at the monogram," Kate exclaimed.

She turns the knife sideways, so we can both see the words etched in by his loving wife. Peter constantly flashes things like this to us and loves to brag about how awesome his wife is to him. They are quite a materialistic pair. He must have dropped the knife while he was sneaking around in here and didn't realize it.

"I don't know why he would snoop on our work. They have more to go through in their area than we do," I say.

"What should I do with it?" Kate asks. "I mean, we can keep it and pretend that we didn't find it, so he won't know that we know, or we tell him and see his reaction."

"Let's mess with him. Tell him we found it. See if he sweats."

I shouldn't be excited about this, but a part of me is. I like Peter, but he annoys me at the same time. And coming into my workspace bothers me for some reason. I don't like sneaking around.

"Okay, let's go," Kate says, motioning me to follow her.

Electricity humming in the air as we leave our room, I can't help but think of the man in the dark hoodie. It could have been him still, even if we know Peter was in there, too. The thought nags at the corners of my mind.

"Hey ladies, what brings you to grace us with your presence?" Brian says as we walk in.

Their workspace is filled with warm sun, as they are facing the East.

"Peter dropped something in our area, not sure when but..."

"Dropped something?" Peter asks, stopping what he is doing to look at us.

His face tinges a soft red, and I notice his hand is beginning to shake.

"Yes, you showed us this before, I think, when we first came and were around the campfire."

"His pocketknife?" Brian asks.

"The one," Kate says, handing it to Peter.

Peter takes it gingerly, his face a darker shade of red at this point.

"Why were you in their work area?" Brian then asks, his face scrunched up in annoyance.

"I wanted to make sure nothing needed to be turned in. I checked at the end of the day because Lily was missing, and Kate was back in the cabin. Just trying to help out the team."

"That was nice of you, Peter, but you should have told me so that I could have helped."

I clear my throat, "Did I leave anything sensitive?"

Peter looks at me and I can see fear in his eyes for a brief moment.

"No. You did a good job clearing things out. Nothing was labeled Top-Secret that I saw."

Liar.

"Okay…" I say.

"How is the work going, ladies?"

Brian continues to sift through an orderly stack in the middle of the room, placed on top of an old desk. This room has more furniture than the one we are currently working in, which I am envious of. Kate and I seem to get the short end of the stick at work. But not with the cabins. The cabins, Brian made sure to give us the best ones, that face the water and the shoreline of the island. Instead of the scary ones skirting the woods.

"Good, on our way to take a break, though. I want to see where the bunker is that Lil found, if that is okay? We are about down to only one quarter left for sorting."

"Of course it is, Kate, you are just as senior as me."

Nodding, she smiles at Peter, and we head back out into the hallway.

"Well, now we know that he stole it," she exclaims quietly.

"Yes, he sure did. But why?"

"Who knows, he can be a little shit sometimes."

I wonder whether there was anything more sinister than Peter just being an asshole. Why? Why would he want to check out our work that particular day? Had he been spying on us? Did he know we had found a Top-Secret document and hadn't called it in? And if he did know, then where was the file? If he'd taken it because he was going to call it in, we'd have been given nine types of hell by Brian and Commander Lessing. If he'd taken the file, it was clear he'd kept it to himself. Why?

Kate pushes the front door to the building open and walks out into the crisp fall air. It is tinted with hints of rain that are still to come, the color a melancholy grey. She follows me down the worn path that so many Navy sailors and officers had used before throughout time. My mind drifts off to images that I had seen online prior to taking this assignment. Black and white pictures of workers dressed in starched whites and blues. Then I fleetingly think of Deception Pass and the words 'Medical experiments,' 'human trafficking' and the missing Top-Secret file.

"So, tell me what possessed you to go walking this direction? Did you know there was a huge bunker there?"

"No, I didn't. You know we haven't had a chance to explore much at all. Only the swimming area that I go to and then Whidbey once you leave the base. But walking, we haven't done it yet."

"That's true. It's like this at most every place I have worked though. We get in, hit the job hard then leave. No time to sight see."

"I came along the shore here..." I say, explaining what we are seeing. "Then a cute path appeared. See?"

Pointing downwards at the cobblestones, Kate nods.

"I can see why you followed it like a dumb kid lost in a store!"

"Hey!" I laugh. "I am not *that* dumb!"

We walk along the stones until the bend comes into view, then the bunker.

"Oh my!" Kate exclaims. "It's *huge*."

And it really is. Getting to see it again for the second time, I notice the size.

"I can see why you wanted to explore it. I do, too. But not go into any rooms that we can get trapped in."

Wandering slowly past me, Kate marvels at the concrete bunker. Tiny rays of sunshine break through the clouds, dappling in and out at various spots along the grass and ground. It's beautiful, just what we need. Careful to step around a large puddle, I see mud has been disturbed next to the cracked concrete sidewalk. A set of large prints trail off towards the foliage in the trees.

Someone was here.

CHAPTER FOURTEEN

"Ghost stories have been around since Roman times in the first century. Ever hear of the story by Plautus? Called The Haunted House?"

Kate takes a bite of a chocolate candy bar, chewing silently as she narrows her eyes at the last stack of documents in front of her.

"I haven't. You're much more versed in scary history than I am," I say, wishing I had also bought a candy bar from the tiny gas station on our way back from lunch.

This time, we opted to take my Jeep to the main town of Whidbey, a longer drive to the other side of the island. Usually, we take the ferry off the island onto the mainland, like most of the workers on the island. But today, Kate wanted to chat and be alone.

"Why do you think the man we saw was a ghost, though?"

Kate scoffs. "He has to have been a ghost. There is no way a man was running around loose here. I mean, the only way on or off the base or fort is by the rickety bridge that you insist on driving across daily to go swimming. Or, by ferry. And the ferry captain would tell us if anyone else rode in or out. The bridge is monitored via closed circuit TV. Remember?"

"Oh. Right."

Recognition hits me, the briefing we had to endure when we first arrived at Naval Air Station Whidbey Island included a safety brief on monitoring. With such a job as we do, we hear a *lot* about operational security. Even for old, abandoned buildings. The US government likes to hold tight to their property.

"I looked at the tapes last night. No one went over the bridge at all except for you, days ago, when you went to swim then returned from the swim."

"I mean, he could have, too?"

"Swam from the other side of the channel? Not likely. The water is freezing! Would you be able to make that swim?" she asks me.

I frown. There is no fucking way. I would drown before then. There are currents, and the temperature.

"No."

"Well," she replies, with a hint of triumph in her voice, "see!"

The idea of a ghost, a real ghost, appearing on the island is just too far-fetched to me. Ghosts don't leave objects behind.

"But Kate, seriously, have you ever known a ghost to move things? Or wear *real* clothing?"

"Move things, yes. When I was in Virginia, I heard doors being shut all the time in one of the buildings where I knew I was alone. And lights would go on and off. The apparitions were doing it. Ghosts. Poltergeists. But wearing real clothing, no."

"Right. So how did we both see a black hoodie on the ground? How could a ghost do that?"

Getting up to throw her candy wrapper in the trash, Kate sighs and then stretches. She is an expert at ghosts, and I trust that she can help us figure this out.

"Lily, there are a lot of things that go unexplained in the spirit world, I've found. Most of it can be debunked or disputed. It's hard to have concrete answers when weird things start happening around you. The command at that Army base, for instance. When I brought it up to them, they treated me like I was insane. Even had the Master Resiliency Trainer who was a certified psychologist talk to me."

I thought about this for a while. "Do you think our command think we are going crazy, too?"

The afternoon light was fading, and dark clouds rolling in. Time for us to clock out.

"Come to my cabin once we get back, I've got chocolate chip

muffins, and I'll make some coffee. I want to go over everything that has been happening. Write it down and dissect it," Kate says, ignoring my question.

Nodding, we make piles for what needs to be turned in and what can be destroyed.

"That sounds perfect." I say, deciding not to push her for an answer.

And really, it does. I need some comfort food and to sit out by Kate's mini fire pit off her porch. Levi is back at work and told me it might be days before I see him again. They probably have a mission that he can't tell me about. I only know when he will be gone for months, as he tells me in the most cryptic way. Never where or for what reason. But I imagine when I check the news and see something going on conflict wise that is big, he is likely there.

"Alrighty, all good. Let's go join the boys and head home. I am ready to be by the fire!" Kate says.

Following her out of the room, I shut the door behind me, the Top-Secret file on my mind. Brian and Peter are already outside, waiting for us so Brian can lock the building door. One of the reasons why he is the unofficial group leader is that they gave him the keys when we first arrived on the assignment.

"You ladies up for some barbeque burgers? I bought some charcoal and have the patties ready in my fridge."

"Maybe later. Lily and I are going to enjoy a fire first," Kate says, as we walk towards the dock. "Not too hungry as yet."

"No problem. Peter and I can enjoy a whiskey first, then."

Peter grins and eyes me sideways. I can tell he is still nervous about what happened earlier. It's bad form to check after each other in this line of work, unless you suspect someone of being dishonest and he has zero reason to think that. Okay, so *we* haven't turned in the folder to be destroyed yet. Our motives are not to sell government secrets, only to read them, which we are supposed to do in our job, anyway.

Then why do I feel sneaky?

Shucking off the thought, I chalk it up to stress. I am one of the most honest people you can meet. I hate lying.

"Ferry is coming." Peter says.

The wind picks up and tosses my hair into my face. I push it back, tucking the bulk into my jacket. Stray leaves from a Japanese maple tree blow over our feet, trailing off into the water where they begin to float and tumble into the incoming surf from the boat. The tendrils of hair left whipping around me are tickling my face as I look back at Peter.

Peter lied though, easily.

The thought begins to disturb me. He has the folder, or the man that Kate and I saw does. Either option is frightening, though I don't know exactly why. I never had a chance to finish reading the contents or understanding what it said.

"You okay?" Kate asks, coming to stand by me.

"Yeah…yeah," I whisper, trying to convince myself.

She frowns and looks at Peter. Then back to me. Our eyes exchange unspoken knowledge, and she nods. The ferry pulls up to the dock and we watch as the gangway is lowered then extended, its metal arms clanking in the wind. Time to get off the island and be taken home to another.

As I walk aboard behind Kate, my mind can't help but wander to the etching along the interior room wall in the bunker. *Deception Pass,* it said.

Why? Why do these two words keep haunting me? I shiver at my own thoughts, glad when I hear Brian's voice break into my ruminations.

"I don't know about you ladies, but I am so hungry I could eat an entire cow. Do you think anyone farms on these islands? The soil has to be fantastic for it, it's always raining," Brian quips, standing near our seats.

"I'm sure they do. Why not?" Kate says.

"Did you ever go exploring when you closed that base in

Germany?" he asks her.

"Germany. Heavens, I haven't thought about that assignment in ages. Yes, I did, as a matter of fact."

"Did you find anything - unusual?"

Both Kate and I raise our eyes to meet Brian's. Why on earth would he ask that sort of question?

"Unusual? In what way?" Kate's voice has a hint of suspicion.

Brian hesitates. "I guess I mean like the weird stuff that keeps happening to Lily; stuff that isn't normal."

"Are you saying I'm not normal?" I challenge him.

Kate intercedes. "Of course you're normal,' she says, tersely. "You can always tell people who aren't normal. There's always something off about them. You can always tell if something is hidden behind their eyes. The eyes don't lie."

CHAPTER FIFTEEN

The fire crackles and sparks, flames dancing in the evening light. Clouds have moved enough to give us a show. Vivid purples and oranges streak upwards onto the cloud cover, illuminating our faces with their brilliance. It's a perfect evening. Only the conversation is dark. Not relaxing, not by a long shot.

"Was there anything before the man in the wood line? Any other time you've swam, that you felt you were being watched?"

Kate scribbles in a small notebook, a large plaid blanket covering her lap and shoulders. She looks like a cozy mummy which I smile at, despite the subject matter.

"No. Not that I can think of. I never felt like I was being watched before. Never here in Washington."

She frowns, tapping her pen on the paper. Sparks crack and shoot upwards like little mini fireworks, the embers fizzling in the fading light. I love outdoor fires. There is just something soothing about them. It brings me back to happy memories, camping as a child.

"Okay. But think back to the morning you swam last. How did the day start? What happened, tell me details."

Leaning back in my Adirondak chair, I snuggle under my own borrowed blanket and close my eyes, thinking. That morning had been a bit of a blur.

"I woke up early, like always; made a quick espresso shot in the kitchen in my cabin, also like always. Then hopped on the six-a.m. ferry, like always."

"I get that it was the same, Lil, but *think*. What minute detail was different? Was everything outside your cabin the same when you left? Did you notice anything off, no matter how small?"

Opening my eyes, I think back. I see the kitchen and my espresso machine. The lighting was soft as I only turned on the hallway light and under the cabinet lights, which are dim, for ambiance. I am dressed in my bikini, wetsuit and a large hoodie, ready to head to the island to swim. Nothing is different.

"No…not really…" I trail off as my mind returns to the morning.

I grab my wet bag that has my towel, keys and clothing to change into after my swim and shower at the main building. Leaving via the front door, I lock up; the porch is still illuminated by the tiny light that looks like an old antique hurricane glass. The cabins are vintage, having been built in the late 1940's. It's craftsmanship you don't see anymore. As I step down the three wooden stairs to the wet grass below, I *do* remember seeing something odd. An old coin. It was off to the side and had been stepped on before. Probably dropped by one of the maintenance workers or cleaners. I didn't stop to pick it up, I just noticed it. The ferry was already waiting for me.

"Well, there was a coin, outside my cabin on the ground as I left."

"A coin? Where?" Kate asks, straightening up in her chair.

"At the base of my stairs, in the grass."

"Where is it? Did you pick it up?" She asks.

"No, I had to get to the ferry, and it was already waiting for me. I chalked it up to a worker dropping it. It looked like it had been there for a while."

Abruptly standing, Kate's excitement is palpable. She wraps her blanket around her shoulders, the excess material bulky.

"Let's go look."

"Okay, but it's dark as shit …"

"I have a flashlight, silly."

Clicking on a small slim flashlight, Kate lights up the dark pathway that connects our two cabins. Mine is offset to the side by thirty feet or so. I leave my blanket on the outdoor chair and shiver at the lack of warmth. Even with a sweatshirt, it's still cold at night.

"Was it a normal coin?" Kate asks over her shoulder.

The flashlight beam bounces precariously along the gravel and stone pathway, casting an eerie glow as we walk. In the distance, I can hear crows or ravens talking to each other. They love our area of the island, probably because the guys can leave scraps of food waste out when they barbecue. This also can attract bears if Brian isn't careful.

"There," I say, pointing in the dark.

Kate finds the half shiny metal and bends down to pick it up. My porch light glows like a beacon in a storm, cutting a soft path through the darkness with its beams. Everything else is in place. A small pot with a flowering plant sits vigil by the door as well as a worn welcome mat. No other furniture is on my porch.

"Lily, this is an old challenge coin. The kind a person gets from work, for achieving something."

Holding it up for inspection, she shines the flashlight directly on the face of the coin. I move closer to get a better look. She is right. A worn phrase in Latin stares back at us. *Mare Secretus*.

"What does that mean?" I ask.

Kate pulls up her phone and types in the words for Google Translate to tell us.

"Seas and Secrets."

"How odd. . ." My voice peters out and I shiver.

The coin is a basic worn silver with a black enamel background on the front. Kate tucks her phone away and returns the flashlight beam to the object, turning it over. We both suck in a breath at what we see.

Fort Warren Special Operations Division – Deception Pass

There's a skull and a snake's head with a long body coiled around it imprinted boldly on the back of the coin. Suddenly I feel as though all the oxygen has left my body. There it is again.

Deception Pass.

"Why does it say Deception Pass?" Kate asks. "And why the scary images?"

I have no idea, and I can't understand why I keep seeing this. Only that we need to go there, in person. And soon.

"Let's go to Deception Pass tomorrow. I'll drive," I suggest, suddenly.

"I'm down. I keep hearing about it and wondered what is there."

"You keep hearing about it?"

"Yeah, well, my internet browser keeps sending me videos on it and ads. It's weird. But it does look beautiful there. I wonder why this coin mentions it, though. I didn't think the Navy had anything near that area. It's state land, not federal."

"That's tracking for you. Everything you say or is said around you is being monitored," I tell Kate, alluding to the search engine.

"Now *that's* a scary thought..." she says, leaving my front yard and following the path back towards her fire pit area.

The glow illuminates about four feet out in all directions, but the rest of the yard is pitch black. It's officially nighttime. The smell of burgers wafts in the air. Brian and Peter are out cooking.

"God, that smells heavenly. I'm getting hungry. But I don't want to go over to Brian's tonight."

"Me either. I just want to sit by the fire."

Each settling down in our spots, we huddle back under the blankets.

"Kate, do you think a ghost left that coin?"

She turns her head to the side, having relaxed back into her chair. As she answers, goosebumps form on my arms.

"Depends on who wants to relay a message to you."

"You believe spirits are only here to give us messages?"

"I believe they do, yeah, when necessary. In Germany I ran

into a spirit. I never told anyone. It's a story I like to forget."

A log shifts in the fire, crumbling into the bigger ones that are burning in the center. The crackle and pops soothe my now heightened nerves. I want to hear what she has to say, but I am afraid it will ignite my own imagination further, making it almost impossible to sleep later tonight. But, as with a slow burning fire, you can hardly stop the momentum once it is lit.

"What happened?" I ask softly.

She bites her lower lip before clearing her throat. Looking up at the stars, she exhales.

"I was in Munich. I took a weekend off instead of hitting the job hard. We had a long contract there and didn't need to work fast. Honestly, it was a good assignment. When else can you say you worked in Europe for six months?" she began.

Another log shifts in the fire, sending sparks up with a tuft of smoke that gently waves in the air. My fingers clutch the softness of the blanket covering me as she continues.

"On the second night there, I decide to take a walk from my hotel. It was well past midnight but not early enough for any of the bakeries or early morning places to be open. Only a few drunk locals were out, and none bothered me."

I glance past the fire out into the waters of Puget Sound. With the moon and stars out, tiny shimmering tips of water can be seen, ethereal in the darkness, like diamonds glistening in the depths of the deep. It should be quite beautiful, only its beauty isn't showing at the moment. Instead, it makes me shiver.

"As I walked down the cobble stone street, I noticed a miniature castle I hadn't seen before. It was small and tucked away down a side street. I wanted to see it, so I decided to explore. Once down the alley though, I felt air so cold I thought it was winter. Only it was late July. Still hot."

"Cold air? Like the stories of air that accompanies ghosts?"

"Yes," she says. "The same."

"I heard a sound behind me, like a scraping of fingers on

metal. When I turned to look, I came face to face with a dark figure."

I glance at Kate's face as she hesitates. There is real fear in her eyes.

"What did it look like?" I ask.

"He looked a lot like the man I saw outside the cabin, only dead."

CHAPTER SIXTEEN

My dreams were fitful.

Ding. Ding.

Notifications ring out softly from my phone on the dresser. I can't open my eyes yet, as I lay cozily under my comforter. These cabins are drafty at best, even though renovated, and early in the morning, it is hard to get up. The inevitable wall of cold will drop you to your knees.

Ding.

"Who is texting me?" I moan.

Braving the chill, I stick my arm out and grab the cell phone. Opening my eyes, I look at the screen. *Levi.*

Good morning, baby girl.

Are you heading out anywhere today on your day off?

Be safe if you do and take mace with you.

Lips in a soft smile, I bite my lower lip. He cares. Texts in the morning are not something he does, even if he isn't out on a mission and gone. He was supposed to be gone right now; he sent a text last night saying that he would be out for a week or so and for me not to worry. This is unexpected, indeed. I send him a reply.

Morning babe. I am going to hang out with Kate, take my Jeep out to town. Maybe do some shopping. Hope you are safe.

He replies almost immediately.

Be safe in town. Bring mace, promise me.

Mace twice? That is odd, even for him.

OK, I will. I love you.

A few minutes pass as I wait for his reply. Just as I give up and begin to sit up in bed, a notification rings out.

I love you more.

Smiling now, I brave the cold and shake off the blankets. He does love me, and he took the time to let me know. A good relationship is probably one of the most overlooked things in this life. Most never get to experience it.

Feet hitting the soft rug under the bed, I grab my fluffy robe and walk out of the bedroom. It's still super early, and the sun isn't up yet. Putting the necessary ingredients into the coffee machine, I hit the start button. Looking out of the front window over the sink, I stare into the darkness that is the front yard. The porch light doesn't even hit this section. I imagine deer out there, munching on early finds before us humans disturb their feast.

Something moves.

Something darker than the shades I see.

"What?" I mutter, leaning closer into the pane.

I know I saw something moving. My heart races as my eyes dart back and forth, searching for what I just witnessed. Then, I see it again. A dark figure runs past in the yard, in the opposite direction. Deep thudding in my chest, I step back quickly. I need to grab something. Now.

Running to the fireplace, I snatch up the long metal poker that is used to stoke the fire. Gripping it hard, I move to the front door and wait, heart going wild.

Thunk, thunk. Thunk, thunk.

My mouth goes dry as time is suspended. Hands shaking, I struggle to hold the poker in a defensive manner.

This can't be happening.

Thoughts race furiously about who is outside. Unable to be a victim, my mind screams, "Check it out!"

Blindly, I walk to the door and decide to be on the offense. The front porch is plenty small enough, I should easily be able to fend off anyone, *before* they try to break in. It's what Levi would want me to do.

Gripping the doorknob firmly, I fling it open as a bead of sweat trickles down my back under my pajamas and robe. The porch is shrouded in a thin layer of fog, as is the front yard. It's spooky just like a horror movie. My heart is thundering. Beads of condensation seem to land on every part of my body, and I can feel the exposed skin become wet.

Then, I see the man. He darts from the wood line to the left, back into my yard. A scream is suspended in the air. I can hear it in my head, but it doesn't manifest into reality. I need to react. I need to do something. *Anything.*

"Who is there?" I shout.

My voice sounds odd, off. Like it's not my own.

"Hello?" I shout again, gripping the poker firmly in my hand.

Ready to swing, I dart my eyes around the yard. The man disappeared in the shadows, and I can't pick him out. If he is watching me, I have no idea. A twig snaps, causing the bushes to rustle. A few birds fly out across the porch, their wings a loud chorus of flaps in the air. I hold the poker up like a baseball bat, ready to strike. The darkness holds fast, dawn still hours away.

"Lily?"

A man's voice rings out across the yard.

"Are you okay?"

I look in all directions, frantically. But I don't see anyone.

"Who is there?" I shout.

More leaves crunch and I hear bushes rustle. This time, louder.

"It's me, Peter."

Suddenly, I can see my coworker in the yard, as if he was an apparition that just materialized. He stares back at me with a look of confusion, and fear. His eyes dart to my arms. Lowering the fireplace poker, I exhale.

"Oh, my God, Peter! Were you just running around back and forth out here?"

My tone is angry and forceful. I want to punch him, for scaring me shitless.

"I have been jogging, yes. Could you see me in the dark?"

"See you! I thought you were some sort of intruder! You darted so fast by my front window. Multiple times!"

Peter exhales this time.

"I'm sorry, I only crossed your path once..."

"What are you doing up so early, Peter?"

Kate's voice cuts him off, startling me. I grip the poker tighter and turn in her direction. She is wearing a cozy sweatsuit and puffy jacket, and tennis shoes on her feet. Not workout gear per se, but something you would wear to go for a walk. And she looks pissed. Glancing at me, she arches an eyebrow.

"I can't run? Is Lily the only one who can?" Peter retorts.

"Are you okay, Lil?" Kate asks me, ignoring him

I nod, trying to figure out what was going on. I know I didn't imagine a man wearing the same clothes that Peter is wearing, running back and forth. It was *real.*

"Where exactly are you running to?" Kate asks.

"Just the perimeter of the island. Obviously, I had to cut through the woods, and there is a small trail I had no idea was there. It's pretty and there's an abandoned cabin on the far side. This island is bigger than we thought. I clocked in six miles from my door clockwise and back to Lily's cabin."

"Six miles? There is no way it's *that* big. I remember in our briefing; they said it was only half that at best!" Kate exclaims.

Putting the poker down on the wooden porch, I shiver in my robe. The cold creeps in now, as my mind begins to come down off of the fear it just experienced. If what Peter is saying is true, then this island is an illusion of sorts. Just like the man I saw.

"I'm really sorry, Lily. I didn't mean to scare you. This is the first time I came by your cabin though; I swear," Peter says, carefully.

Awkward silence fills the air as our eyes lock. I have no choice but to believe him. Or at the very least, act like I do.

"Don't worry about it. I just didn't sleep well, and I was

probably still half asleep for all I know when I went into my kitchen."

"Gonna go grab a shower and get some breakfast at Brian's. He's making biscuits and gravy. I think he could've been a chef in another life." Peter does not know how his choice of words disturbs Kate and me.

Nervously laughing, we wave him off. Then she hurries up onto the porch, grabbing the poker that I had set down.

"Let's go inside!" she hisses, in a sort of whisper.

I let us both in and collapse on the leather couch by the fireplace. Fatigue setting in from the adrenaline is wearing off. This is not how I saw the morning going, not even close.

"What the fuck happened?" Kate demands.

Taking a mug from my open kitchen shelf, she busies herself with making coffee for us both.

"I don't know…I woke up, got texts from Levi, which is so not like him but was incredibly nice. Then I put on my robe and came into here," I gesture, pointing to the open kitchen.

"You looked out the window and saw Peter's deranged ass running around?" Kate asked.

"Yeah. I mean, it *had* to be him. It was a man the exact same height, same clothing to include shorts even. Hood up, black hat on. Exact same as Peter! Why would he lie? Is he trying to scare us?"

Kate brings both mugs over to the couch and sits opposite me, handing me one of the steaming cups. Taking a sip, she thoughtfully ponders my question.

"It could be him. Or it could be…"

She trails off, looking beyond me into the rest of the house. I get goosebumps at the thought. The unspoken one that neither of us wants to consider.

"The man in the hoodie," I whisper.

CHAPTER SEVENTEEN

Driving through the woods is cathartic. There is just something about it. Especially up in this part of Washington. Every tree, with its massive moss-covered trunks and branches that reach the sky, speaks to me. Whispering to my soul. Beckoning me to stay and explore.

"You're awful quiet."

Kate tucks a candy wrapper into a paper bag that we had just gotten at a small convenience store along the route. I am beginning to think she has some sort of addiction to confectionery sweets. At least I haven't seen anyone consume so much chocolate before. *And* stay thin.

"Mmm," I hum.

The radio is playing soft alternative hits. Moody songs that match my inner vibe. I want to get some answers on this trip.

"I know you want to figure out if that man was Peter or not but honestly, Lil, I think we both need to relax today. Enjoy the water and forests."

"We do," I say, sighing.

I hope I don't look too guilty as I think of the research I have been doing. The Navy had been up to no good here for a long time, secret things and whispers online. Plus, the human trafficking.

I bring my mind back to the present. Hell, I w*ant* to enjoy myself. Stomach grumbling, I instinctively clutch my abdomen. Lunch time is almost here. It took a long while to get calmed down after the morning and to get ready. Kate and I spent a few hours going over what might be happening, to no avail.

"Like, look, that place looks delicious. And it's overlooking the river!"

I look up the road a way towards the object of Kate's admiration.

"That is a cute pizza place," I agree, readying my turn signal so we can pull over.

Another grumble leaves my stomach. I can almost taste the pizza.

"My favorite food as a kid was pizza. Did I tell you that I only ate three things up until the age of nine?" Kate says.

I laugh. "Seriously?"

"Oh, yeah. My parents both worked corporate jobs and didn't cook much except what was in the freezer isle and quick. Pizza, chicken nuggets and those hot pocket things that had ham and cheese in them. Those were my diet staples. My mom would give me fresh fruit, of course, whatever trays were already cut up from the deli. But yeah. I am lucky to be healthy after such a bad diet growing up."

"Did you also eat a lot of chocolate as a kid?"

She blushes a shade as we get out of my Jeep, doors slamming.

"Well, no. I only started eating so much chocolate after my ghost encounter in Germany. It helps me when I am stressed."

Feeling bad for assuming she just loved the sweet treat, I apologize.

"I'm sorry, Kate, I can only imagine how scary that was."

"It w*as*. But it's in the past. We just need to figure out what's going on now, to both of us."

Her mannerisms as we walk up to eat suggest that I don't need to press her on what she experienced. It was *that bad*. The front of the restaurant has plants and more plants. So many they almost block the walkway in.

"Someone likes to garden." Kate laughs.

"Indeed. I always envied people who can keep plants alive. I have a brown thumb. Levi jokes that if we ever do live together, he will buy fake plants."

"Speaking of Levi, how are you two doing?"

I push the door open to the pizza place and a wall of heavenly smells hit our faces, causing us to moan in succession. There is nothing quite like good Italian food.

"Doing good. Other than he wants me to quit my job, my career, and move in with him."

A waitress interrupts our chat. "Would you like a window table? It has the best view in the place."

"Yes, please," I say.

Once seated, Kate launches directly in.

"Did he propose?"

"Propose? No, no. But he did say that he isn't asking me to move in and just date me."

Kate chuckles. "He didn't. That's a half-ass proposal. Like a pre-proposal. Test your response. But not having to commit. Yet. What did you say to him?"

"Well, I said I couldn't quit my job, of course! I mean, there is no way. I love what I do. I need to work. And I am not ready to give up all my financial independence, not just yet."

"Oh, God no! I think that would be a huge mistake. I am all for marriage, don't get me wrong. I was married once upon a time. It can be beautiful. But if you don't have a child yet, stay in your job. It's quite hard to go back to work after taking such a long absence like a lot of young women do for a man."

She is making valid points.

"I agree. Plus, Levi is gone so much. I would spend most of the time alone. It would drive me absolutely nuts."

"Men like to control, sometimes it's innocent, other times it's not. It's good you are sticking to your career. Plus, I want to try and get our next assignment together! There is one at the joint base, JBLM. It's closer to Seattle. They aren't closing the base, of course, but a section of it. It sounds interesting and we should both apply for it."

"That sounds good!"

Our waitress comes back with a very simple menu that has only eight items on it, all pizzas. We order one to share and resume looking around. Out the large picture window where we are seated, there is a tumbling river below. It must connect to Puget Sound as all the island rivers do. A memory of us floating in the water flashes across my mind. I can *feel* the cold again. It is terrifying.

"You okay?" Kate asks, her face locked onto mine.

I hadn't realized how long I was staring out the window.

"Yeah. Yeah, I'm okay. Just remembering the ferry capsizing. The water."

"It was horrible," she says, firmly. "Do you wonder if, well, if someone had tampered with the ferry engine? I've been thinking about it and how incredibly easy it would be to do something like that. Those boats are just moored on base, where they aren't guarded or anything."

Her comment redirects my mind almost instantly.

"On purpose? Why, though?"

"I don't know. I just have a weird gut feeling."

"Do you think one of us is in danger?"

The waitress brings out our pizza as the question hangs in the air. The pizza is gorgeous, bubbling with aromas and steam. The cheese makes my mouth water as I take a slice and place it on my plate. Too hot to hold for very long, I use my fork to cut a piece. Heaven explodes in my mouth as I take a bite. Kate does the same, moaning out loud.

"Oh my….!" she exclaims, chewing. "This is so good."

Once the 'foodgasm' wears off, Kate begins to answer me.

"Do I think we are in danger here? I get a weird feeling, Lily. And my feelings are usually right. I don't think we are being stalked per se, but there are ghosts or something here. Maybe it has to do with things the Navy has done."

"Has done? Like in the past? Military operations?" My mind instantly returns to Deception Pass and my findings. Human Trafficking, medical experiments. What happened to the people? Were they, our ghosts?

Kate nods.

"Exactly. Spirits can become stuck. Or in limbo. I think that and then other things, can come through the veil and be seen by us."

Not being overly religious, I have heard of the 'veil' but don't necessarily believe it.

"I don't know, maybe Peter *was* telling the truth. Maybe he wasn't who I saw running in the yard. It could be a spirit. One from long ago," I say.

The thought sends goosebumps up my arms and takes the excitement of the pizza away, almost instantly.

"I don't think we need to be scared though, Lil."

"I saw a bear, a man watching me then chasing me, I got locked in a concrete bunker with a ghost and I saw another man running around. *Twice.*"

"I know, but you have been so stressed lately. And you did hit your head, in the bathroom, remember? You could have effects from a slight concussion."

She was right, I *had* hit my head in the bathroom. I forgot about that. It's where I saw the dark figure in the bathroom too, in the corner. Kate and I ran from it…or so I thought. I had been dreaming. Or had I? I look at Kate and I cannot fathom the look on her face.

"There is another thought I have been considering, though," Kate says, her voice an octave lower. "What if this place is like Skinwalker Ranch? Haunted."

"I've heard of that place. It's in Utah, right?"

"Yes ma'am. And strange things happen all the time to the workers there. Not unlike what is happening here."

Before she can tell me more, her phone rings. A knot forms in my stomach thinking about the ranch and its supernatural goings on. I had watched an episode of the show that is filmed there on the History channel once with Levi. *You know there is a lot out there that the government is not telling people, right Lil?* Levi had warned me.

"Yes sir, we have the documents ready to go and..."

Kate frowns, an anger line forming in between her eyes.

"Well, yes, we can bring them in today, but we are all off and scattered in different directions. Plus, our contract says we get a day off a week..."

Her cheeks tinge a red that I have rarely seen.

"Yes sir. We will head back."

Hanging up abruptly, she looks at me.

"We have to drop off our Secret and Top-Secret pile *now*. Today."

"Who was that?" I ask in disbelief.

"Commander Lessing himself."

CHAPTER EIGHTEEN

Naval Air Station, Whidbey Island is big. Bigger than I thought. I pull through one of the lanes at the main gate, having just had our IDs checked and verified by the Naval security forces. Kate is still upset over our day off being ruined. I am, too, but for a different reason. I had really wanted to see Deception Pass in person. For myself.

"The weather is finally sunny, too. Look at this shit!" she laments, pointing through the windshield.

"Just our luck, I guess," I answer, merging with traffic.

Lots of people are out. Families pass us with their windows down, eager to get fresh fall air. A large SUV crammed with screaming kids passes by and I glance over.

"My God. I can't even imagine having that many kids. There has to be … what, twelve kids in that monstrosity?" Kate says.

I cluck my tongue. "No kidding."

The lane merges with another as we pass a large area of unit buildings. As I glance over my shoulder and then back, I am now behind the SUV. The light ahead turns yellow and the driver guns it. I brake to avoid getting pulled over by the Navy Police. As I do, I see something that makes my blood run cold.

A man, in a black hoodie, stares at me from the very back of the SUV.

"Shit," I mutter.

My pulse begins to pound, and my palms sweat, immediately. Before they speed off, I focus on the man's face and see a sinister grin. I blink, then the man is gone.

"Lil?" Kate asks.

I can't react. Heart racing, I can only grip the steering wheel. The grin is imprinted in my mind, like if I had just stared directly into the sun, a phantom image that won't go away. He looked evil, and he was looking *at me.*

"Lily, are you okay? You look like you've seen a ghost."

She reaches out with a thin hand and touches my arm.

"Huh?" I mutter.

The light changes to green and I sit with my foot on the brake, still jarred by the grinning man in the back of the SUV. Someone honks behind us.

"Lil, the light is green. It's green." She says firmly.

Coming to, just barely, I step on the gas and continue the drive towards the headquarters where Commander Lessing is waiting.

"Do you need to pull over so I can drive the rest of the way?"

I shake my head, "No, I'm fine. I just saw something. Someone, in the back of the SUV."

"What SUV?" Kate asks. "The one with all the kids?"

I nod.

"Oh, for God's sake, the man won't quit!"

Her phone rings and she picks it up to answer.

"Yes, Commander Lessing, we are on our way. We have *all* the documents. Nothing was left that is Secret or Top Secret. No. Well, that particular room is done anyways, swept of those highly sensitive docs. Yes."

Half listening, half not, I wonder why he is calling for a second time. We already said we were on our way earlier. Finally, Kate hangs up, frustration evident by the way she jams the end call button.

"My *GOD*. That freaking man. He is acting like we aren't professional. Like I don't take safeguarding documents seriously. Or we are hiding something. Which is ridiculous! You know as well as me that we make piles and drop them with Brain's load weekly, on time and like clockwork."

I turn towards the building where the offending man is waiting for us and exhale, letting Kate vent. An idea pops up in my head.

"I bet the Navy is hiding something. That or they think I am crazy now. They *all* didn't believe me when I said what I saw in the bunker. They *all* acted like I had hit my head or something. Maybe he is testing me, to see how I will act or react."

Kate purses her lips, deep in thought at what I had just said.

"If I were you, I would keep that sort of talk to only me. I believe you. And we can't tell anyone about the man either, the one we keep seeing. Have you told anyone else?"

"Just Brian. Oh, and Levi."

"Great. Brian will forget, as he does most things," she laughs. "But Levi won't. Good thing we are not working under him. Has he brought it up at all?"

"No. Just told me to be careful and bring mace with me wherever I go. Normal boyfriend stuff. I don't think he is too concerned. I can take care of myself. And he knows I am smart."

I find a close parking spot and we both get out to stretch. Already the day has brought a lot of driving, and my butt is a bit numb. Kate opens up the back of my Jeep and hefts one of the black canvas bags on her shoulders, leaving the second bag for me. All we need to do is carry them inside and up to Commander Lessing. Easy work.

"That's good. He cares but doesn't sound like he thinks you are nuts."

I laugh, shutting the back of my jeep and beeping it locked. The canvas bag is heavier than I thought it would be.

"Oh, he thinks I am nuts! For wanting to work this job. It's not glamorous and ladylike. But I love it."

"You'll find, Lil, that men have a hard time understanding women who like such a nomadic career. It's not for everyone. I've worked with women who had families even and still traveled to all the bases for months at a time. Majority of them ended up quitting and moving to a more stable contractor job or even just go GS."

103

"Be a General Schedule employee, you mean? Yeah, that is the cushy route, no doubt. Set salary and an office with all holidays off and the healthcare benefits. Yeah." I say.

We reach the front door, and Kate pushes the automatic opener on the wall with her knee.

"I could never stand a permanent office. I tried it decades ago. This lifestyle is all I want to do until I retire for good," she says.

"Here with the documents?" A man in full uniform asks, waiting for us by the front reception desk.

"For Commander Lessing, yes," Kate answers, an eyebrow arched.

We have never had an escort when dropping off our weekly hauls. Something is definitely up. The officer simply nods and begins to walk down the hallway we use to deposit the documents. Only this time, we pass the room and go to the Naval Commander's office. I have only been here once.

"Ladies," the Commander says, greeting us from behind a huge desk.

Kate drops her bag where the escort officer motions, and I do the same.

"Thank you for stopping what you were doing to come in. With the bear incident we are going to ramp up our security protocols for document drops. I will add these into your contract so there isn't any confusion. You can also be comped with a half day for coming in, as well. Tomorrow, there is no need to go in to work at Fort Warren as your team is moving cabins to a different island. Closer to Warren."

"We officially move tomorrow, Sir?" Kate clarifies.

"That is correct, a team will meet you at your current cabins tomorrow to help box and ferry things over."

A beat of silence fills the room, indicating that Commander Lessing was done speaking with us. Kate nods and we exit his office, minus the officer following. We stay silent until we have exited the building and entered back out into the fall sunshine. Halfway to my jeep, Kate coughs, clearing her throat.

"Is it just me, or did the commander seem to be feeding us a bullshit story?"

"No, I noticed it too. If they are really changing or tightening up the turn in protocols, then why aren't Brian and Peter here also? Why just us and *our* documents?"

"Exactly," Kate says.

Climbing back into my ride, I can't help but wonder if the missing folder has something to do with it. Somehow. The thought is fleeting but there.

"Coffee? I'm buying. It's too late to go back out to Deception Pass now, or we will be there in the dark," Kate grins.

"I know. Dang it. I wanted to go today. Coffee sounds nice. They have the best at the Naval Exchange. Is that okay?"

"You read my mind."

I motor us out of the headquarters parking lot and back into the busy traffic of the base. The sun is starting its late afternoon descent, like Kate said, it will be dark soon. Looking at the color of the sky, there will be a spectacular sunset tonight, which we should be able to make, if we finish our coffee and get back on the road within the hour.

"I don't think I could have ever been a Naval spouse, or an Army or Airforce one."

"No?" I ask.

"No. They do travel a lot which is cool, but the being stuck and having to find a new job at every location? No, thanks."

"That is definitely hard. I think the majority choose to be stay at home spouses or moms, though."

Pulling into the Naval Exchange, Kate pulls out another chocolate candy square from her purse, offering me one. I shake my head, having a dislike for the confection.

"Indeed. Like the mom in the SUV with the twelve kids."

We both laugh as we park and get out. The imagine of the

man in the back comes back to mind. The sinister grin.

"Lil?"

"Yeah?" I reply, as we walk up to the large shopping center.

"If anything else happens, I do want you to tell me. Promise? No matter how crazy it seems."

Arching an eyebrow, I nod at her. I am grateful for her friendship, but I thought that was already understood.

You've been acting weird lately, that's why she said it.

My inner monologue was right, I reassured myself. We enter the building to be greeted by throngs of people. Luckily, the line for coffee looked small so we wind our way over. Bumping shoulders with people as we do, I apologize each time. Until I bump into a tall man wearing all black.

"Sorry..." I say, looking up.

He turns his head and looks back at me. The same man from the back of the SUV.

"Oh, that's alright. *Lily.*"

CHAPTER NINETEEN

The man is staring out at me with daggers of brilliant light in the bluest eyes I have ever seen. They distract from the sinister sneer of his thin lips. I look up and his eyes meet mine. Taken aback by the intensity, I gasp I can't remember the last time I saw eyes this blue. Have I ever seen this shade of blue before? They remind me of a glacial pool. He stares wildly at me. My heart races in a rhythmic pattern. It hurts my chest.

"Am I dreaming?" I gasp.

The man chuffs, an otherworldly sound.

"No. This is real." His voice is ragged, almost muffled. It's hard to understand what he's saying.

If it's real, then why has time stopped? I look beyond the man's arms and see that everyone has been suspended. Frozen. People that were once walking are now standing like statues, some in mid-movement.

What is happening?

"Lily Morgan.," the man says.

"How – how do you know my name?" I stammer; fear drenches every word.

"I don't want you to be scared. No, no. That has never been what I want," he says, in his odd, ghoulish voice.

"Who… who are you?" I manage to ask.

He tightens his lips, then grins again, and I see immediately that his face is just like the face I saw in the back of the SUV. There is no doubt in my mind that this is the exact same man.

"Just someone who wants you to carry on, Lily. You must carry on…" his voice peters out, disappears into the sounds that I am becoming aware of around us. I shake my head and open my mouth to speak, but as I do, I watch as the man literally begins to fade in front of me. In a split second he had gone, if he had ever been there at all. *Beep, beep, beep.*

Beep, beep, beep.

Sharp rings echo as I slowly open my eyes. It was a dream. It must have been a dream. But what did he mean, I must carry on? For some reason, I think immediately of Deception Pass and the research I have been doing. Maybe that is what he wants. He wants me to find out things that nobody wants me to know.

He's a ghost.

He *was* a real ghost; I'm convinced of it. The hardest part is going to be not telling Kate. Guilt washes over me as I stretch I'm not going to tell her because something inside me is saying to keep it to myself. An instinct. Or gut feeling. Knowing that this is a survival mechanism, I listened. I don't plan to hide it forever. Just for now. If I am suffering from concussion syndrome, then I need to give my head time to rest.

Suddenly, there is Kate's voice, sharp and urgent.

"Lil! Are you awake?"

Kate raps at my front door. I realize that it is still dark out, and I panic. How did I get in bed? What is going on. I glance at the time on my cell phone; I groan and realize that it's time to get up and get moving. The Navy movers will be here in an hour.

I realize that I have no idea how I got here. What happened after Kate, and I were in the queue for coffee? I hear Kate shout again and I begin to move, to function.

"Coming!" I shout in response.

Struggling to get out of bed, I forgo the robe and make my way quickly to unlock the front door to the cabin. Kate greets me with two mugs of steaming coffee and a bag that smells like delicious muffins.

"I couldn't sleep, so I've been baking and packing up my stuff," she says, handing me coffee.

"Baking? Already?" I laugh.

Taking a long sip, I savor the flavor. Kate is the best cook. In fact, I secretly wish she and Brian would get together. They would make the best power foodie couple.

"When I am stressed, I make food. Not just any food, but *good* food. You should know this about me by now."

"I do; I just slept like crap. Need to wake up," I explain.

Not a total lie. I do feel exhausted. Mostly though, I feel haunted. And I have no one to tell.

"Okay, spill."

"Spill?" I ask.

Kate grunts, beginning to put boxes together for me with a roll of packing tape. The sound is loud and snaps in the space, waking me up.

"Something is wrong, and you aren't telling me. You went a bit funky last night at the Naval Exchange and you wouldn't talk to me about it, so spill."

I decide to tell her some of my worries, but still not what happened at the Naval Exchange.

'So, I've been doing some research – about Deception Pass, this place, what was in that document – the whole thing, really."

Kate begins to pile a stack of my belongings into a box. She is silent. I get the strangest feeling that she's not really very pleased with what I've just told her.

"Do you think that's wise, Lil? Don't you have enough to cope with, having all these strange things happen to you?"

"We have to – I have to find out what's going on here, Kate. Something is going on and I don't think it's just about the document, getting moved from one place to another – it's like the Navy has something to hide." I pause. "Something unexplainable is happening here, too and I think the man we saw is a ghost and is trying to tell us to find out."

"Do you think he is for sure a ghost?" Kate asks, careful to sound nonchalant.

Taping up a box, she begins working on a second as I join

her. Thankfully, I didn't bring too much with me. The job should be done before the movers arrive.

"I hope so," I reply, watching my friend. Her movements are sharp and edgy. "I highly doubt that a random man would actually be running around on the islands by himself. This place is full of security." I think of Levi. He's here, somewhere. "I think there are spirits here. And the one in the woods was watching you somehow. Have you ever looked to see if any secret missions were carried out in this area? Naval ones?" Kate asks. "Is that in any of your research?"

Naval missions? Does she know? Or has she been asked to find out what I know? Sudden suspicion washes over my whole being.

"What sort of missions?"

"Like the type that Levi does but would never tell you about. We do have access to the databases. Our clearances allow it." Kate replies, her eyes fixed on mine.

Blood runs out of my face at what Kate is suggesting. There is no way. We would get caught searching for that. Secret SEAL missions were highly classified. And yes, we could find them online, but I certainly don't want to risk that. Losing our jobs was only *one* possibility if caught. Levi hinted enough times that mission data is being monitored, I know it's virtually impossible.

"Where are you going with this?" I finally ask.

Kate takes a large drink of her coffee before finishing the last box.

"I am thinking that more than meets the eye is going on in this area, Lil. And I want to find out what and why."

A knock at my front door interrupts the conversation.

"Naval movers!"

"Coming, one second!" I answer back.

Nerves suddenly take over. I hadn't expected to ever move from this cabin until it was time to move to the next job in a few months. It's weird actually. Why move us now?

"Beautiful island. If only the Navy took better care of it."

I overhear one of the workers remark as I open my door. Odd thing to say. This island is *very* well taken care of. Only the cabins are old.

"Ready to have these out?" The lead worker asks me.

I nod and let them get to it. Kate and I watch as all my things are whisked away.

"Better get ready. I'll meet you outside," she says.

Hurriedly, I dress in the bathroom then gather my duffle bag and purse, taking my stuff down to the dock where Kate is waiting. The sun is out and shining brightly, only a few clouds in the sky. But it is cold, probably only in the mid-fifties. If that.

"Well, look who is up! Today is an exciting day! Apparently, the new cabins are 'smart' equipped. That's what the workers are saying. The Navy put them together for higher up visitors. No idea why *we're* getting to live in them but I'm not complaining!" Brian greets me.

"Smart cabins?"

"Yeah, like high tech..." Peter interjects.

No shit.

"I know what it is, but I don't get why we would be put in them either."

"Well," Kate finally joins in. "Maybe we are the test subjects, sounds like they are brand new."

As everyone chats about various things, I turn my attention to the water and the thoughts swirling in my head. I can't help but wonder if something else is going to happen. Hopefully, nothing to do with bears, ghosts and sinking in Puget Sound. The passenger ferry is loaded up and the captain calls out as I scan the shoreline. We embark as a crisp wind blows through the area. I shiver, finding our usual seats with Kate.

"At least it's a day without rain. Can you imagine doing this in a downpour? Or even a slow drizzle."

111

"You're right," I say, watching as Peter brings his duffle bag over.

"Hey, can you ladies watch this for me? I have money in it and don't trust the workers. I need to use the men's room."

Kate laughs. "Yeah, of course. But the workers won't do anything."

"Better to be safe than sorry. My wife would so upset if I lost what I am carrying."

I shrug as he walks towards the cabin area where there is the only tiny bathroom on board.

"Why is he carrying money of any large quantity?" I ask Kate.

"He is shady, Lil. I can't pinpoint it exactly, but I have a feeling. Maybe he is taking kickbacks somehow, I don't know."

Kickbacks.

The ferry doesn't take long to take us to the shore of the island where we are now staying. The dock looks new, though, making what Kate said true. It is a new place indeed. Just for us.

Why?

"The cabins here are all spaced a bit further apart, but each has shoreline views and there is a trail system that skirts the boundaries. In the middle is forest."

We listen as the leader of the movers describes the island from a piece of paper he is holding.

"That's about it. We will take your stuff to the designated cabins. Commander Lessing said your names are on the front door, in clear plaques."

Marveling at the simple but modern construction of the cabins, our little working group walks around, checking out the outside of each.

As before, the movers work fast and before we know it, they are done. After bidding them goodbye, Kate and I walk to our respective cabins, passing by Peter's. He and Brian are busy on the shore, looking at the outdoor fire pit area that their cabins share. I glance at Peter's duffle which is now unzipped on the porch. A few clothing items are spilling out.

Black hoodies.

"Do you see what I see?" Kate whispers loudly, pointing.

A lump instantly forms in my throat.

"Yes…"

"You know what those look like? And Peter has *never* worn one that I have seen…"

Fear trickles through my veins as I answer.

"The mystery man's hoodie."

CHAPTER TWENTY

Lifting my arms, one at a time, I cut swiftly through the water. With each stroke, my mind is put further at ease. The water is cold and bites; even wearing a wetsuit, your face isn't covered. It's darker on this island, indicating there is more depth here. Trying not to think of creatures that might accompany such deep water, I stroke more. One arm then the other. Over and over, in a rhythm that propels my body smoothly.

I don't need to take the early ferry to Fort Warren. I can swim right outside of my front door. Which I intend to keep doing. So far, I love the current here. Imagining Kate watching from her porch, I feel at ease and like I can relax. More strokes, as Levi comes to mind. He is out there, somewhere, operating in secret. And he texted me again this morning.

Hey baby, glad you are at the new cabin. Much safer. Enjoy it and I miss you.

He said he misses me. He never says that. Usually, our texts are not about emotions, but practical stuff. Maybe he *is* thinking more seriously about me. Smiling at the thought, I stop to tread water. Something suddenly feels off.

Turning to look in all directions, I only see small waves and currents as the dark water moves around me. The woods are to the far right and stretch down the coastline of the island. Then the cabins dot the left along with people. I see three. Brian, Peter and Kate. They are too far to actually identify but their heights are right. I know it's them. Nothing looks off, so why do I feel like it is?

I miss you.

The words Levi ended the text with pop back up. He misses me. And I know he meant it. Legs kicking slowly, I continue to move my arms in large swirling motions, to keep myself afloat. Still scanning, I see nothing out of the ordinary. And definitely no men in black hoodies watching me. I shrug and start to stroke again, beginning to swim. Only a bit more to go and I will turn around and head back.

Peter's hoodies swirl in my mind as my arm cuts through the water. He had them but never wears them. Unless he sleeps in a hoodie, which isn't likely. No, it has to mean something. I will find out too, somehow. I just need to be clever about it. So, he won't think I am digging. As I feel that I should stop and turn around, I slow my strokes and begin to tread water again, turning in the water. I am down by the woods now. The cabins are not in sight anymore.

Something large brushes along my right leg. Freezing, I look down. The water is pitch dark and I can't see anything. Before I can even react, it touches me again. Rubbing hard against my lower leg now.

"Shit!" I say, frantic.

It's too large to be a fish, way too large. It can only be a handful of things, and the ones I am thinking of are predators. Something splashes from behind. I whip around slowly, so as to not act like a wounded fish. I see nothing.

"Fuck..." I mutter.

Heart racing, I slow my legs down and focus on keeping my arm movement softer.

A whale, a shark?

If one of those is touching me, it means they are curious and that is not a good thing. Especially if they make multiple passes. I need to get to shore. I need to get to shore now. Slowly, I turn my attention to the woods and the beach in front of it. It's a good distance away from me still. I will have to swim farther than I want against the current.

As I begin to do so, I feel a nudge on my back.

"Shit!" I yell instinctively.

What is touching me? I'm thinking of the worst scenario, and it's not keeping me calm. Thudding in my chest intensifies with each passing minute. Swimming has always been good, and I've never encountered any animals before. Nothing more than a few jellyfish or small fish. Certainly nothing like this.

Dampening my emotions, I move in the direction I need to go to reach the shore, arms cutting through the water as I slowly kick. Water splashes in front of me. I think I see an arm come up, but I am not sure. Now my mind is playing tricks on me, and I can't figure out why. A wave hits my face, and I close my eyes. When I open them again to gasp for air, I notice the sky has darkened to an almost black hue. Another storm has suddenly blown in. The atmosphere surrounding me is inky and bleak. Not knowing what to do as panic sets in, I repeat the phrase that bursts in my chest.

Keep swimming, keep swimming.

Another splash crashes next to me, but not as close as before. My heart is racing so hard I know I am in the middle of an adrenaline attack. It's keeping me alive and my mind sharp. But it won't last forever. As soon as I reach the beach, I will feel the infamous 'dump'. Suddenly, I can't think, my mind becomes hazy. The cold water is taking hold. I am getting closer now. I flinch as I kick underwater, my limbs expecting to feel the thing trying to grab me again.

Then I see it again, an arm, then torso surfaces next to me.

The man! The one from the Naval Exchange!

He turns and looks into my eyes as we both keep pace with strokes in the water. I can't speak and I am stricken with fear. His mouth opens as if to say something only for him to be dragged under the water. I yelp and swim faster. Something else was in the water with us and it took the man. Frantically, I increase my speed.

Anticipation building, I finally see the beach in front of me. I kick and stroke until I can touch the rocks beneath my feet. The moment my feet contact the rocky surface under the water I exhale and gasp, as a wave laps at my face. I look down and can sort of see now through the water. There is no-one in sight. As quickly as I can, I trudge heavy footed until I am up completely from Puget Sound. Wind bites at my exposed skin on my face, hands and feet.

"Fuck..." I say, shivering.

Looking around, I see no one. Nothing but the empty stretch of shore that meets the woods. I turn back to the water. I can see a black silhouette, another swimmer sticks up a hand a few yards out, they're swimming backwards and forwards, backwards and forwards. The little blood I have left in my face drains at the sight. He had followed me all the way in.

"My God."

The figure bobs up then down as whoever or whatever it is swims closer then farther away before finally, disappearing all together. Shivering, I stand still as water beads roll down my face and I watch the water. Time ticks by until I am satisfied that the thing is gone.

You are safe. Walk back.

Inner thoughts spurring me on, I trudge through the sand and small rocks. I have a good mile to go to get back to my coworkers at the cabins. The ferry will come soon, and I might miss it. The Navy sticks to firm schedules for toting us back and forth. Which means I will probably have to take a sick day. The prospect makes me feel upset. I don't want to do that.

I wonder if Kate could see me, or what happened, from her porch. Trying to keep my balance is proving hard without shoes on. I slip every few steps. The rocks are wet and slimy from algae that is growing on them. The weather is thankfully holding out though, so I'm not walking in the rain as well.

The woods to my right, I glance over every few minutes. Just checking to see if anyone is there. Or a bear.

"Don't think that!" I scold myself out loud.

Seeing another bear would be unthinkable. Not again. Levi comes to mind as I continue on, and how he would re-act if

117

I tell him about this swim.

It's best I keep it to myself, for now.

Filing this away as just another thing I have to hide, I resolve to not tell him. It wouldn't be a good thing, and he would only get upset at me. He never likes me to swim in the first place, and especially alone. Looking up, I can see the cabins in the distance. No one is outside though, so they all must be getting ready or about to board the ferry. I knew this would happen.

The beach area gradually loses rocks and becomes mostly sand. I can see my cabin first, at the end. Instead of walking to Kate's, I make my way home. I left the door unlocked. There are only four of us here and Kate was outside when I left. She would keep my place safe. Feet finally touching the wood of the porch, I can tell how cold I am. I have barely any feeling left in my skin.

"I'll just shoot Kate a text..."

Opening my front door, I am hit with heat from the wall mounted heating system. It feels glorious. Cellphone visible on the kitchen counter, I reach for it and begin to send a message.

Are you guys still here or did you leave already?

Kate messages back almost immediately.

Where the hell have you been? You got back from your swim, and we didn't see you again!

Confusion hits my brain. I had already gotten back. Did she just see me?

What do you mean? I just got back, had to walk a long way from down the beach.

Little dots appear as Kate types.

No, I saw you come in and you waved at me.

I did what?

I saw you guys watching me...but that was the last I saw you.

I wait for Kate's reply. When it arrives, it makes my skin crawl. *Watching you? I never watched you go out or swim, just when you came in.*

118

The phone slips from my hands as I try to take in what she is saying to me.

"Who did I see then standing on the shore?"

Images of the three people come back to mind.

"This can't be happening..."

CHAPTER TWENTY-ONE

Ferry rides used to be mundane.

They were a part of the day that I enjoyed a lot, but nothing too special. In themselves, it's a lot like taking a taxi ride. But not this morning. This morning the ferry feels like a prison. A prison in my own mind. I haven't been this confused in a long time. This island chain is hiding things. Deceptive things.

"Deception Pass."

"It's a creepy place, that's for sure. Took the Mrs. fishing last weekend. And we felt like someone was watching us the entire time."

Listening to the Captain talk to another worker, I eavesdrop, though I don't really want to. I am already scared enough.

"Watching you, what do you mean?"

Another worker, holding a drippy breakfast burrito, joins the conversation.

"You guys talking about Deception Pass? That place is fucking weird! I camped there…"

"You can't camp there, can you?"

"I wasn't *trying* to camp there. I *had* to. I nearly drowned one day when I was taking the sea kayak out to fish. Something chased me and then I hit a rock. I couldn't see it and it put a hole in the bottom of my kayak."

"Christ! What was it? A shark?!" The captain marveled.

"Not sure…" the guy said, nodding. "It could have been, but if I was to lay bets, I'd have said it was a man. A huge man. Something about him scared the daylight out of me. I ran aground and it was already dark, so I had to camp om the embankment, in a cluster of trees until morning. I was able to hike out to the park area and then borrow a phone. I won't go back there."

As they continue their conversation, my mind remembers my

encounter from this morning. We are not that far from Deception Pass. Was the mysterious swimmer who'd chased me the same one who had chased this man who was still talking to the captain about his encounter. Shivering in the air, I realize my body is covered in goosebumps. But not from being cold. From being scared.

Watching you? We never watched you.

Kate's words return to my crowded mind as I think about the people who were watching me from the shore. The people I had thought were Kate, Brian and Peter. Who were they? And who was the person they saw, and thought it was me? I think of Levi and something he once told me. Losing your mind can occur through deep bouts of stress; maybe this is what is happening to me. Maybe Levi is right.

Maybe you need to take a break from work.

The ferry is approaching Fort Warren now. I can see the dock in the distance. It's practically covered in leaves. Huge orange and brown leaves from the nearby trees dot the woody surface, trailing off into the grass and then the forest beyond. It looks like a master painter has created the scenery.

"Fall here is pretty though, I will give it that," the captain says, readying the boat for letting us off.

"You guys watch out for bears. After the last one, I would be nervous working there with so few people."

I only nod as his warning sinks in, stepping off to head to work. He isn't wrong. We *do* need to be careful. None of us carries a gun though, and beyond the bear spray we now have thanks to the Navy leaving us a few cans, we can't defend ourselves. The prospect is depressing if I think about it too hard. So, I don't.

Making my way through larger leaves then tiny yellow ones, I come to the main building where we are still working. Soon, we will switch to a different one. Only about ten buildings left to go. I want to get inside, get warm, and focus on boring work.

"Finally! Brian had me wait for you."

As I look up, I see Peter. He is indeed, waiting for me outside the front door just as he said.

"Why are you waiting for me?" I ask.

This is weird.

"We are all starting in a new room. Kate finished up the one you were in, and we finished ours, too. Brian wants it to go faster so we can get out of this building finally."

"Okay, but why wait for me?"

"Oh," he says, holding the door open so I can go before him. "We can't wander around outside alone. The Navy wants to be cautious because of the bear. It's coming from higher than Commander Lessing."

"Ugh. Makes sense. Like the buddy system...great."

Our shoes make squeaky sounds on the wood in the hallway as we both walk to the only room with light coming from it. The building feels creepy now for some reason. More so than usual.

"I could never have been in the military. Doing stupid stuff like always having a buddy with you. It's like they treat grownups as children," Peter says.

He motions for me to go into the room before him, so I walk past. He's wearing too much cologne today, the scent hitting my nose as I pass.

"This place probably *is* haunted. I mean, I thought I saw a guy last night by the shoreline. It wasn't Peter, either."

"Who wasn't me?"

We walk into the room to catch the conversation between Kate and Brian. Stacks of documents are all over the place as are a few empty bookcases.

"Oh, hey, Lily. Glad the ferry could still get you!" Brain says. "And just some man, obviously the figment of my imagination. Or a ghost."

I nod at Brian and look at Kate, who pats a chair next to her.

We haven't worked together like this before. I don't mind at the moment, though. The more the safer. Brian has just said he thinks he saw a man, or a ghost. Is it the same one I have seen?

"A ghost? You believe in those?" Peter scoffs.

As I sit, Kate glances at me and mouths, 'You okay?' I mouth back. 'Yes'. I can't tell her anything else about the morning than I already did on the phone via text.

"Of course I do! I never told you about my ghost story on Fort Hood?"

"It's called Fort Cavazos now…"

"Yeah, I'll never call it that. It's always going to be Hood to me. And I saw a few ghosts while I worked on my first contract. We were shutting down a section of buildings, old ones."

"I always wanted to go there, is it as big as they say?" Peter asks. "My wife would love it."

"Yes, it's massive. The biggest US military installation."

"Why would she love it?" Kate asks.

"She has a fascination with the desert and bigger bases. I don't really know beyond that."

"What ghosts did you see?" I ask Brian.

He smiles, never one to back down from sharing stories.

"Well, there are a lot of deceased in that area. A lot of old battles fought there in that area. And Texas used to be part of Mexico. I say all this to give a backdrop to the ghosts I saw. They weren't like regular ones you might see on a base."

Sorting through a pile slowly, I feel my pulse quicken. Thinking of the people on shore, the trio I saw, and thought were my colleagues, I can't help but think they were ghosts.

Brian takes up his story.

"I worked alone mostly on that assignment. We didn't have a lot of help, and I volunteered to take a building by myself. I would go in early, before physical fitness training began, as the base loved to shut down most of the roads for the first few hours of the day."

Kate hands me another stack of documents, as I finish with the one in front of me. Absentmindedly, I take it and skim the first few papers.

"I came in one morning, after a few months of being there, and I settled into work. After about an hour of being in that creepy old building, I had to pee. Drank too much coffee. They have the best coffee places on Hood," he continues.

Goosebumps stick up on my arms. I can feel them through my shirt. I have no idea what Brian is about to say but I am anxious to hear it.

"So, I get up to go the bathroom and have to walk down a long, dark hallway. Just like something out of a movie. Most of the lights were not operable in that building. Instead of bringing a flashlight, which I usually did, I opted to use the flashlight on my phone. Come in handy those things, and bright too."

"We did that before in the bathroom here," Kate interrupts.

"Yep. Super handy. I went into the men's bathroom, and it didn't have any windows, so no outside light to help me see."

Hairs on the back of my neck stand up at the mention of no windows in the bathroom. I flash back to the bathroom here when the lights went out. I could see absolutely nothing.

"Tried the power in there but it still was out. I balanced my phone on the sink, used the urinal and then right as I went to wash my hands, I felt something."

"Felt something?" Peter laughs.

Brian didn't laugh back, though. He kept a serious face.

"Yes. Something touched my shoulder and even left a mark. I checked afterwards."

"Holy crap!" Peter says.

"Who touched you?" Kate asks.

"Well, I turned around and saw a shadow behind me. It was

tall and it was a man."

I stopped looking at the document I was holding and locked eyes with Brain.

"What did he look like?" I ask.

"He was part transparent but also had the weirdest feature…" he trails off, then after a while he says, "He had a wide creepy grin and the bluest eyes I'd ever seen."

CHAPTER TWENTY-TWO

Coffee hits my nose with an assault I can only describe as brutal.

"Ow, so *hot!*" I exclaim, taking a sip.

I made a full thermos to take with me as I rode the ferry and then to drink after my run. Only I delayed running until I make sure there are no mysterious people, be they ghosts, or maybe even bears, along the beach. So far, so good. Nothing but fog and leaves for miles. Fort Warren is a pretty location; I will definitely give it that. Shutting the thermos lid, I glance in all directions as I make my way back to the Jeep. Still, I see nothing. I am alone.

Satisfied that I am safe, I take my phone out of my jacket pocket and go to my text messages. I touch Levi's name. We haven't talked for a few days, just that text telling me to be careful and safe when we were going to go to Deception Pass. But I feel like sending him one. I know eventually he will see it and read it.

Thinking of you, babe. I miss you. It's not the same running without you.

Time to run. I have about an hour and a half until I need to be back in the buildings, and where I can shower before work. Void of rain, the fog isn't so bad. But it does make you wet regardless, if you stay in it for too long. I plan to run a straight two miles out and then back. Nothing too strenuous or hard. Just enough to replace the cardio I was getting from swimming. No way will I ever go back into the water here after that last encounter.

I don't know if I can ever swim again.

Brushing the thoughts aside, I lock my stuff in the Jeep, pocket the key and do one last stretch before heading out. I made sure to have a keychain version of mace in my jacket this time. One cursory glance behind my shoulder and I take off at a jog. My lungs inhale the air around me; it's a nice morning to run.

Brian's story comes to mind, and I push it back. No way I am thinking about the creepy ghost and the possibility of one here. Not now. Not while I exercise. Picking up the pace I am at a full run along the hard sand. It's pretty stable, more so than you'd think. Shoving everything out of my mind, I only focus on the scenery.

Washington has always been a place I have found beautiful. Birds circle overhead and I hear eagles chatter from the trees high above, which makes me smile. They will begin to dive for fish at some point, which is always a beautiful sight. Taking sharp breaths in, I exhale as slowly as I can. I haven't been running in a while, and the first run after a break is hell, totally different from hiking or walking. It feels like you're dying, to be honest. Muscles begin to burn as I traverse the beach. I will be sore after this; there is no doubt. As I continue on, the leaves from nearby trees blow in the wind, causing me to have to crunch them on the sand. Fall is so gorgeous.

I am near the two-mile turnaround point, according to my watch, but I notice something through the trees. Something big.

What is that?

Deciding that I have to investigate, I slow to a jog, becoming parallel to the object. It looks like a train car. A bunch of train cars. I didn't know there were train tracks here, let alone active ones. The cars are sleek and not at all old. Before I know it, I have left the beach and am coming to a standstill in the woods.

"What is this?" I whisper to myself.

Something moves in the cars. Or so I think. I can't really see. Moving on autopilot, I crunch the forest floor beneath my feet with each step towards the train cars. The tracks are seemingly buried beneath the moss on the ground. I can barely view the old metal tracks below. Bending down next to them, I see that they aren't old. The metal is black but very new.

"The hell?"

Reaching down, I touch the metal only to feel a low-level shock enter my fingers. I yelp and pull my arm back. It's *electrified*. Why? I hear something crunching behind me.

"Who's there?" I say loudly.

The crunching stops. Heart thudding, I whip my head around, looking for what is behind me. I see nothing, though, only the dark woods with wet tree branches and trunks. Water drips from each one in soft, rhythmic patterns. Had someone followed me?

Suddenly, a large deer steps out from the darkness. It blinks, brown fur standing out amongst the green. Clutching my chest, I sigh. Just an animal. Not a person. The deer stands staring for a few seconds before it turns back to the woods and heads back to its home. Once I can't see it anymore, I redirect my attention back to the train car. I can see movement again, however slight. It's coming from between the metal slats. The cars are a muted grey, almost the color of the darkest moss. They blend in very well, as if they were a military grade.

Military. Could these be military?

The question is frightening. Never had I expected to see this in the woods while I ran! Thinking it had been here the entire time, every day that I swam, scares me even more.

I need to see what is in the cars.

Creeping slowly, I approach the first box car with care, peering through the slats. Something dark and small moves, causing the entire thing to jostle a little. Sucking in air, I get closer. I don't even realize I am holding my breath until I loudly exhale. It startles me but I am determined to see what is inside. I can't view it properly though; I need to be closer still. Mindful of the electricity that lies on the tracks below, I position my feet, so I am not touching them. Then, I gently grasp the metal

128

slats and push my face as close in as I can. This is by far the most reckless thing I could do in this situation, but here I am. Doing it anyway.

Just need to get a glimpse…

No sooner had the thought come into my mind than someone comes into view. A person!

"Hey!" I say, watching the person turn back into a shadow in the car, out of view.

A freaking person!!

"Who, who are you? Are you okay?" I yell, straining to see into the boxcar.

Only faint scratching can be heard. Then, nothing. My pulse thuds wildly as I slowly walk down the length of the car. A few times my feet hit the tracks, sending electricity up my legs. Not enough to stop me but what I would imagine a low voltage electric fence to feel like. I have to see it, though. Who is in there and how to get them out.

After looking for what feels like ten minutes, I realize the person is intentionally hiding from me. I turn to long slats on the walls of the car, running my hands along them to see if any seams that open exist. The person had to get in somehow. I just need to find the door and get them out. As I explore, I hear crunching sounds again. Thinking the deer had come back, I turn slowly, my hands still on the metal.

It's not the deer, but a few men in black uniforms, through the woods a ways.

"Shit!" I whisper softly, dropping my arms.

Quickly I move around in between two box cars. I try to hide as best I can, ducking behind a tree. The men approach, chatting about work.

"Fuck me, I don't want to have duty all weekend. Why can't they switch us out?"

"Because, dumbass, there aren't any replacements. We are it. No one else on the team knows about this project."

Team?

"O'Neill won't let anyone else know..."

"As he shouldn't."

O'Neill!. Levi! They are talking about my Levi!

These men must be SEAL members. I feel anxiety well up as my heart accelerates. I am having a panic attack. A massive one. There are scratching noises coming from the train cars. *Both* of them. There are more people in them!

What is this? What the fuck is going on?

Feeling as though I will suffocate, I slide down the tree I am hiding behind and grip the leaves and forest floor below, trying to maintain control. But it's no use. This is the worst panic attack yet. I need Levi. I need to hear his words, to know what to do. He would help me. I can't let his team members see me. They can't know I am here.

Suddenly, my vision goes black, and I pass out.

CHAPTER TWENTY-THREE

I come to, water dripping off my face.

"Ugh..."

Opening my eyes, I see light, misty rain in the air, dampening the forest. My hair and my face are damp. The overhead canopy of branches is soaking, and the leaves are dripping rainwater onto me. Looking down at my clothing, I see the black running tights are also wet. I remember passing out as voices of Levi's teammates talked nearby. How long have I been here?

Unzipping my running jacket pocket, I take out my phone and look at the time. An hour.

Did the SEALS find me?

Glancing around, I stay as still as I can. And I listen. Listen to all the sounds around me. If the men are still here, they have definitely spotted me and are probably watching, waiting for me to wake. It hits me that I might even *know* who the men are, after all, I have met all of his team on multiple occasions. A cold chill runs down my spine at the thought. Would they hurt me?

Could they ever?

The team was about the mission, whatever that was at the time. If they were asked to watch these train cars, then they would be prepared to defend them. Hands down. I am in a bad situation, worse than anything else that has happened here in Washington so far. The seriousness is not lost on me.

The wind softly blows through the branches up above my head. Droplets of water plink plunk to the ground.

I am grateful that I can't hear any animals except for a few birds in the far distance. More importantly, I don't hear any scratching sounds coming from the train cars that I can't see.

131

I need to move and survey them again. If I can help the people inside, I will. If there is one person trapped, there have to be others.

Gathering courage, finally, I hold my breath and slowly stand, keeping my hands on the tree trunk I was resting against. So far, so good. No voices telling me 'Don't move.' I step forward and turn. What I see makes my pulse race again. The train cars are *missing*. Gone. Not here anymore. Forgetting about the Navy SEALs, I walk over to the area where the train cars were standing not more than an hour ago. The ground cover looks like nothing was ever there. Train tracks are buried under leaves and moss and bits of grass. I reach down to dig for them and then touch them without hesitation.

No shock.

Only cold to the touch metal. Just metal. Not electrified. How? Why? I begin to look for footprints from anyone else besides me that would have been in this area. But I can't find any. The mud looks completely undisturbed. Even from me. I step into a section of it and then test, to see if my footprints will be visible. They are, thankfully. Running shoe prints follow as I walk.

"How come they weren't visible then where I walked in?" I ask no one.

It doesn't make sense. Unless...

Unless the SEALS swept the area. Got rid of every trace of the train cars. But not me. They left me alive. Why?

Because of Levi.

The answer is obvious.

No way they could dispose of me without Levi finding out. And he loves me. Even the mission would take a backseat to him if it meant it would cost my life. More leaves crunch in the distance and I suddenly feel the urge to run. I can't hide here any longer. I need to get back to my Jeep. There is still time to shower and make it to work. But only if I hurry. Taking off

132

towards the beach, I run. The image of the dark figure in the train car comes to mind. The person looked *sick*. Or too thin. Were they being held prisoner?

Running faster now, I feel like I am flying. I just want to get to my Jeep. I want to shower and to talk to Levi. I need to ask him about all of this. Eagles call from above as I fly down onto the beach, shoes kicking rocks as I hit the last five hundred yards before the parking lot. Finally, I am back to my SUV.

"I can't tell Levi..." I decide. Some innate sixth sense tells me this.

Unlocking my Jeep, I climb in and shut the door quickly. The SEALs could still be here, watching me. The thought sends a fresh shiver up my spine. Turning the heat on, I reverse out of the parking spot and get back onto the small road that takes me to Fort Warren. The journey doesn't take long; it's only a few miles away from the park. Checking the time, I see I have about thirty minutes until I need to be at work.

The Fort still has a small gate entry point, and I drive through it slowly, looking into the guard shack. No one is there, but I am paranoid now and want to check anyway. Only a dark room stares back as I look, then proceed through the opened barriers. The Fort is still monitored via security cameras, too. So, I really don't need to worry so much.

Then how come the man with the black hoodie got in?

Shaking the thought off, I drive to the main building. The one with showers. Parking, I hurry inside with my gym bag. I shower quickly, as I want to get into work before I am late and talk to Kate. Something tells me I can trust her with this. I just won't tell her I passed out. Or mention that the guys I heard were SEALs. It's possible she will be able to help me research and figure out what tracks go through the island. Or at least listen to my tale and nod. Really, I don't know what else to think.

This island is haunted.

"The entire area is haunted..." I mutter, once I'm dressed and walking back to my Jeep.

I have five minutes to spare. Still gonna make it! Parking in my usual spot near the work buildings, I jog to the one we are currently working in. The door swings open and the smell of muffins hits my nose. Kate cooked, or at least it smells like she has.

"Hey, Lil. Brian brought us breakfast from Whidbey, chocolate chip muffins. They are *heavenly*."

Kate greets me, her mouth full of a bite of delicious smelling food. Brian brought breakfast. He never does that.

"I saved you one..." Brian says, pointing to my chair.

There is a brown paper bag sitting with a cute green napkin underneath. I pick up the bag and look at the name embossed on the napkin. *Deception Pass Bakery*. I swallow spit that is stuck in my throat. Did I read this right?

"You got these in Whidbey?" I ask hoarsely.

"Sure did. I know the name says Deception Pass. There is a new bakery on the base with the name. Cutesy napkins, huh? They had tons of bridge pictures and Puget Sound pictures blown up in the store, too. Pretty cool gimmick."

I can only nod. What a weird coincidence.

Kate swallows her bite and looks at me. "How was your run?"

"Good, I..."

"Peter! Let's take the load to the next building. It's pretty heavy already," Brian interrupts.

"Alright."

The two men struggle to lift the canvas bag that we had been filling, proving to be a two-man job. Peter whines as they leave the room, asking why we don't have carts to help us. Brian gruffly explains that lifting the bags is in our job description.

"Wow, Peter has been a pain in the ass lately. He has been complaining nonstop about work," says Kate, in a slightly petulant tone. "I mean, I get he misses his wife, but damn!"

"What happened on your run? You look like you've seen a ghost."

Checking to see that the men have left the building, I shut the room door. Kate looks concerned, and rightfully so. I am definitely not myself right now. I begin to slowly pace the room. The events from this morning were weighing heavily on my mind.

"I started my run, and everything was fine, until I hit the turnaround point."

"What happened?"

"I saw something in between the trees, in the woods off to the right of the beach. I'm telling you, Kate, I saw them." I am doubting myself. Did I see them? What really happened there?

Goosebumps form on my arms and I subconsciously rub them. Kate notices and looks even more concerned.

"Okay, tell me. What did you see, Lil?"

"I saw train cars. Not the normal kind either. Not passenger trains. But like cattle cars." I whisper. I can hear the plea in my voice. I want her to believe me. Hell, I want to believe in myself, too. "With people in them."

"*People?*"

"People..." I nod.

Fear wells in my chest. It is just beginning to really hit me, what I stumbled upon. Like something out of a horror movie. Something I wasn't supposed to see. Something no one was supposed to see.

"What the fuck? Packed in them like cattle?" Kate asks.

"No. I don't know. I could only see one and then other shadows. And scratching. I heard lots of scratching coming from inside."

We hear the outer front door shut and Brian and Peter's muffled voices floating down the hallway. Kate gives me a look of acknowledgement that she understands, and nods.

"Talk more after work," she says quickly, as our coworkers

open the door to the room.

I nod back, trying to calm myself down.

"You cold?" Brian asks, noticing my arms.

I am still rubbing them vigorously.

"Y…yes. It's cold in here."

"That it is. Let me adjust the thermostat. Better to work in a comfortable environment than one you are freezing in."

As he exits the room, heading for the thermostat Peter eyes me suspiciously. His body language is off. I don't know why but I feel uneasy.

"I should have brought you a hoodie," he says, still looking in my direction. "Though I don't know if black is your color.

"Is it *your* color?" Kate asks.

She glances at me, both of us thinking of the hoodies we found and the man we both keep seeing.

Peter chuckles. "Sometimes."

CHAPTER TWENTY-FOUR

Peter is chasing me down to the beach, his face fraught with delight. I scream as I see the glint of the knife in his hand. He is enjoying this, and he intends to hurt me. As I run, my tennis shoes get wet; the tide has come in. It's getting late. I wanted to eat barbeque with Brian and Kate, but Peter asked for my help with something for his wife. Then he lured me to the woods, to the place where I go swimming. To where I swam before.

"You can run, but I will find you. I've been watching you this whole time," he shouts back.

Our voices echo in the air, bouncing off the trees. No one is coming to help. No one is going to hear me scream when he catches me. My only hope is to run faster. To get away. Eagles scream from the trees above. Just like on this morning's run. My mind races with options for how to get out of this. What to do. My phone is in my pocket, but I can't dial. I am running too fast.

"I've been training, Lily; you know I am going to catch up eventually!"

He screams louder now and still, I run. I am flying down the beach. Sand kicks up everywhere as I feel the water numb my skin. I won't be able to feel my feet at all pretty soon. But that doesn't matter. My mind is keeping me alive. Then I hear it.

A train whistle.

Looking to my right, I see box cars moving slowly. They are the same ones that I saw before. Muted grey and silver that blend in with the woods somehow.

"Help!" I shriek, turning towards the trees, which loom above me, dark, foreboding, and unhelpful.

I don't slow, even as I slide a bit on the muddy path. I have to get help. One of the car doors clanks open, the metal scraping as the car moves slowly through the woods. I can catch it, I can jump in.

"That isn't going to help you!" Peter shouts.

I ignore him. A hand sticks out from the darkened train car. A blackened, skeletal, filthy hand.. My mind screams *get in, get in*. Without a second thought, I catapult myself into the opening of the car. Right into the arms of the black hoodie man. He has a wide creepy grin on his face and the bluest eyes I have ever seen. Then everything goes black.

Cologne hits my senses sharply, like a bomb going off. I cough and slowly open my eyes. There is a black hoodie on the chair next to my bed in the cabin. I'd woken from a nightmare about Peter. And this is his smell. *His* cologne. I know it very well, from working with him for months now. It is his. Why is this smell in my cabin? Sitting up in bed, I touch a warm arm. Yelping, the arm moves to hold my leg, taking it captive.

"Morning, beautiful."

From under the covers, the other arm pulls the comforter down. My boyfriend stares at me.

"Levi?"

"Uh, huh. Got it in one."

"How? How did you..."

He reaches out to tuck a strand of unruly hair behind my ear.

"Well, babe, I came back early. I can't talk about my missions. You know that."

Nodding, I look at the hoodie as he clicks on the lamp by the bed. Peter's shit grin as he chased me, a knife in his hand, is seared in my mind. It wasn't real. It was a nightmare. But his hoodie is here. And it felt real. It definitely felt real.

"That hoodie was on the porch when I came up to your cabin around two this morning. It's not yours, that much I know. Did you have someone over?" Levi asks.

"Over?" I say again, turning to look at him.

The look on his face tells me that he thinks I've cheated on him.

God, no!

"No. No, babe. I haven't had anyone over. It's Peter's. His hoodie."

"Peter?" he asks, grinding his jaw. "He was here?"

"I don't know. I didn't see him. But that is his hoodie," I gesture. "And that smell is his cologne. That hoodie is coated in it."

Levi touches my arm one more time as he gets out of bed to inspect the hoodie.

"You actually thought I had a man over?" I ask, in disbelief.

He was never the overly jealous type. In fact, he hardly ever got jealous at all.

"Well, no man wants to think that. But I came to surprise you," he says, holding up the hoodie, looking at it closely. "And you have a man's hoodie reeking of cologne on your porch. So yeah, I kind of had a moment of doubt."

"I would *never* cheat on you, Levi. Never."

He puts his thumb through a loose seam in the armpit area then feels in the front lower pocket where you put your hands. Some sand falls out. When I see the grains tumbling onto the hardwood, I flash to the dream I had. It felt so real. Peter, with a knife, chasing me on the beach.

It was just a dream.

Wasn't it?

"I know that babe. I know you wouldn't. I *do* want to find out if this is Peter's hoodie. Get him to eat a candy bar today. Take the wrapper when he is done. Or better yet, take coffee for everyone, and then take his cup when he is done. That will give me the DNA I need to see if it matches this."

"DNA?" I say, wide eyed.

He can't be serious!

"Yes, Lil. I need to know if my girlfriend is being stalked or harassed."

139

I nod, realizing he is serious and won't let this go. I could easily bring in coffee. There is a drive-thru place about ten minutes outside of Fort Warren. And my Jeep is just sitting there, waiting to be driven. Plus, Brian did bring in muffins yesterday. It won't look weird.

"What time is it? Am I late?" I ask, whilst looking for my phone.

"It's exactly two hours until you need to leave on the ferry," Levi answers, tugging me to the edge of the bed. His eyes alight. "You need to relax, baby. You are tense as hell."

I rest my face on his abs as he begins to rub my shoulders and upper back. It feels heavenly. And he isn't wrong; I am terribly tense.

"Have you been swimming lately?" he asks softly.

"Yes..."

I don't want to tell him about anything that happened on the beach, whether real or imaginary. No way in hell, he will flip if I do.

"Be careful. Promise me, okay?"

"I will."

He continues to work on my muscles and even finds a few knots to rub. It hurts and I want to tell him to stop, but I don't. It will help me out in the long run to let him work his magic.

"Do you want to go on a vacation once this job is done for you?" Levi asks.

I groan, moving my face to the side against his bare skin.

"Yeah, babe. Where to?"

"I was thinking about London. We can stay in some old hotels, see historic things, do tourist stuff. I've been with the team numerous times but never for personal reasons. You will love it. We can even make a short trip to Ireland on the way out. Want to stay in one of the oldest castles there? I know the owner."

The description is intriguing and sounds downright perfect.

"Of course! I'd love that. But I don't know how much downtime I will have between this and the next job. Kate says there is one on JBLM. Near Seattle. I want to apply for that so I can stay in the area at least."

He stops rubbing my shoulders.

"You are still set on working past this job?"

"Levi, I can't just quit. I can't. I explained this to you, I thought you understood."

Sensing his frustration, I stop talking. I know he wants more from me. But he has to also give me more in return. As if reading my mind, he pulls me up and proceeds to get on one knee.

He can't be serious.

I suck in my breath.

"Lily Morgan. Will you marry me? Not today, not tomorrow, but in the future?"

I can't think. He isn't holding a ring, and the proposal is confusing. He wants me to feel secure, and this is how he does it? Before I can react, a loud knock sounds on my cabin door. Levi frowns, breaking eye contact, and gets up to answer it. I'm still shocked that he proposed. I thought he might, in the future. But not *right now.*

"Oh, Levi. Is Lily here? I need to talk to her. It's important. About work." It's Kate.

"Yeah, she is, come in," he says, gesturing for her to enter. I stand in the bedroom doorway, having pulled my robe on.

"No, I'll just wait on the porch. I don't want to interrupt."

Kate's eyes meet mine. I can tell she is scared of something.

"Levi, you are shirtless. Let me go outside for a sec."

He shrugs and stands aside to let me go out onto the porch.

"I'll be right back," I whisper, leaning up to kiss him as I pass by.

He squeezes my ass as his eyes linger on me, even as I exit the cabin.

141

We are going to need to talk quietly, or he will hear. And I am keeping quite a bit from Levi right now.

"I found another one!" Kate says, pacing on the porch.

"Another what?"

"Another coin."

CHAPTER TWENTY-FIVE

Kate hands me her cell phone, the screen open to Latin pronunciations. We are on the ferry, trying to figure out the meaning inscribed on the coin she found on her porch. It isn't a coincidence either, the hoodie left on mine and now the coin on hers. Someone is trying to send us a message. But who?

The man in black. The one who I saw on base.

That toothy grin as he smiled at me from the back of the SUV and then again when I bumped into him in the food court, it wouldn't leave my mind. And those eyes. Those too blue eyes.

"Who do you think left it?" Kate whispers, scrolling the page.

Landing on the correct words, she covertly shows me the coin face again and then compares the writing to her screen. *Secretum locum.* Secret Place. There is a skull, and some sort of maritime symbol embossed in the background of the coin. Neither of us has any idea what the hell this means though, just like the first coin.

"I don't know. I keep thinking of the man, though. The one with the…"

"Black hoodie."

"I was going to say the blue eyes, but yeah, the black hoodie. I didn't tell you yet, but Levi is going to take DNA off of it," I say.

Kate tugs on my sleeve, her eyes narrowed.

"What do you mean, Levi is taking DNA? Off what?"

We keep our voices low as Peter and Brian walk by. Peter glances backwards, his eyes catching mine. I feel uneasy, then he turns around.

"Lil! Tell me!"

Looking back at Kate's phone, I sigh.

"There was a black hoodie left on my porch last night sometime and it reeked of Peter's cologne! Levi found it."

"Holy shit, are you serious?" she asks, her voice strained.

I nod, watching my male coworkers as they lean over the ferry rail, and wonder what Peter could be capable of. Terrorizing coworkers? Possibly. Chasing me with a knife? Did it really happen? I don't like to think that it did because I trust him, and he came off as very upstanding when we first started working this job together but looks can be deceiving. You can't ever really know anyone. Can you?

I turn my attention back to Kate's question, "Yes. And I'm telling you; the hoodie is the same one we saw in Peter's bag! It's soaked in his cologne."

"Did Levi freak out?" she asks.

"He played it cool like he always does but he was clearly jealous and wondered what the hell was going on. He proposed to me, even."

"He what?"

She rubbed her temples.

"He got on one knee right as you knocked..."

"This is making my head spin, Lil," she nervously laughed. "But you aren't wearing a ring, did you say no?"

I shake my head.

"No, I didn't say anything, you knocked. Plus, he didn't ask with a ring. He didn't have one."

Her face looks shocked, "No ring? What the hell? No way, girl. He has to have a ring."

"I know. I know."

Brian wanders over before we can discuss it further.

"Ladies, we all got here early, do we start early and then get off early or..."

"That's a lot of early," Kate says, tucking the coin back into her pocket discreetly. "Let's just start on time. Gives us a minute to breathe."

"Fair enough," Brian says, as the ferry approaches the dock on Fort Warren.

144

Leaves blanket the area, like a thick carpet of orange and red. I look to Kate.

"I am gonna get some coffees for everyone. Won't take me long."

"For everyone?" she asks, arching an eyebrow.

I mouth, 'Levi, DNA' and she nods. My partner in secrets. Kate is readily becoming the only person I trust. Even more than Levi. I just hope that my confidence in her remains as it is. Brian and Peter wander off into the building as Kate takes a walk by the beach. I briskly make my way to my Jeep parked a few blocks away. I brought it over on the ferry when we started this job because it was convenient to have it on the island for short trips. If Levi is correct, and he *does* get Peter's DNA from the sweatshirt, then I have a much bigger problem. And he will be the number one suspect for leaving the coin on Kate's porch as well.

"But *why*? Why would he do all of this?" I say out loud, once I get into my Jeep.

Either he is a psychopath, or he has some sort of vendetta. Neither are good.

I make good time getting the coffees, and rush back with them, not wanting to waste any time getting Peter's DNA.. The thought is making my anxiety run high. I don't want Peter to sense anything.

"You brought us coffee! Bless you..." Brian exclaims, taking the warm paper cup that I offer him.

"Thanks, Lily," Peter says, giving me a fake smile that makes my pulse quicken with unease and I hope my face isn't giving my anxiety away.

"Welcome."

As I give Kate her cup, she gestures to the filing cabinet in the back of the room. Not sure of what she has found, I glance over my shoulder to see if Peter is looking. He isn't.

"Look..." Kate says, opening a drawer carefully.

She picks up a large stack from the top of the filing cabinet and begins to rifle through it so as not to alert the guys to anything unusual. With my heart thudding in my chest, I peer into the drawer. The file folder that I lost is there! The one that Kate found which contained details of experiments on Navy Personnel! It is in the filing cabinet, all neat and tidy. It was missing. And so were some of the sections of it. But not anymore.

It's time to do some digging. I casually flip through and skim the contents. Everything appears to be here now. Which is weird. Who had this and why did they put the complete pile back?

"See?" Kate whispers.

"I do. How did you find this?" I hiss.

She clears her throat and shows one of the papers in her hand, so I nod and cluck my tongue. Brian and Peter look over then go back to what they are doing.

"I just opened the drawer, and it was here. Tonight. Tonight, we are combing through this, are you up for an all-nighter?"

I meet her eyes and nod. We have the complete file; we need to finally go through it. Look up anything that is in it. Figure this out, once and for all.

"Did anyone hear any strange sounds last night?" Brian asks, breaking the silence in the room.

Kate and I both grab a pile of papers and sit down at the large table, to begin working. I take a sip of my coffee as Peter looks taken aback momentarily. His face colors.

"Sounds? What sounds?" he asks, with a slight edge to his voice.

"It was bizarre, really. I mean, I heard what sounded like scratching on the screen to my bedroom window. Then when I went to look, no one was there. And the sounds stopped. But they resumed at the front door. You guys noticed that we don't have peep holes? How are we supposed to see out?"

"Scratching? Like an animal?" Kate asks.

"Well, yeah, I mean, it was like an animal, I suppose, pawing at something. That sort of sound. But the window is up pretty high. It's got to be at least six feet off the ground."

"True. Did you look for prints?"

Peter interjects. "Probably a bear. There are so many on these islands..."

I can sort of agree with him on that. I have seen a bear at this point already. Kate questions him.

"Naw, Peter. No way. There would be prints. And why would a bear go for the bedroom window? Especially one that high up?"

Peter flashes anger, which is uncharacteristic of him.

"I don't know, Kate, probably because they smelt his barbeque inside."

"I can assure you; I had nothing left. We ate everything but one burger, and I had that later. No, it wasn't food," Brain says.

Peter gets up in a huff and drops his stack of papers on the table, abandoning his paper coffee cup.

"I'll be back," he mutters, walking out of the room.

Brian doesn't seem phased by his actions. "Want to know what I think it was?"

Kate nods and so do I.

"I think it was a ghost. I've experienced it before, as I told you. I don't know why, but I felt like someone was trying to get to me. But not a physical person."

The hair on the back of my neck stands up as he says he feels like someone is coming for him. I feel the same.

"I need to go to the bathroom," I say, standing to leave the room as Peter had done.

Kate and Brian resume talking about ghosts and what they think about the islands here. And the things that keep happening to us. Only Kate holds back on the things we have kept to ourselves.

As I exit into the dark main hallway, I hear Peter talking in an angry tone from another room. He is not happy. I need to hear what he is talking about, given he's the prime suspect in most of the things going on. Slowly I creep nearer until I am outside the door. Ensuring I am not visible, I try to slow my heart rate down. I hadn't realized it was thundering in my chest.

"No! Commander Lessing, no. I just want to get the position, that's all."

I can hear him pacing the floor.

"It's all of them. But mostly Lily. Yes, her."

Me? What about me?

CHAPTER TWENTY-SIX

A warm fire crackles in the fireplace.

"He is a snake, Lily. One hundred percent. I thought I had seen it all in this job, too."

"I don't know what he meant, though..."

"Oh, I do! He means to try and move up into your position, Lil! Move *up*. That means you have to go."

Kate's words hit me like a brick in the face. If I have to go, that means Peter definitely could be messing with me. And I need to be careful.

"I have a sinister feeling, Lily. I just do."

She stokes her fireplace with the long metal poker, sending the logs to settle, bright red sparks crackle and pop. I used to find the sounds comforting, but right now they are anything but.

"By 'go' what do you mean?"

Kate puts the poker into its metal holder and looks back at me. Her face is tired, and I'm sure I look tired, too.

"Do you think he would try to hurt me?"

"I have a bad feeling, Lil. It's hard to explain. We should stick together. No more swimming for you or running. That I *do* think is a bad idea. But I don't know. I just don't."

"I can't believe we are having this conversation. It's wild. Feeling this way at work is insane."

I glance over at Kate, she appears as concerned as I am.

"I agree. But here we are," she muses, sitting down on the easy chair nearest the fire. I am curled up on the couch, my feet tucked underneath myself. It's cozy in Kate's cabin. A sliver of comfort in a sky of dark clouds. We are working on kicking off the agreed all-nighter. The first step is to go over the Top-Secret folder, document by document. This is going to be rough. And we both know it. Picking up the said folder, Kate takes out the documents as I sit alert, ready with a blank notebook, pen in my hand.

"The first page is nothing of interest. Second is table of contents and to whom the document addresses," she says.

Nodding, I take notes, annotating each page and its contents. When she gets to the fifth page, that is when she brings up the locations.

"Gold Mountain. That's the code for whatever it is they were or are doing. Let's get online and look up what is there."

I open my laptop, typing into the search bar the special location. Right away there are links that detail the exact location of the mountain. It's not on one of the islands. But on mainland Washington. Just past where the coast ends. It has something that stands out, though.

"A railway runs into it."

"Into it?" Kate asks, unable to view my laptop screen.

"*Into* it. As in the tracks go through the mountain. Completely."

I marvel at the photos on an explorer's webpage. A man has taken a 'tour', meaning, he broke into the area and took illegal photos. The mountain is owned by someone. I just need to find out who. It doesn't specify online. Anywhere. At least, there is no mention of an owner in any area I can view.

"How in the hell can train tracks go through a literal mountain? Someone had to hollow it out!"

"It's called Gold Mountain for a reason though. . . I see there is mining there. Or was."

I click on the article the man wrote, skimming the content. Suddenly, something sticks out. My skin crawls as I read the words.

"What Lil? Tell me..."

My voice is caught in my throat. This can't be. There is no way.

"The man, he saw what I did," I say slowly.

"Saw what?" Kate asks.

I read feverishly until I reach the end of the blog entry. It validates my experience on the beach when I ran.

"He saw a train. It was there outside of the mountain. The same set of cars that I saw, down to the material and construction. Then the hidden tracks as well. With electricity. I don't know, Kate; this has to be a government thing. But what are they doing with cars of people in them?"

"Wait, someone online saw a train just like you did? Where, at Gold Mountain or here on the islands?"

Realizing again that Kate can't see the screen, I begin to explain the page to her.

"Yes. A travel blogger or local explorer, he went to Gold Mountain to hike, and he wrote about it. Seeing the same train described in the *exact* same way as what I saw. I mean exactly. What does this mean? For the train to appear over by the mountain? I didn't think any trains were on the island!"

Her face appears tired suddenly, lines appearing to make her look older.

"You must have seen where its origins were, then. Or you saw where it stops. But it doesn't make sense. There shouldn't be trains here and even if there are, why stop in the woods? For what purpose?"

It doesn't make sense. All I know is that someone else has seen what I have seen, and they shared it online. It wasn't hard to find either. So, the government would have already seen it, meaning it isn't a threat to anything.

"I don't know..." I say, trailing off.

"Well, okay. We know that Gold Mountain is extremely important. What else is in the documents, though. Let's see."

She turns the page and reads. I turn my attention to the fire; it's crackling startling me a few times. Orange and red glow back at me. What if the man I keep seeing has something to do with the trains? Another thought creeps in.

151

What if the train cars were ghosts as well.

"Well now, this is interesting. The word 'paranormal' is here. Only once, though. And mentioned in a set of briefs that were referenced. It's odd. Usually what happens in a briefing wouldn't be mentioned in another briefing. At least not like this."

"It wouldn't?" I ask, my eyes are still focused on the fire.

"No," Kate says. "And plus, this thing reads like a sophisticated code."

"It's that jumbled?"

Something cracks and instinctively I know it isn't the fire. I direct my attention to the front door. Kate doesn't pick up on the distinction in sounds and continues to scan the documents. All the tiny hair on my arms stands up. I stare at the door, sensing there is something there on the other side. As if in slow motion, I move off the couch.. Kate is still engrossed and doesn't notice.

As I creep past the living room towards the front door, I feel the coldness of the hard wood through my socks. An owl hoots loudly from outside. The fire crackles again and so does whatever is out there. Remembering there are no peepholes on these modern doors, I decide to look out the window. Taking a deep breath, I pull the curtain aside and peer into the darkness.

I see nothing. Emptiness. I shiver. My instincts still scream at me that there is someone out there. Someone or something. The last thought makes my heart thud loudly and I can feel the palms of my hands growing sweaty, slick with anxiety.

Then I see it.

A dark figure is standing about a good yard away, by the water. A very *tall* one. It moves. It begins to walk towards the cabin. I drop the curtain and back up quickly, towards the living room.

"Lil?" It's Kate's voice. "Lil, what's wrong?"

152

Dropping the papers, she stands up, and stares towards the front door.

"What did you see?"

"I saw a dark figure, out by the water. He started walking towards the cabin. It's coming for us, Kate." My voice is high, strangled with fear.

"No one is getting in, Lily. They can try, and they will be shot."

Walking to the kitchen, Kate takes out a sidearm from one of the drawers. I'm uncomfortable with guns, usually, but not now. She readies it and stands in a protective stance a few feet back from the door, ready in case the person tries getting in. Suddenly, the sound of boots come onto the porch. The fire crackles in the fireplace as we both wait. I can't breathe or move.

The heavy footsteps walk across the porch, back and forth. Kate and I stand frozen, listening to each thud and thump. My mind races with who this could be. Peter's face flashes front and center. The sneer he had while chasing me in the dream I had. It can't be him, can it? The sound of walking stops.

"Where is he?" Kate whispers softly, adjusting her stance.

We wait for what seems like ages before Kate gets frustrated and decides to do something.

"I need to check out the window."

She walks softly to the curtains, and taking a deep breath, moves them aside to see who is outside.

"What do you see?" I whisper, hoarsely.

She holds the sidearm down to her side, and peers out in all directions.

"I don't see..." she stops speaking abruptly. My heart is thudding wildly in my chest and the tension ripping though me is so great I want to scream.

Kate freezes, her body rigid.

"What is it?"

I can't move, even though I want to. My heart is caught in my throat, and my legs are going numb slowly as the anxiety takes hold.

"He is smiling at me. The man."

"What? Where the heck is he? What's going on?"

"He's in the yard. Just off the porch."

I see the face of the other man in my mind. The one from the SUV and the Naval exchange. The ghost with blue eyes.

"Kate...." I gasp.

She turns to look at me, before glancing back out of the window and then she drops the curtains.

"He's gone."

CHAPTER TWENTY-SEVEN

It's almost six in the morning and Kate is finally on the last page. I should be ready to sleep but I'm not. Instead, I am wide awake. Sipping a coffee, I walk towards the fireplace and stretch. A yawn escaping my mouth, I listen to the crackling within the wood that is burning. The familiarity of the fire is bringing me comfort finally, after a long night of fear.

Whoever was outside of Kate's cabin didn't bother us again the rest of the night, after they 'disappeared'. Though I wondered if they were watching us still or lurking around outside in the darkness. Kate kept the gun on the living room coffee table, just in case.

"I don't know about you, but I am not a bit tired. Weird, huh? A few hours ago, I could've fallen dead asleep." I hear Kate's voice piercing the early morning stillness.

"It's the adrenaline. Finding out everything we have so far, and it's the strong as fuck coffee you made us! I mean, the beans coming directly from Columbia, it's like being hooked to a coffee tree!"

Kate laughs. "I knew it would help. I save that for dire times. It's got so much caffeine in it; I don't think it would be legal to sell here."

She wasn't kidding. The coffee has a kick.

"The last page is nothing of consequence. It's done."

"So, we think the Navy discovered paranormal activities associated with their bases and they were experimenting on sick sailors and civilians that had been trafficked into the US. That's the gist of it, after all our research and decoding that Top-Secret document. And it all happened on Fort Warren," I summarize.

"Pretty much!" Kate agrees.

"Maybe, just maybe, the Navy decided to expose the living to

155

the dead..." I say, thoughtfully.

The idea flew into my mind and wouldn't leave. Could this be true? Could experiments have been conducted to see what the dead would do?

"I don't enjoy thinking of one of our armed forces branches in such a sinister light," Kate says, frowning.

"I don't either, I just wonder, is all. It's individual leaders who can be shitty, I would imagine. What if the doctor in charge of the program... what if he turned evil or wanted to push some crazy boundaries?"

"That could happen, I guess. I don't like it, but if what we read is true, they were crossing lines for sure."

One of the logs falls over and crumbles. Having burned all night, it was nearing its end. Kind of like each of us at some point in life.

That's it!

"Kate! What if...what *if,* the sailors they experimented on were already dying? What if – what if they are conducting experiments at the point of death, when the soul is supposed to leave the body."

"Like tampering with the soul? Girl, the human soul becomes more aware of its own mortality nearer to death..."

"Exactly. The stories we read on hospice patients, and don't forget the Philadelphia experiment. The US Navy was supposed to have made a whole ship and its passengers disappear!" I say, emphatically.

We had spent hours researching various topics last night and might have gotten seriously carried away. But the idea of experiments at the point of death sticks out in my mind.

"The train car. What if the people inside, who were being trafficked, what if they were also sick? I mean, it would be impossible to traffic a boatload of people into the US without questions being raised, so what if the majority, who weren't sick, were transported elsewhere and the ones who were kept in the US by the navy were kept specifically for experimentation?"

Kate puts the document down and looks at me. I know she agrees that I have hit the jackpot with this theory. The implications of naval research into human souls at the point of death are so far-reaching, I don't even want to think about them. I mean, what if their experiments made it possible for them to transplant a human soul into a ghost? Or re-use a human soul on something that wasn't – human! My God!

"I think we should burn this. We read it in full. We can't take it back to work and honestly, I don't want to get caught with it. It's just a copy, anyways," Kate says, decisively.

The idea is shocking, burning a Top-Secret packet. But she is right, we cannot risk bringing it back. What if Brian sees it, or worse, Peter. He is looking to get rid of me, too.

"Burn it," I say.

Taking the poker, Kate stokes the fire just a bit more, then places the thick document on the top of the pile. It catches instantly, just as there is a knock at her front door.

Who is outside?

My pulse quickens. Dark thoughts about who is out there penetrate my already full mind. I don't want to get worked up, but I can't help it. The damn coffee isn't helping either. Creeping carefully to the door, Kate talks loudly.

"Who is there?"

Instead of answering, footsteps can be heard on the porch. Kate takes a step backwards, glancing at me. Her face is white. Neither of us knows what to do. We listen in silence as the person on the porch walks back and forth slowly.

Do something!

My mind kicking into gear from the caffeine, I walk to the door and yell, startling myself and Kate.

"WHO IS THERE?"

The footsteps stop. Then they move to the door.

A soft knock resounds on the wood.

"Hello?" A man's voice says.

I don't recognize it and am tired of feeling like a mouse in a maze, so I unlock and rip the door open as Kate screams, 'Lily, no!'

"Peter?" I say, in puzzled amazement.

Standing a foot away from me is my coworker, and he is wearing a black hoodie.

"You ladies want to eat some biscuits and gravy? Brian made a huge batch..."

Kate pushes past me onto the porch, looking around frantically.

"Who else was out here with you?" she barks.

"Out here with me?" Peter replies, shrinking away from her livid face. "No one was with me. I came by to offer breakfast because Brian asked me to."

"We heard someone walk across the porch and we heard it last night, too!"

Kate is getting too worked up. It might be more than just fatigue. Not wanting Peter to lash out or say something sarcastic, I jump in to interject.

"Were you out running?" I ask in my sweetest voice.

Peter looks at both of us then casually walks off the porch.

"I was. It's cold out and Brian caught me right as I finished my run. You should try running here, Lily, you'd like it. There is a nice trail that goes around the island."

Before I can answer, he jogs off, leaving us both watching his receding figure disappear into the frigid air. He wasn't kidding, it's indeed freezing. And I can't help but think he might just have been the man from last night that we saw.

"That piece of crap. He was probably here last night! Did you *see him* in the black hoodie? He is pretty tall and honestly, in the dark, anyone can appear taller than they really are."

Kate shivers as she looks over the side of the deck, into the

158

grass below.

"Well, I don't know if it was him or not, I mean, the figure I saw was big," I say.

"That's also true," she continues, before pausing for a split second. "It could have been a ghost, too."

Walking closer to the left side of the deck, Kate stops cold, leaning over the rail. I want to see what she is looking at, so I join her.

"Are those fresh?"

"Yes. They have to be." Kate mutters.

We stare at a set of huge footprints in the grass. Bigger than I have ever seen. Much bigger than Peter's feet, by far.

"Lil. What are we looking at?"

"The biggest footprints I have ever come upon..."

I literally have never seen anything this large before. They can't be from a real person. There is no way.

"Hang on, let me get my shoes."

Kate goes back inside as I stare at the prints in the frost on the grass. The stride is also massive, and it trails off into the forest. Exactly where the man we both saw last night was coming from. The question is, was he *real* or not. I keep going back and forth. It doesn't make sense either way. Unless his size was something to do with the experiments, and he really was a ghost! Do ghosts leave footprints?

"Okay, I'm going to walk around. See where these prints lead."

"Hang on a minute, I don't think that is a good idea," I say.

Kate is nuts to go out there and see what might be lurking around. If it's real, the human that belongs to these prints is a giant!

"We have to figure this out, Lily. I am not just going to let someone fuck around and keep tormenting us. I have had enough." When Kate gets upset, nothing and almost no one can stop her.

159

I run back inside to grab my tennis shoes and wool coat, then take off after her. She is already at the wood line, about to walk further into the trees when something catches my eye. Something shiny. A coin!

I bend low to pick it up and realize it's identical to the coin we found on Kate's porch the other day. Kate takes it from me and grunts.

"This is the exact same coin..."

"Do you think someone is doing this to give us clues?" I ask.

"That or to further fuck with us."

We walk into the woods, becoming fully engulfed in the forest in the process. The trees are massive, their greenery rich and abundant. Leaves stretch across our heads, high above us, creating a magnificent canopy of foliage that forms shadows and shapes in the semi darkness. It smells like the most wonderful evergreen candle, but I know it's dangerous to be walking around here, just the two of us, without any sort of protection. Bears and wildlife are plentiful. And the large man could still be here.

"I am beginning to think the Navy did this," Kate says.

"Did what?"

"This. The stalking us with that man, the train cars, the documents we found. I am starting to really believe that the Navy has secret stuff, Lily, and we have just stumbled into the world where it exists."

I want to tell her about the stuff I've kept hidden from her, like seeing members of Levi's team near the train cars, but I can't. If I do, she might think I am going nuts. And my sanity is currently hanging on by a thread.

"If we have, wouldn't they know already?" I ask quietly, afraid. My words are more of a statement to myself than a question to Kate.

Suddenly, a twig snaps behind us. We both freeze, slowly turn around and run.

CHAPTER TWENTY-EIGHT

Lungs burning, we run.

Déjà vu hits. We've done this before, even if it was in my dream. But this time is real.

"Lil!"

Kate labors in front of me. Her breathing is shallow and rapid. If she doesn't get her breath under control, she could pass out. But still, we run.

"Yes…keep running!" I shout back.

I have no idea what is behind us. I dare not look back. All I can focus on is my breathing. And running. I can hear twigs snapping beneath our flying feet; Kate groaning in between gasping for breath; foliage slaps at our faces and tries to entangle our wrists as we surge forward.

Thud. Thud. Thud.

Whatever is behind us, it is still chasing us. It sounds large, judging by the stomping noise its feet are making on the ground.

"Which way?" Kate shouts, in terror.

There is a small fork on the trail in front of us. Left or right. If we go right, it will lead by the water. To the left, we will go deeper into the woods. But that could lead us back towards the cabins. I have a strong feeling that I do not want to be near the water with whatever is following us hard on our heels.

"Left!" I shout back.

We reach the fork and veer left, our tennis shoes catching in the mud where the trail turns.

"Shit!" Kate cries, stumbling.

In an effort to not crash into her, I push her forward roughly, so she will keep going.

Thud. Thud. Thud.

Do the footsteps of our assailant sound closer?

We have to keep going!

Water splatters down my neck as I brush against the wet, sticking out foliage. It gives a frigid shock to my system. The path is gravel and it's not wide at all, in fact, it's actually narrowing.

"How much farther?" Kate shouts.

Good question.

"I don't know!" I yell back.

Running solely on adrenaline, my brain tries to work out what to do. Other than running, I have nothing. Whatever is chasing us is not giving up. It is eventually going to catch us. We could split up and try to confuse it. But if it chose to follow Kate, that would be bad. She is on the verge of collapse and the slower and or injured will be its prey first. No. We have to keep running.

"Don't stop though!" I scream at her.

Kate groans as she huffs and puffs. I know she can do it. We have to do it.

We have no choice.

The forest seems to close in as we run along the trail. Dirt and loose, small rocks underfoot, we fly through the path. My jacket is soaking wet at this point, and I am freezing cold. I don't know if it started raining or not, the tree canopy is too thick above for me to tell. But the smell of evergreens is still slamming my senses, along with another smell that I can't really place. Whatever it is, it smells rank. Like rotting flesh. Goosebumps form all along my arms and a pulse inside my head starts to throb at this thought.

What the fuck is chasing us? A corpse?

162

"Girls! Kate! Lily!"

Someone is shouting. I hear a man's voice, sharp and urgent, coming through the trees, but I don't know who it is.

"Here!" Kate shrieks, but not loud enough for whoever it is to respond. They can't hear us!

At this point we are both ready to collapse. The trail narrows even more then suddenly opens up. I risk a glance back. There is no-one there! I stare wildly, listening to the thud, thud, thud of the footsteps, getting faster.

"Hurry!"

Kate is yelling at me.

She flaps her arms as we find ourselves back out of the woods and into the clearing at the back of the cabins. Brain is holding a shotgun, and he pumps the barrel in the signature style, that sound we all know from movies.

"To the left, girls!" he shouts.

As if in a dream, I jump to the left and follow Kate's lead. Then the loud crack of the shotgun rings out. It blasts over and over as we fly to the side of my cabin, hands touching the wet wood planks. I turn my head to see what's happening. Has Brian shot something?

Blood rushes to my head, throbbing with each heartbeat.

"Lil...Lil," Kate chokes out.

I turn to her, and our wild eyes meet. Identical terror. Both of us are traumatized. Neither can breathe correctly, though we are trying. All I can do is nod.

"Ladies! Ladies! What's the problem? Peter and I heard you girls screaming and then, as you got closer, we could see you were running like two people possessed! I thought someone was following you, so I got my shotgun and fired some warning shots. But there's no-one there." Brian's voice is concerned but puzzled.

Both Kate and I are now collapsing onto the ground. We are spent, our chests heave, our leg muscles are screaming at us.

163

Kate rolls over onto her back and eventually sits up. I lay there waiting for my breathing and my heart rate to return to normal.

"I wanted to see why shoe prints were all over the grass by my porch and they led to the woods." Kate explains. 'So, we followed them."

"Wait, shoe prints in the grass?" Peter asks, his face slightly flushed.

"Yeah. From a man's shoes. Big shoes."

Kate glances down at Peters shoes and Brian looks down at his own.

"How big are we talking?" Brian asks her.

"Bigger than yours by far," she answers. "Honestly, bigger than *both* of yours."

We both get to our feet as Peter snorts. We make our way back to Kate's cabin, all of us gathering on her porch again.

"I keep thinking this place is haunted. I mean it. No idea why, but I get the heebie-jeebies. And now I can't run in the morning." I say, clutching my sides, which are aching.

"No one should go for runs or swims, not alone. I think that has been proved. We need to stick to our cabins and the boat launch area," Brian says.

"I agree," Kate grunts, rubbing her legs. "As much as I hate to admit it. I don't relish having freedom taken away, but something was following us. Something big and I guess it was the same thing that made the footprints on the grass outside of my porch. If there is some ghost or person or whatever running around with a gun or other weapon, we can't be unsafe with our actions."

"Well, I have this old girl with me," Brian pats his shotgun. "You still have your piece, Kate?"

"Sure do."

"Good. Keep it out and loaded. The ferry comes in thirty minutes, we better hurry and get ready."

Nodding, we head back to Kate's cabin and shut the door,

leaving the men to go to their cabins.

"I am scared now, Lily. Genuinely."

The fire is smoldering, only embers glowing. It still emits a mean warmth as I lean against the mantle and swallow the lump in my throat. My thoughts are scattered, and I try to put them together before speaking.

"The prints were too big to be real. That is a fact. No man alive is that large unless he's related to famous basketball players. It could be a ghost. Or the Navy…"

"The Navy? Why though, we haven't spilled any secrets, Lil. We burned the documents even."

"We did. But we also know now. We know about the experiments that took place here in the past."

"Okay, but who would ever believe us? We would be deemed crazy."

"Exactly. Maybe they want us to leave."

"I am *not* leaving until the job is done."

"Me neither."

"I think we should talk to Levi. He is the only one who could help us with it," Kate finally says.

"I can't. It sounds, well, he wouldn't like it, Kate."

"Lil. Please. We should tell him."

Looking back into the fireplace, my mind swirls. If it's something to do with his team, this will backfire. And it could place my boyfriend in danger. But really, now I have no choice.

"I'll text him."

CHAPTER TWENTY-NINE

Rain splatters on the thick glass windowpanes. Staring out into the trees beyond, all I can see is a watercolor of water, as if in a carwash. The sound is soothing, though. I need to feel safe for a moment.

"This freaking place also rains too much," Peter grumbled.

"Peter, you are driving me nuts. We know it's raining. We can all hear it and see it." Kate barked back at him.

"Kate's right. It's not helping to complain. I think it sounds nice, actually. Did I ever tell you guys about the time I got caught in a flood in Spain?" Brian, ever the peacemaker, intervenes.

"Spain?" Kate asks. "When were you there?"

"On vacation, after an assignment. I dated a Spanish lady, long distance, and she invited me to go over for a week."

The rain is drumming against the roof and the windows of the cabin, but it sounds soothing, despite the deluge. I am only half listening to the conversation inside.

"You dated online? I can't picture you doing that, honestly!"

Brian laughs. "Well, I did. It didn't last, as most long-distance relationships don't. But she was the nicest woman you could ever meet. Lived in an old, haunted farmhouse in the country."

"Wow, that's pretty cool. Tell me about the haunting?"

"It was weird," Brian begins. "The farmhouse was fantastic. Crumbling ruins, mostly, but all painted white and rustic looking. Tiled terracotta floors and big wooden beams on the ceiling. But the atmosphere was – strange, tense. The lady I was dating seemed nervous all the time. After a couple of days, the ghost, or ghosts, made an appearance. Strange knockings at the door, indecipherable figures spotted in dark corners, footsteps outside of the building –"

"Exactly like what's going on here," I interrupt, in a hoarse whisper.

It goes quiet in the room except for the sound of the insistent rain and Peter clearing his throat.

"That's some coincidence," says Kate, watching me as I stare out of the window. Raindrops run down the panes in rivulets making the outside blurry and hazy. Nothing is as it seems. Trance like, I remain silent. Nothing is as it seems, I repeat in my head until my phone vibrates, and I snap out of my strange reverie.

Looking down at the screen, I see that Levi is finally able to reply.

Babe, what is going on there? What do you mean, something chased you?

I see the words and try to formulate my response to what Levi is asking. I sent him a vague message about Kate, and I, having seen footprints, but I focused more on whatever was chasing us.

We exchange a few brief texts; I'm trying to get information from him, but he stonewalls me. Guys are good at that, especially Navy SEALs.

"Lil, you good?" Kate gently asks, coming to sit by me in her metal folding chair.

I nod. I am and I'm not.

"He's not answering me, Kate," I tell her. "Well, he is texting back and replying to me but he's not giving anything away, which tells me he knows more than he is letting on."

Kate shrugs. "I suppose it was worth a try, Lil. Back off for now, then. Don't make him suspicious."

I nod and then her voice brightens.

"I was thinking, I want to rent a kayak this weekend. Well, a couple. One for each of us. Then we can check the area out more. See if anything odd is there lurking around. After all the references to it in the documents..."

"I guess you're right," I say, absently, still staring at the screen, wondering if Levi will add anything more.

167

Lil, I don't get this! What is it you are trying to say? That you think the place is haunted. That you think I am somehow involved.

I could be honest with him or deflect. My mind feels uneasy about laying all our suspicions bare, about the medical experiments and the trafficking of people and the involvement of the Navy. I love Levi, and I don't want to hide things from him. But then I remember the men in the woods. They were scary, not like the normal SEAL team members that I met in the past. These ones were on a mission, and they were there to mess with whoever was trapped in the train car. I can still see the shadow-people's faces, flashing briefly in the darkness as they looked at me. And the man in the hoodie, with the bluest eyes. Who is he? Would Levi tell me if he knew?

Better to not antagonize him. Swallowing the lump in my throat, I put my phone down and look at Kate. She is eyeing me over top of a large stack of documents.

"I don't want to worry him when he is out training or doing God knows what," I say softly.

This time *she* nods and continues working.

A clock ticks on the wall closer to the door. It's one of the old ones that probably has been in this building since the 1950's, the paint on it weathered beyond repair. With each tiny turn of the clock hands, my heart beats with thoughts. Jumbled and swirled, I try to make sense of it all. The man with the creepy smile, the tall one with giant feet, the people I saw on shore who weren't my coworkers, bears and incidents happening in the water. This place is undoubtably haunted. There is no other explanation for it, and I don't like it.

"You know what I think we should do?" Brian suddenly breaks the silence.

"What?" Kate answers.

He clears his throat.

"We need to do a good old fashioned 'fire guard' at night. I heard they do that in the military while in boot camp. Take shifts to guard the area around the cabins. What do you think?"

No one speaks for a beat, each of us thinking. Finally, Peter clears his throat again.

"I am game for that, but only if we can share the shotgun. I can't roam around unarmed. My wife needs me to stay alive. There could be more bears out there or ..."

"Well of course, we would hand off the shotgun, I'd light a fire outside in the firepit and then put a chair on say, Lily's porch. Perfect location?"

He looks at me and I nod, agreeing. It's not a bad idea.

"How many hours are we talking though? There are only four of us and eight hours of sleep time roughly."

"Then two hours only should do it," Brian says. "Are we all in? I think we should give you ladies the last shift though, because you look exhausted. And this way you can sleep as soon as we get back tonight."

"Sounds good to me, Lil?"

"Yep. I am good with it," I agree.

"Will you help me carry the bag out to the collection point?" Kate asks me, standing.

Her eyes say more than her words, so I stand and help her as the men continue to work, oblivious to our silent looks. We grab on opposite ends of the burlap bag and heft it up to carry outside. Workers will load them up when the ferry comes in a few hours. Once we make it out of the building Kate exhales loudly.

"Finally, we are going to do something about this crap. I was trying to think of a way to surveil at night."

"Yeah, it's good, but do you think it's really going to matter? And can we trust Peter?"

Wind whips my ponytail around the side of my face, a chill hitting my skin.

"We don't trust anyone, Lil. But each other. And I am going to do the shift with you, you go first, and I'll wait until either

169

Brian or Peter hand over the shotgun, then I'll come out. We are *not* doing anything out here alone anymore. Not if we can help it."

"Okay."

Dropping the bag off by the ferry ramp, I glance at the choppy dark depths of Puget Sound. Something flicks in the water a few yards out, but I see nothing. Only the dark froth of the waves.

CHAPTER THIRTY

What are you doing babe?

Levi texts again as I try to close my eyes. I need sleep, as our shift will come before we know it. Never thought I would pull guard over any area, that is Levi's job. But here we are.

You must be busy with Kate or going to bed early. I'll try you again later. Be safe Lily. Don't go outside alone.

Fluttering my eyelids softly, I let my hand go slack and my phone rest on the comforter. Sleep claims me instantly. Then I wake up in the forest. Opening my eyes slowly, I feel the chill of the outside night air. My body forms goosebumps and water drips onto my head. I look up and see the tree boughs above. It's raining lightly, and the forest channels the water like a sieve, directing it where it wants it to go.

A moan escapes my body, and I sit up. I am wet from the ground, and it feels real, though a part of my consciousness knows this is a dream. Feeling pulled to something deeper in the forest, I stand and begin to slowly walk towards the fog, down a gravel path. I don't know where I am at. It looks nothing like the path on the island we are now staying at, but it is still in Washington. At least that much I know.

Winding, turning and losing some elevation, I follow the path as the fog gets even closer. Water drips on my neck from the trees and I shudder at the feel of it. My pulse begins to slow; each beat a hard thud in rhythm with the droplets. Approaching the edge of the thick grey curtain, I stop briefly before stepping in. Then I am engulfed.

"There you are. Finally," a male voice says.

Instead of terror, I only feel numb. My mind goes blank as I search for the man's identity in the recesses of my mind. To no avail. I have no idea who he is only that he is calling to me through the fog.

"Don't be scared. I've been waiting for you, Lily."

He knows me.

But how?

"Fog is beautiful, isn't it? We can stay here for a while."

Turning my head in all directions, I search for the man. But he is nowhere. Is he real? The fog is so thick on my fingertips I can almost grasp it, as if a blanket that you pull under your chin. The water molecules swirl with each movement I make in the air. I stand mesmerized, in a dream state.

"See. It's magic, isn't it?" the man asks.

I can only nod, my voice won't come. Turning my head, I search again for the man. I should be scared but oddly, I'm not. Whatever is happening, it has a hold over me. Then I hear footsteps, as if from heavy boots approaching. I drop my arms and blink. Waiting. Waiting for the man to get to me. The air stills so there is nothing but my heartbeat and the sound of the man's boots.

"Are you paying attention, Lily?"

He asks the question not to hear an answer but to give me a warning of what was about to happen. I open my lips and inhale the fog softly, ready to reply.

Knock, knock!

Exhaling, I open my eyes again.

I am back in my bed, a spare comforter draped over me, cell phone still in hand. And there is someone knocking at my cabin door.

"It's time." I mutter, getting up to answer.

Having slept in fresh clothes after a hasty shower, I am dressed already for the night shift. Only my mind is still suspended in the dream world. I need to know who the man was, the one who had been coming for me.

"Hey, Lil. All has been quiet, except for the hoot of some owls and a few splashes in the water. Most likely whales or something moving along the channel."

172

Brain greets me on the porch as I close my door to keep the cold outside. I slip on boots waiting under the porch light and shrug into my heavy parka.

"Okay. Good," I reply quietly.

"Did you sleep enough?" He asks, handing me the shotgun and a box of extra shells.

"A few hours."

"Okay, good. Listen, I know this has been horrendous for you. I can tell that you're stressed about the bear and work and maybe other things, all this talk about ghosts and hauntings. We are doing good with the buildings, though, and should be done with this job in I'd say a few weeks. Only two left to sort through and they don't have near the volume that the last ones did."

"Hmm?" I reply, feeling the weight of the weapon in my arms. Shotguns are usually lighter I thought. Brian's must be an antique.

"The assignment. It's almost done. We are making fast work of it, the four of us."

"Oh, work," I quip, realizing what he just said. "That fast?"

"Yes. I was talking to Commander Lessing once I got to my cabin earlier, he said we will be done soon. Then we don't have to worry about the damn wildlife anymore or anything else bothering us."

"You didn't tell him that we are staying up in shifts with your shotgun, did you?" I ask as he steps off my porch and into the dewy grass below.

"Course not. He wouldn't like that," he says deadpan, disappearing in the darkness.

I watch as his shadow blends in with the landscape. Commander Lessing would definitely not want us to do this, with a gun no less, on Naval property. Or property they are leasing if they don't actually own it. The government is weird about their land and what can and should go on in it.

Kate exits her cabin and steps onto her porch in virtual silence, waving to me. I wave back. It brings me an enormous amount of comfort knowing she will be out here, too. As if on cue, an owl hoots in the distance. Checking that there is a round in the shotgun, I carefully walk out to the grass to meet Kate. A cold breeze whips at my face as I do.

"Gosh, it's cold. Did you even sleep?"

I nod, "Some."

"Good. I did, too. This shouldn't be too bad. Only have to make it through four hours of this. Then I have some bacon that has our names on it and coffee."

"Sounds good. Should we go sit by the fire for a bit?" I ask.

"Mmhmm. Let's go."

We walk down the path towards the water, keeping in mind to be as quiet as possible so we can listen for any sounds. Flashes of my dream fill my mind, but I push the thoughts away. I can't deal with it right now.

"I don't know what it is with fires outdoors. Nothing beats it," Kate says.

"I know. They are comforting, warm, put you in a trance and they smell good," I reply.

She laughs, "Touché. You should become a writer in your spare time. That was the perfect way to describe it."

"Speaking of work," I say, settling onto a bench by the fire. "Brian said that in two weeks or so we will be *done*. Did you know that? He said he was talking to Commander Lessing and that's what was said."

"That is awfully fast. I guess I kind of thought, a month or maybe less, but really around a month. Two weeks. That commander rushes things. I haven't seen one be this pushy to be honest."

Another owl hoots in the distance as the fire crackles in the dark.

"Lily, have you thought more about applying for the job on

JBLM? It's so close to here but in a far more populated area. Closer to Seattle, and we could potentially get the job together."

I hadn't thought of it again, the only thing I can think about is here and what could be happening around me.

"Not really. I need to talk to Levi more. I need to know if he meant what he said in wanting to marry me. I couldn't go to Joint Base Lewis-McChord if we were to get married, I don't think."

"Shit, that's right! He *did* ask you to marry him. I forgot, with all this crazy stuff going on. Has he brought it up again? Or is he still gone at the moment?"

"Gone. But he sends me sporadic texts."

"Well, what do you want to do? Deep down, just your first gut instinct."

"Marry him but I…"

A large crack comes from the woods behind the cabins, interrupting our conversation and my train of thought. Kate immediately stands, her body rigid. I grip the shotgun and freeze, eyes scanning the woods. The waters of Puget Sound are behind me.

"Lil…"

Loud noises keep resounding from the woods. It sounds like metal on metal, or something industrial.

"Lil. What is that?" Kate hisses softly.

"I don't…" I begin, gripping the gun hard in my hands. "I don't know…"

As suddenly as it began, the noises stop.

Silence settles over the forest and the sounds of the water lapping behind me come back into focus. The trees are shrouded in darkness except for ambient light from the cabins softly glowing on the forest's edge. Just enough for us to see if anyone is there. Slowly, I scan. Standing so I can see better, my palms sweat underneath the shotgun, I hold my breath.

175

Then I see it.
A tall man in a black hoodie.

CHAPTER **THIRTY-ONE**

"I saw him Kate, I'm telling you, I did."

"I believe you, Lil. But I didn't see him…"

"He was directly behind my cabin. I saw him, but maybe I didn't. Shit, I don't know now."

Kate hands me a stack of documents that are half damp and smell of mold. Wrinkling my nose, I wish I had brought throw away gloves. Like the ones that doctors and nurses wear when you go to a medical appointment.

"Eww, why are these wet?" I ask.

"There is a leak in the corner where they were stacked. From the wall. I'm guessing it stems from the roof. The Department of Defense never fails to shock me about how they treat buildings. I mean, they spend billions on training and weapons but can't keep things free of mold, so their personnel don't get sick?"

I snort, "I agree. In Virginia I had to work with an industrial style mask in one building. It was *that* hazardous. And they had soldiers working in it just a few months prior."

Settling in a chair, I begin to slowly peel the papers apart. Nothing so far is of a high enough classification to warrant it going in the 'turn in' pile. And even wet, if a document is marked Secret or above, we *must* turn it in to be destroyed.

"It's a damn shame. Hey, you know what this makes me think of? The experiments."

"What about them?" I ask, sorting more as my fingers become coated in bled out ink.

"Well, if the Navy has no issues poisoning sailors in these moldy health hazardous buildings, then they sure as hell have no issues doing things on a bigger scale as well!"

"Bigger scale? Like beyond what they've done here?"

"Of course! You can't think that it's not happening at other bases, can you?"

Levi pops up in my mind and I can't think that he would condone such actions. Could he? If his team was really a part of such madness, with people trapped in train cars, how could I think of marrying him?

"You okay, Lil? Your face turned a few shades whiter. Do you know something I don't?"

That is precisely the problem, but I will sound insane if I tell her. And it's too dangerous.

"No, I just think about Levi. I can't imagine anyone doing that to *him*. Or anyone else's loved one."

"It's happening, Lily, and it has been for a long time. I just want you to take another job, away from here."

Reaching the end of my pile, I throw the last bits away and glance out the window by the trashcan. The rain keeps coming down outside. I wonder how the earth here can absorb so much water. Any other area of the US would be flooded. And Kate's words are burning into my mind. Experiments on sailors. How could this still be happening? How could no one stop it?

"So, I went online, and I rented two kayaks. They are for Saturday, and I got them for the entire day. We can take our time exploring Deception Pass. Are you still game?"

"You did?" I say, still looking out the window at the area near the buildings. "Yes. I still want to go."

"Okay, good."

"What if...what if we see something there though?" I ask.

"Like what we keep seeing? The ghost?"

"Yeah."

"Well, I'm not about to approach it. But we won't run either. I refuse to run again. Only from wildlife!"

I sigh. She is right, we can't run from ghosts. What good is that? In the end, they can follow you anywhere you go.

Like the man.

178

"Kate, do you think that spirits or ghosts could just be figments of our imagination? Or do you really, and I mean really, think they are real?"

Kate hands me another soggy stack as she takes one for herself. We both grimace at the dampness and smell.

"They aren't paying us enough for this. That is interesting, just figments of our imaginations?"

I shift the pages one wet piece at a time as I try to formulate my words. Shaking off the water after getting through a couple, I frown.

"I don't know. No one saw the figure that came into the bunker. Everyone thought I was hallucinating. But I wasn't. I had a handprint on my arm. And it was a very old structure. It probably holds other spirits that are trapped in it. Or maybe, whatever it was could have been a hallucination instead of being real."

"I wasn't with you. I can't say one way or the other. But I do know you. And you tell the truth, always. If you say you heard it, felt it, that is real to me. Ghosts can smell though. The one I encountered in Germany; it had an odor to it. I used to think I saw a demon to be honest."

A demon? Now this had taken a turn.

"What do you mean?" I ask quietly, getting to the last bit of paper in my soggy stack.

"After the incident, I researched the town. Specifically, paying attention to its history. It was so old. Stories popped up of hauntings. Not just simple ghost stories, either, but demonic activity. Or suspected at least."

She stands and shakes her hands off, sending tiny droplets onto the wood floor. I stare at her, not wanting to hear what she has to say, but wanting to know at the same time.

"That is an area I have zero interest in, so I didn't pursue studying it or anything. The occult is scary to me. Regular ghosts, not so much. But I have heard of stories where a person smells something baking that isn't and then sees a ghostly apparition."

"Me, too. I have heard of that, too."

"So, it's possible," she says, "that the thing in the bunker with you was a real ghost. I mean, what if it was a person who got killed, like Naval personnel decades ago, and it got trapped or stuck in that place? It happens to people, Lil."

I mull over the concept. It does make sense. This entire area could just be a conduit for the paranormal. The base is closing, maybe it's closing for this reason. We sort through the piles until we reach a few that aren't wet. Kate hands me a dry stack and I happily take it. Finally, back to regular business.

The building's front door opens in the distance. We can hear people talking, men. I glance at Kate. She mouths 'Be right back,' and gets up to check. As she leaves, I look towards the windows in the room. Water begins to sprinkle on the panes. Definitely another normal fall day in the Pacific Northwest.

"Sir, we are going as fast as we can. I can guarantee that. But a lot of the documents are wet and moldy. This isn't a normal job," Kate says.

I can hear their conversation now as the group moves down the hallway.

"I understand that there are certain challenges here on Fort Warren. Rising to meet them is part of your job description but we do need to support your team. What can you use to help for the last few days?"

Commander Lessing is here. Great.

Why would he come here in person? He's never been here since we started the job.

"Sir, we don't need anything. We just need time to get the job done, and we are working hard," Brain interjects.

"Can you use more bags? I can arrange two pickups a day."

"That is not necessary. But why the sudden push to finish quickly?" Kate asks.

She is super bold by challenging the Commander. No one does that, and for good reasons. He can mess up even a contractor's career with just a phone call.

"Variety of reasons, mostly above me. I have to get this base turned over ASAP."

"Give us a few more weeks, sir, and it will be thoroughly swept of all documents," Brian says.

Boots and footsteps fill the air as the group passes by the room where I am. I can't see them, and they can't see me, as I am hidden in the corner.

"Alright. Your team has ten more working days. No more. I have *my* team working on finalizing the contract adjustments for your agency."

Even the Commander has to get this approved though, which is our saving grace. Kate and Brian leave the hallway as I then hear another familiar voice.

Peter.

"She is here somewhere, sir; I saw her with Kate."

"Okay. Have you filled out the forms yet to report her taking a Top-Secret document?"

"I haven't yet, I need to…"

"I said it before, and I'll say it again; it's a serious accusation to say a coworker stole Top-Secret documents. You can be prosecuted for lying. So, you better be one hundred percent sure that is what you are saying before filling it out."

"Yes, sir."

Boots pivot on the wooden floor as I feel the color drain from my face. I can't believe that Peter is accusing me of stealing documents. How did he know we took them? He has no credible proof.

"Oh, and Peter," Commander Lessing calls out, "You guys are almost out of here. Think about that, too."

The door bangs shut as our veritable boss leaves. Silence fills the room, though I can hear my coworkers chatting in another one. I feel sick to my stomach and the air is hard to take in. This can't be happening. Only one person comes to mind. The only one I want right now.

Levi.

CHAPTER THIRTY-TWO

Days pass, thankfully mostly in silence. I've been worried that something would happen, but nothing has. Kate and I have done our night shift together, which has forced us to go to sleep earlier. Which, oddly enough, has been nice. I haven't heard from Levi in a few days either. I miss him, but this is rather normal for us. His texting while out on a mission is not. Overall, I've been able to calm down.

I roll the windows down a crack, letting the fresh air come in. The road is dry for once and temperatures are in the mid-fifties. Perfect day to go kayaking.

"It's not raining. We got so lucky!" Kate says with a big smile on her face.

"Indeed."

The road narrows to where there is no shoulder at all, and the sides are flanked by deep forest. On any other day, this would have made me nervous, but today it brings me happiness. I love being outside and in nature. As we drive along, I picture doing this with Levi. And how nice it would be. I miss him.

A deer darts into the road. It runs so fast, I miss it. Thankfully so.

"Oh my God, Lil! The deer!"

"That was close… have you never had a deer run out in the road anywhere?" I ask, my voice is an octave higher than normal.

"Yes I have, in Texas once and somewhere up on the east coast. But not here. I assumed we would see some wildlife today, though. I watched a few videos online last night about the basics of kayaking. We have to go slow so that way we don't capsize ourselves."

"I do *not* want to capsize and be strapped into something. We most definitely will go slow!"

The trees pass by as my thoughts return to the figures in the Sound that day that I swam. The man came out of nowhere and whatever was with him was relentless, pulling him under the water. What if more of them are out there and we see them?

No, don't think about that.

"It must have been so crazy for the early settlers coming here when no roads existed."

I grunt. "For sure. It had to have been thick, the woods."

"When we learned about the Oregon Trail and the earliest settlers, they didn't say that the Natives who lived here were violent. Not like in the plains of the US."

"No, they weren't the same. Plus, they had permanent structures here, instead of moving all the time."

"That's a good point. Hey, that reminds me of ghosts. What if they have certain types? Ones that are fixed to certain locations and then some that can follow you and move all over the place?"

"Do you think the ones here are fixed?" I ask.

"Yes and no. If we saw the tall man in the hoodie on the base, then both saw him on different islands, he could be able to go anywhere. But the others, they would be fixed."

"I can't believe we stumbled upon this, Kate; I mean what are the odds?"

"I know."

I turn to look at Kate, her face an odd shade of pale.

"Like in Germany, those things are all around us, you just don't know about it. I think ghosts pick and choose who to appear to sometimes."

Pick and choose who they appear to.

Something about her statement hits me, and my stomach knots up.

"Almost there," she says, pointing.

A large brown State Park sign appears on the side of the road. 'Deception Pass Recreation Area'. We are only a mile away! I can feel my pulse begin to quicken. I have wanted to come here since I saw the name on the documents in the first building we worked in, then also etched into the bunker wall. There is something here. I have no idea what, but we need to check it out. And what better way than from the water?

"There isn't much I am afraid of, except for drowning, Lil."

Kate's strange statement settles in my mind.

"Drowning?"

"Yeah. I have been scared of that since I was a child. I nearly drowned once in the town public pool. My dad threw me in to teach me how to swim."

"He what?" I ask in horror, getting ready to turn down the road we needed to go on.

"Don't get me started about my horrible father. But yes, he threw me in. I sunk, of course. And he refused to dive and get me until I started taking in water. So since then, I have kind of been terrified of water."

"But you did so good when the ferry capsized. You kept super calm. And wanting to kayak…"

"Oh, I know. I have been practicing mastering my mental focus for years. Especially for things that scare me. After all, we can't live in fear forever. I refuse to die with that mindset."

Her outlook never ceases to amaze me. And it's one I struggle with. But I do my best to face fears.

"There!" she says, quickly, pointing to the rental shack to the left of the parking area.

"Okay, let me park."

Finding a good spot, we both marvel at the giant bridge nearby that cars are driving on. It connects the islands and Puget Sound. I didn't expect it to be this *large*. Taking the keys out of the ignition, Kate hands me a chocolate square.

"Eat this. You are gonna need the bit of energy."

I take it and pop it in my mouth as we exit the Jeep with our small wet bags. It does taste divine. The air is rather temperate for the season, and I am grateful. Sunshine even peeks out of the clouds for a few minutes. The *perfect* day to be here. We walk to the kayak rentals and meet with a younger man who has them staged for us on the shore.

"Let's head over and I will give you a short instruction block on how to get in and how to keep yourself upright. I am Will, by the way."

"Nice to meet you, Will. I'm Kate, as you know, and this is Lily, my coworker."

"Kate, Lily," he says. "What brings you out to Deception Pass today?"

My tongue is suddenly tied so I let Kate answer. How do you say that you aren't searching for government experiments without saying that you are?

"Oh, it was highly recommended to us from the cute new coffee shop on Naval Air Station Whidbey Island. They have the most beautiful photos in their shop from here."

Damn, she is clever.

"Oh yeah! I know the owner of that shop! My dad is retired Navy. Small world. Did you try their fall cinnamon latte?"

As the two keep chatting, I scan the wood line along the edge of the shore to the left. The wood is thick in that area, being away from the road. I don't see anyone, but half expect one of the ghosts to be there. Especially the man in the black hoodie. Instead, I see trees and shadows. Nothing more. Shaking my head, I turn back to the water.

"Lil, see, it's not too hard."

I grunt and pay attention to the lesson Will was giving us. He demonstrates getting into the kayak and then getting out, showing us how to strap in around our lap and then what to do if it tips over.

"Your turn girls ..."

Gingerly, I climb into the kayak and settle in, getting the belt to work and my dry bag tucked in securely. Then we get back

186

out and ready ourselves to actually get into the water. I try to not fixate on the thoughts of figures in the water.

They might not be here. It might have been a hallucination.

Knowing my anxiety is just that, anxiety, I ease into thoughts of feeling the sun on my skin for once. It's glorious and warm.

"Okay, climb in and get ready, then I will push you out."

Will stands behind, readying to get us in the water. Once Kate is ready we feel the kayaks bumping into Puget Sound and then we are off. At first the waves are choppy, and I feel very unstable. Anxiety returns and it brings my heart rate up instantly.

"Kate, I don't know about…"

"Calm down, Lil. The water evens out to the right, follow me. Take it slow."

Now it's *her* turn to help *me* in the water. I try to think back to floating in these waters when the ferry went down and how calm I was then. My mind switched instantly to what Levi taught me. I just need to do that now. It can't be that hard, can it?

I paddle slowly, taking care to move in smooth motions and not choppy like the water. The kayak pitches but it stays upright, despite feeing like I will tip at any moment. Kate is in front of me, and I continue to follow her. Keeping my eyes on her is hard though as I want to focus on the water and the shoreline at the same time. I didn't realize how overwhelming kayaking would be. But it's too late to turn back.

"Do you see that? What is that?" Kate calls over her shoulder.

She stops paddling to point out further in the water. Something dark is floating. I strain my eyes to get a better look, but I can't tell what it could be. We paddle closer and then it becomes clear. Blood running cold, I call out to Kate.

"It's a black hoodie!"

CHAPTER THIRTY-THREE

"Pick it up with your paddle!" Kate calls me over her shoulder.

The sweatshirt has floated my way, unfortunately. I am numb from shock and can't get the smiling man out of my mind. The very last thing I want to do is pick up this garment. But I have to. I stop moving, letting the mild waves pitch and toss me slightly as I eye the black cotton floating towards my kayak.

The closer it gets, the more clearly I can see it. It's not all black, like we thought. There is something else on it. Some kind of embroidery. Reaching out as it comes close enough, my paddle picks it up. I raise it in the air slightly and keep my legs braced on the floor of the kayak, so I keep upright as the water tumbles more. Then I bring it into the kayak with me, dropping it in between my knees.

"Is it a black hoodie?" Kate asks loudly.

I nod, absentmindedly.

"Is that what I think..." I whisper.

Touching the graphic printed on the fabric, I remember the first coin we found outside of Kate's cabin. The same image is on the sweatshirt. But how could that be?

"Someone is messing with us.."

Kate beckons for me to join her up ahead, so I leave the garment where it is and paddle slowly up to her until I am close enough to hold it up and show her. Her face goes pale with recognition. She knows what the graphics are as well as I do.

"Lil. My God. How in the fuck is *that* floating out here?"

Her eyes meet mine and we both look scared. Instinctively, I begin to scan the shoreline, looking at the groups of people that have now also arrived at the parking lot. There are a few dozen men that look clean cut, most likely Naval personnel. Or Coast Guard, as they also have a few stations out here. None are looking our way, though.

"We have to keep that. Don't throw it back."

"I won't," I say, retuning my gaze back at Kate.

She usually has a no-nonsense air about her but right now, she looks frightened. The only thing we can do on the water, though, is pretend nothing has happened. If anyone is watching us, it's imperative that we hide what we have. As Levi would say 'always look like you are supposed to be there'.

"Let's go around the bend so we can go under the bridge," I say, pointing up with a nod of my chin.

Kate nods back and without a word, proceeds to paddle towards the bend. Before I follow, I look back at the shore. The group of men are milling by the kayak stand. I notice a lone raven haired one on the edge. He is tall. *Very* tall. And he turns towards me; his face fixed with a grin.

The man….

I swallow and close my eyes, heart racing. Opening them after a beat, the man is gone. Blinking, I scan fervently. He is just gone.

Did I actually see him? Was that real?

Kate's paddle jars me out of my train of thought. I need to paddle. So, I do, turning my back on the shoreline. Hairs prick at the back of my neck, and I feel that we are being watched settles over me. I think it's probably paranoia. And to deal with that you have to keep going. There is no other cure for it.

The water takes over my senses as I catch up. It's dark at the depth we are at, and I can't see more than a foot down. There are most likely a lot of fish and other creatures below. Thinking of them swimming and diving distracts my mind. I wonder if the whales are fully out of the area now. If they aren't, we might see one or two.

Kate was right. The water is less choppy the further out we go. It feels more like being in the slowest wave machine at the water park. And I honestly feel stable now and not like I am going to be thrown out of the kayak.

"Lil, oh my God, look!"

I look up as we approach the base of the bridge. It is *much larger* than it looked from the parking lot. Much.

"It's magnificent," I spout, my mouth dropping open.

"Yes, it is! To think, men built this. Can you imagine how they did it? I bet some died even."

"Died?" I ask, my gaze returning to my coworker.

"Well yeah, it was built in 1934. I bet they had a few workers slip and fall."

She has a point. I look up again at the underbelly of the metal. It arches upwards in the middle and has multiple spindles of steel connecting to the upper bridge section where the cars can drive across. I picture what Kate suggested. If men had fallen, their bones would literally be underneath us. A shark circling the depths comes to mind, as possible remains lay on the ocean floor. Shaking my head at what my imagination conjured, I keep a slow and steady paddle, now parallel to Kate.

"So, I was thinking," she begins. "The coins. The image on the first one is on that hoodie. The second one was obviously military related as well. I think, and it is just a theory, that someone from Commander Lessing's office is messing with us. Because of Peter."

"Peter?"

"Yes. Think about it. He told the Commander that you took a Top-Secret document. How he even knew about it is beyond me, but he somehow did."

"Yeah…" I muse, defeat in my voice.

I hate remembering the conversation I overheard. It makes me sad to think that a coworker would try and report me without even talking to me first. And also, that I had made an enemy somehow with Peter. It has never happened before in my work life.

"So, then someone at Commander Lessing's office knew, too. I bet a few people know. And one of those assholes has decided to mess with us."

"To what end, though, Kate?"

"Get you to quit. Possibly me as well."

"There is no shortage of men wanting women out of contracting..." I mutter.

"Exactly," Kate replies.

It's a possibility that I haven't thought of before. Could she be right?

"I am only saying it, so we are aware. 'Cause a ghost didn't throw that hoodie in the water. Let's skirt the embankment on the other side."

"Cross the middle? The current looks fast..."

"We will go slow," she assures me.

"Okay."

We begin to paddle out and I notice very quickly that the water is massively deep. The color turns a shade of navy blue that resembles a night sky. It sends adrenaline shooting up my arms with every stroke of the paddle.

How is Kate tolerating this with a fear of drowning?

Glancing up, I see her paddling faster than I am. Maybe she is regretting this decision and wants to get across fast. I follow suit, picking up my speed, trying not to look down at the water for very long. Even when I swim in Puget Sound, I don't go so deep that I can't see. The sun begins to hide behind a cropping of clouds, making it useless for happiness. We continue to paddle. I try to think happy thoughts. The air is chilly, and I shiver in the breeze. One thing about being on the water, you have to prepare for the weather to change at any given moment.

Finally, we reach the middle of the channel.

"Lil! Lil!"

"What?" I shout.

Kate struggles to paddle as the current grips us, threatening to send us down from where we just came.

"To the right!"

I look as I paddle and see a shocking sight.

People.

People are suddenly with us. A group of Asian women in kayaks paddle full force towards us. Their movements wild, paddles ripping through the water, I react in confusion. Where did they come from? They are about to collide with us!

"Paddle! Paddle faster!" I shout.

Realizing the panic in my voice, Kate ramps up her efforts. Raindrops hit my face as the weather begins to worsen. We are moving but it feels like we aren't. That is the deception of deep water. It can jar your senses. The mariners describe it in old books. Precisely what is happening now.

"They are going to hit us!" Kate yells.

We are in small pieces of plastic out in deep water in the middle of the channel. If they hit us, we will fall out.

"Lil!"

Furiously, I stare helplessly at the strangers. Their eyes are vacant and black, as if not there. I paddle, but not fast enough. Shock hits my body like a Mack truck. I am sent up in the air as two of the kayaks collide with mine.

Then the world goes black as I hit the water.

CHAPTER THIRTY-FOUR

"Lily Ann Morgan, I promise to love you, cherish you, take care of you and never leave your side."

Levi stares into my eyes as the room appears as a watercolor painting, melted in the background. All I can see is him. I realize this is a dream of some sorts and I try to speak. When I open my mouth though, water gushes out. Then Levi fades away, to be replaced by darkness. I'm trapped under the kayak, under the dark blue of plastic. And I can't go anywhere.

Sucking in air, I realize the capsized kayak has created an air pocket. My feet dangle below me, into the abyss. The life jacket I have on is keeping me afloat.

Kate.

Where is she?

I begin to focus on what I need to do. I have to get out from under the kayak. It hits me how I even got into this situation to begin with. The Asian women. They looked so intent, so hell bent on ploughing into me. Maybe they didn't hit Kate; it's possible. Lifting up my arms, I push on the Kayak seat. It moves up and I get a glimpse of the sky, but the seat is heavy, and I can't keep it up. Dropping it back into the water, I groan. My teeth are chattering.

The water temperature has to only be around fifty degrees, probably colder. Unsure of how long I have been in the water, I pray that help will come soon. Dying in Puget Sound is not the way I am going to go out. It's just not. I still want to get married, and experience more of life. I don't feel fear, oddly enough, but rather resolve.

I need to swim under this.

I have to swim, I tell myself. Come on, Lil!

To get out from under the kayak I need to swim. But that means taking off the life jacket. I can't do that. It is the only thing that is keeping me alive. Fighting against the urge to swim, I continue to float under the kayak. I'm stuck.

"Where are the whales?" I whisper to myself.

They must have kept moving. My feet aren't touching anything, only dangling in the water below. The water is darker than I remember, even from moments ago. And it's freezing cold. I can barely feel my legs. Once again, I need to worry about hypothermia. Muffled sounds fill my ears as I look for the source, but the kayak is in the way.

"H.., help! Help!" I yell out.

Panic overtakes me. Which is ridiculous, as I am literally stuck under the kayak, and it stands out very well in the water. There is no need for me to yell. Anyone looking would just overrun this and find me.

The voices get closer, as does the sound of a motor engine. Someone is nearby in a boat. Hopefully, for me. Panic quickly shifts to need. I *need* to get out of here. Thoughts race all over the place, how this even happened in the first place.

"There? She is probably not under it anymore. She can't be."

A female voice rings out loudly but still muffled.

"There! Yes! She has to be there!"

I shout again, in a vain effort to get the people to hear me.

"I am here! I am here!"

My voice sounds foreign, like I am hearing it from another person and not myself. Legs numb now, there is nothing more I can do but bob like a sitting duck in the water and offer up a fragmented prayer that I am found. More motor sounds come closer, and the kayak begins to violently toss along with the water. I reach up my hands to brace it, so my head won't get slammed by the impact.

"Kate! Where is she?"

I think I hear Levi, but I can't be sure.

"Under the kayak!"

The definite sound, unmistakenly, of a boat engine roars right by me. Before I can blink, the kayak is ripped out of the water, and I am blinded by the light. My eyes instantly shut as I feel myself going up into the air then into someone's arms.

"I've got you, Lily. Don't worry."

I cuddle instinctively into the warm chest I find myself pressed against and arms encircle back around in response.

Levi came. Again.

My brain trained on the thought, I sigh and shiver.

"Lily! I'm here! We are heading to the shore. Hang on."

Levi doesn't say anything else like he normally would but instead holds me close. Maybe he is done with my antics, and this is the last straw with him. After this, he will one-hundred percent expect me to quit. And honestly, at this moment, I don't blame him.

"You need to be careful, Lily. You need to get away from the island."

A voice I recognize, whispers near my ear. It is the same voice as the man in the hoodie. I open my eyes, but the light is too bright, so I close them shut. Confusion hits again. Is the man holding me? How could this be? The boat speeds through the water and reaches the shore very quickly. With a large bump, I feel it hitting the rocks. Probably shallow enough for us to not get very wet as we get out.

"I've got you..." Levi says, hugging me tight before leading me off.

I barely open my eyes, struggling to walk. My legs are number than I thought, and they aren't cooperating. Instantly I am hefted into strong arms, and I let my head fall onto my boyfriend's shoulder as I close my eyes again. Too weak to think straight, I settle into his body as I feel myself being carried off the boat.

"She is going into shock..."

"Call the ambulance!"

"Lil!"

195

"Lil. I'm so sorry."

"Where is she?!"

Voices melt and drip like candle wax in my ears. Confused, I sigh and listen to Levi's heartbeat. It pounds loudly in a heavy rhythm.

"I've got her," another male voice booms.

Suddenly I am jostled and transferred to another man's arms.

Why would Levi let me go?

This new pair of arms feels stronger, and more muscled. My eyes are still closed with a heaviness I seem to be not in control of. Mummering, I try to stay awake.

"I am taking her, fuck the ambulance. Kate, get in."

This other man is more familiar. I think he might be Levi. But who was carrying me earlier? My body is cradled tightly and then I hear car doors slamming. Then we are moving again. Heat blasts onto my face and I moan. It feels good.

"Baby girl. I am here…" a voice whispers.

Levi. Not the man in the hoodie.

"God, that was wild!" Kate wails. "They came out of nowhere!"

"It's not your fault. Crazy people are everywhere Kate, and they probably had no idea how to kayak."

"We never should have gone out on the water."

"Stop. It's *not* your fault."

As the love of my life talks to my coworker, my mind blanks and I succumb to sleep.

Beep. Beep. Beep. Beep.

Rhythmic sounds softly resound in the darkened room. Slowly my eyelids flutter until they open. I am laying in a soft bed with a tight sheet and banket tucked over me, like a burrito. There is a TV up on the wall, turned on, but without any sound. It bathes the room in a soft blue glow. Turning my head, I feel a soft pain and groan.

"Lil…"

Levi leans forward and takes my hand in his. I smile softly until I see his handsome gaze boring into mine. He looks tired and worried. Not his normal self.

"Babe," is all I can manage to say, weakly.

He exhales and blinks, staring at me.

"You scared me. Again."

Closing my eyes once more, I feel his hand stroking mine. Then his phone rings. He keeps a grip on me as he answers with his other.

"Yoh. Uh huh. Uh huh. Yep. The mission has to halt. We can't continue right now. It's compromised. That's what I said."

I am not focusing on what he is saying, not really. I just want to know what happened once I was rescued. I can't remember much. Or even about the moments that the women overturned me. My memory is virtually blank, just fragments left. Only the memory of the cold water and being under the kayak is sticking. And those thoughts I can stand forgetting. I don't think I will want to be in the water ever again after I get out of the hospital, if that is where I am.

"I said *we halt*. Effective immediately."

His voice became agitated, and I frown. What is he even discussing, and with whom? I hate it when work stresses him to this point.

"Levi…" I whisper.

He hangs up and responds.

"Yeah Lil? It's okay. You are in the hospital on the base. I brought you here instead of the local one. I know the docs here."

Giving him a soft nod, I open my eyes again and turn my head so I can stare at him again. He softens and lifts my hand to give it a gentle kiss. The gesture is so sweet.

"Work okay?" I whisper.

"Yeah," he exhales. "It will be fine."

197

Mustering up strength to talk, I decide to ask.

"Is there a train car system on the islands?" I ask weakly, the question startling even myself.

His hand stills and he stares at me in disbelief.

"What train car system?"

Silence fills the air as I hear my heart beating in my ears, whooshing with sudden anxiety.

"What do you know?"

CHAPTER THIRTY-FIVE

Levi's bed is warm with the scent of him and his body heat. Probably the best part of being in a long-term relationship is just this. Having someone to sleep next to. I am grateful that he came to the water to look for me but also wonder how he even knew at all. He was supposed to have been out on a mission somewhere. Rolling over, I stretch and yawn, keeping my body entirely under the thick blanket. Levi stirs next to me. His warm hand finds my waist and tugs me to him.

"Lil," he murmurs.

His voice is husky from sleep. We haven't been at his place for that long, as the hospital on the base took forever to discharge me.

"Hmm?" I respond, closing my eyes.

"We need to talk."

I swallow a lump in my throat. We do need to talk.

"Yes?"

"This assignment," he begins. "It's turning out to be so hazardous that my boss even said you need to quit."

"I know," I quietly say. "I know. It's been awful."

"More than awful, babe. How many times have I had to divert the team's training in the past weeks? Too many to count. None of your other assignments were like this. None."

I feel bad. He is right. I haven't encountered anything like I have since being here. The ghosts, the figures, the man in the hoodie. All of them. And only here in Washington state, here on these islands. I have no idea why.

"I am trying to get through a day where something doesn't happen." I say, weakly.

"You asked about the trains. I told you that…"

Interrupting, I want to soothe his worries, "I'm sorry for telling you what I probably saw when I was experiencing hypothermia. I believe you when you say it's nothing bad."

"Lil, listen. I told you that it was nothing. Those trains were moving Top-Secret stuff but only weapons that the public can't know about. Standard. Only that was not entirely true."

Not entirely true?

My pulse quickens at what he is saying, my brain suddenly alert.

"What do you mean, 'not entirely true'?"

"I mean I shouldn't be telling you this. The truth."

"Go on..."

What is he about to tell me?

"If you are going to marry me, then I need to tell you a few things. But you have to answer my question. You never did. And we didn't talk about it again."

"Do you mean will I marry you?"

"Yes," he softly says, his hand grazing my forearm under the blanket.

I turn my head to look into his eyes, to see how serious he actually is. Softness stares back at me. He is serious all right.

"Of course I will marry you, Levi. I mean, I love you. You surprised me is all, I wasn't expecting you to ask. And you didn't have an actual ring."

"I know, Lil. I do have one, though. It just wasn't on me at the time."

He reaches over towards the nightstand and brandishes a small leather box, which he hands to me. I hold my breath as I remove my arms from the blanket and take it from him,. Opening it slowly, I see a large yellow diamond set on a simple silver band. It's beautiful.

"Levi..."

"It's made for you," he says, taking it out of the box and sliding it on my finger. "Yes?"

"Yes," I reply.

Leaning down, he kisses me.

Now we are engaged.

"*Now* we are engaged," he chuckles, reading my mind.

The mood quickly turns somber though as he sits up, leaning back on the headboard. I have seen this look before on his face, usually when things at work are not going as planned for reasons he never divulges to me. This time is different, though. He is about to talk. The gravity of which I know is serious.

"I can't tell you anything Top-Secret. You know that. But I have to tell you that you aren't crazy. You did see a train car with people in it."

The room goes eerily quiet.

I feel my heart thumping faster in my chest. I wasn't imagining it. I *did* see what I saw in the woods. It was real. Not hypothermia. Not me going crazy. Real. And the ghosts or other spirits were real, too. They had to have been…

"You probably want to know who the people were." It's a statement, not a question.

I nod but don't say anything. Levi looks at me, his eyes no longer soft.

"They are of no consequence, Lil. I can promise you that."

What is he saying?

"All life is of consequence."

"Not all, Lil."

"Who are they?"

"All that I can say is the Navy is working with other government agencies. We are just the transporters for them. It's on our land, the train tracks."

He reaches for me, and I let him pull me onto his lap. I trust him, but what he is implying sends a pit into my gut. Suddenly I feel different.

"Lil. There are devils in the world. Who do the worst of the worst. And our government, instead of executing them, can use them for the development of things that keep us safe. Keep the world safe. Understand?"

201

I shake my head.

"It's Top-Secret. I can't tell you anymore. But you are not crazy."

The SEALs that I heard in the woods. They sounded like they didn't want Levi to know something. I try to recall the things they said that I overheard before passing out. It had sounded more sinister that what Levi just explained. He isn't telling me everything. Not even close.

"Okay," I whisper.

Tracing his chest with my fingers, I muster a bit of bravery. I want to put together the pieces that are rattling loose in my brain.

"What is so important about Deception Pass?"

He stiffens under my touch. There is something to that place, I just know it. And his reaction is telling.

"What about Deception Pass, babe?" His voice is light, belying his stance.

"Well, I have seen it on a bunch of documents on Fort Warren. A bunch. Then it was scrawled on the wall in the bunker, and it's just seemingly everywhere."

I don't mention that I know he named a mission after it. He doesn't need to know I was eavesdropping after being rescued from the ferry sinking.

"It's just a place here on the islands. A strait, connecting the islands. As you saw."

"But why was it listed on documents on the Fort, then?"

"I don't know, babe. You never mentioned it before. What were the documents about?"

"Random briefings. We just skim things; we don't read them."

"Except Top-Secret ones," he says, thumbing my chin up to make our eyes meet. "I heard from Commander Lessing that you took something from Warren."

My face pales. How did he find out?

"Babe…"

"I… We…"

"You and Kate?"

I nod.

"We read it, like we are allowed to do. We skim things, yes, but *sometimes* we read things. Depends on if we are confused on the classification."

"I know you, Lil. You are as honest as they come. What did the document say? What piqued your interest to the point of taking a Top-Secret document off site?"

"It talked about experiments. Carried out on Naval personnel, those that were sick, already on sick call. They tested things out on them."

Now it was his turn to have the blood rush from his face.

"Where did you find this document?"

"In one of the buildings, just sitting in a pile of old musty stuff we had to go through."

"Just sitting there?" he asks incredulously.

"Yes. Why?"

"That shouldn't have been there."

"Well, of course not! Do you know the times I can count finding anything Top-Secret? On only one of my hands. For my entire career. Trust me, it made no sense. For Kate either. Actually, Kate found it first. And she was the one wanting to take it to our cabins to read it."

"Kate?" He becomes guarded again.

"Yes. She is super into stuff like that. Conspiracy stuff that the government is doing. And we did take it, I did. But then after we read it, we burned it."

"I know."

"You know?"

He traces my cheek with a finger.

"I know, babe. I checked your cabin. Remember my job? Well, Lessing asked me to check. I know that you burned it.

Evidence in the fireplace at Kate's."

"God…" I say, embarrassment on my face.

"Be glad he asked me instead of someone else. I always have your back.

"I overheard him talking to Peter. About getting rid of me. Trying to anyways."

"Peter? Lessing just asked me to investigate. I did and told him that you are not in possession of any documents. Which now, you are not. Why would Peter have anything to say?"

"What did Lessing say?" I ask, worry evident in my voice.

"He is still watching you, but not suspicious anymore."

I try to push off Levi to get out of his bed, but he holds me on his lap out of care and concern. Something that used to perturb me, but I appreciate it now.

"I didn't do anything other than take the file, then look at it. We didn't make a copy or distribute it or anything. I swear, Levi."

"I know, babe. I know and I told Lessing that."

"I feel sick now Levi…"

"You don't need to feel sick, come here, relax. This assignment is almost over. Lessing said there are only a few weeks left, or less. Then you can take another one or take some time off. I am okay with either."

Laying back down, I think about everything and my mind wanders. I wonder who has been leaving black hoodies and coins. Who exactly is the man with the smile. Or if he is even real at all.

CHAPTER THIRTY-SIX

"We are gonna need to encircle you with bubble wrap."

"She needs more than that, this place isn't for you, Lily…"

"Peter, shut up. Respectfully."

I grunt under the weight of the stack I am carrying, listening to my coworkers. Paper weighs a lot more than you would think. It smells, too; a stench of mold and mildew. I plod along the hallway with the bulk while Brian and Peter two man carry a full bag, and Kate handles a dolly with a small filing cabinet. We are in a rush to get through this building.

"I am *fine*!" I say gruffly to the group.

"We just need to get this job done, before my phone rings off the hook," Brain says, kicking the door open to the last room we need to tackle.

"Lessing still onto you?" Kate asks loudly.

"Uh huh. He is, indeed. The weirdest work experience of my life. I have never had a boss rush a job like this. It's not like they are going to use these buildings. Or even tear them down yet. It doesn't make sense."

"We are just a pain in his ass. That's all. He wants us to go and also, he wants this project over. Probably the reports of us almost drowning, too, have added to the urgency. It is a headache to him."

"Most likely. Officers care about image above all else. Glad I went the contractor route and never joined."

"I wouldn't have minded joining. My wife…"

"Your wife would have *hated* it. Deploying? Training? You would be gone," Brian interrupts.

We all know his wife is obsessed with him and being near her constantly. She doesn't trust him either, calling and texting nonstop. I suppose she has my sympathy. I don't trust him either. Then it hits me, what if his *wife* is the one who pushed him to report me? He has to tell her literally everything. If that is true, then it makes sense.

"My wife just likes to have me around. That's all. What's wrong with that?" Peter asks, defensively.

He is mad. We touched a nerve. Furthering my suspicions.

"Nothing. Unless you want any amount of personal freedom," Kate retorts.

"I don't need freedom; I love my wife."

"Nobody is saying you don't," Brian says. "We should all be focusing on finishing this job, and fast."

"Your boyfriend…"

"Fiancé, Peter," I say.

The men drop their bag and turn to stare, mouths agape. Kate even stops wheeling the filing cabinet to look.

"What?"

I stare back, wondering what had just happened.

"You are engaged?" Kate asks, a slow smile on her face.

Holding up my left hand, I show my engagement ring. Kate lights up like a bonfire.

"Congratulations!"

"My! That is a gorgeous ring!" Brian exclaims. "Love the yellow. Congratulations!"

The only one who hasn't said anything yet is Peter, but I expected that. He is probably calculating the cost of my ring out of jealousy.

"Was it last night?" Kate asks.

I nod and she smiles, turning back to the dolly. Peter picks up the bag and so does Brian.

"Congrats," Peter mumbles, begrudgingly.

"Thank you, Peter."

A part of me feels bad for him. He might be close in age to me, but we are vastly different people. And he is trapped in his circumstances, whether happy or not. Marriage does that to people. I can tell he has a ton of pressure on him as the man

206

of the household. But it doesn't excuse him from wanting me to get fired in the way he has.

We continue our trek to the last room. It's in a precarious spot, around a tight corner and down a set of stairs. Almost in the basement. The heady scent of mold hits our noses as we descend the stairs. Another hazard of working in such old buildings.

"God, this is gonna get us all sick…" Peter exclaims.

Brian grunts, "Good thing we have the best healthcare."

Kate juggles the dolly down the steps. "We should be fine. It's only for a day or two. Think of the sailors that have to live in buildings like these. Can you imagine?"

"I can. And it's horrifying. So many bases are like this across the US. You'd think with all that money, they would be able to overhaul all the buildings and not one service member would sleep or work in mold."

"It's the DOD. Money goes where it's not needed," Peter says, kicking the door so it opens.

Each step in, we let out a collective gasp. There is a horrid stench here.

"Out come the masks. I had a feeling this was gonna happen. Here, put these on."

Brian takes out a baggie with Covid era face masks and hands us one each. The surgical blue brings back memories. Ones I would rather forget, as I am sure we all would. Once mine is secure, I take normal breaths and feel the heat hit my eyes. Wearing a mask sucks.

"Alright, let's get to it. Then we can take the bag out as we fill it."

This room is by far the worst in the entire building. It has so many documents stacked in it, floor to ceiling, almost. The people who used to work here must have designated it as the dumping ground. The place where documents go to die. Only they aren't dead, it's us who are tasked with giving them their final burial. I help Kate get the filing cabinet off the dolly and propped up against the wall. Brian and Peter start at opposite corners, tackling the first stacks. This is a massive amount of work. It will take a few days.

"He asked you again and with a gorgeous ring!"

I nod at Kate.

"I am so glad, Lily. You deserve the best. Did you hesitate this time or..."

Opening the cabinet to reveal a trove of Secret documents in old musty folders we both grunt. These will need to be hauled out to get destroyed. And she had just carted it all down here. Sometimes our jobs are full of irony.

"Getting our exercise in today," I quip. "And no, I didn't hesitate. I said 'yes'."

"Good. I am glad. I know how much you love him."

"Oh, damn it. I left the secret sleeves in the other building. We will need them for this. There are too many folders to let loose in the bag."

"And with how angry Commander Lessing is being, we have to do it by the book."

"Yep," Kate sighs through her mask.

"No prob. I will go get them. I could use a bit of fresh air. I hate masks and it's rank in here."

Kate nods and joins Brian with his stack. Working together goes faster. No one looks up when I leave but I do catch Peter eyeing me when I walk out the doorway and step onto the stairs. He didn't appear happy. I tell myself it could be any number of things. He is just an overall angry guy. But still, something feels off about him. I can't place my finger on it.

Stay on task so we can finish this job.

After my night with Levi, I only want to stay at home and enjoy our life together. I am not ready to quit working, by any means, but I may need to think harder about the assignments I go for. The one at JBLM, up by Seattle, might be my last for a while. Deep in thought, I leave the building where we have worked for months and exit into the cold air. Images of the bear that was shot flash in my mind. Its blood was all over the ground that I am standing on right now.

Glancing down, I see nothing but moss and water. The Navy cleaned every single trace of the bear away. I wonder if any paw prints from the beast are left behind in the wood line. Not sure why I even care, but feeling compelled to look, I wander between the building next door and an old, rickety one. The ground is soft and slightly squishy, being raised slightly by massive evergreen tree roots that are nearby. They form a network that you can't see and actually tangle together in such a way that the trees can communicate.

I walk further into the trees and find a game trail of sorts. Bits of brown fur are scattered along the sides. This has to be from the bear that came into the building.

Right?

The slight stench of bear hangs in the air, though. That wouldn't still be here. Not from the trace amounts of fur that I am looking at. It hits me that I might have made a mistake with coming into the trees.

Snap….

A twig or branch breaks in the distance.

My mind races and I feel my body cease up. I don't have anything on me to help myself. If it is a bear.

Crack….

More sounds. Something is coming closer. Frantically, I look for what could be in the trees around me. But I can't see anything. It is too dark; it's like looking into a scene from a German dark fairytale. Fear barely describes it. Branches rustle and I hear the sound no one wants to hear while outside. I heard it in the concrete bunker. Heavy breathing.

I turn and run.

CHAPTER THIRTY-SEVEN

My feet fly and then slip.

I fall and hit the ground hard, mud coating my hands. The noises grow closer behind me, so I cry out and scramble to stand, then continue to run. I know which building I need to get into to get Kate's document items, and it's not far. I can make it.

Someone is in the woods behind me.

Looking over my shoulder as I speed between buildings, I see a dark figure, shrouded in the branches, but moving fast. *Is it a ghost?* Whoever it is, it is coming at me like a freight train. Yelping, I race faster until I reach the building. The front door is unlocked, so I yank the heavy wooden door open and then slam it shut, locking it behind me. Expecting to hear the sound of breathing, I pause, listening. The only sound audible is *my* ragged breath. I can barely breathe. My chest burns.

After waiting a few minutes, I exhale. Whoever was chasing me didn't see what building I went into. Brian, Kate and Peter come to mind. I don't want them to wander outside with the dark figure, but I left my cell phone with my bag in the other building.

"Shit," I curse under my breath.

The realization isn't good. Of course, this would happen. And now I am stuck again. Waiting a few minutes more, I finally give up and look around the entryway. It's dark and dank but doesn't smell like mold, oddly enough. Probably just feels this way from not having heat in this building. That and time compounding. The floor creaks as I take a few tentative steps away from the front door.

My surroundings hit as I struggle to focus. Feeling like I am in a scary movie set, I swallow the lump in my throat. Suddenly, I forget about how I will get out of here and make it back to the other building. This building holds a sinister air to it. When working here it felt okay, but right now, it doesn't. Not at all. Something is off.

"Hello?" I call out.

I am alone. I know no one will answer. I am vulnerable and anything can get me, the realization hits. Staring down the long hallway, I see darkness moving. Like being in a cave with shadows that shift and change. There's no light source in sight. I blink, and stare, listening to any noises. But all I hear is rustling from the wind outside.

Then there is a soft creak.

"Shit!" I whisper.

I can't help it. My nerves are shot. I heard it. I know I did. Slowly, I walk away from the door and onto the carpet runner. My shoes make zero sounds. Looking left then right, I see empty rooms on each side. The windows are covered in a film of dirt, and they're wet from condensation. They failed to function properly for years, if not decades.

Another creak. It sounds far off. From somewhere else in the building. It is two stories, so it could be from upstairs.

"Please be no one."

My voice is soft, almost not audible. I stop walking and listen. Nothing. No sounds. Nothing except the thump of my heart whooshing in my ears.

Continuing down the hallway, I feel cold air hitting me. It's freezing and makes my teeth chatter.

Cold air. Like a ghost. Exactly as Kate described it in Germany.

This *can't* be happening to me. The carpet's hue, a dirty red, sends my mind into overdrive. What if it is waiting for me? Waiting for me to come here today so it can finally harm me?

Creak…creak.

More sounds. Like someone is moving slightly or walking. The carpet runner covers the hallway only; the rest of the rooms have old plank style hardwood flooring. And the sound

211

is getting closer now. Definitely not from upstairs. Horror movies are set like this. Alone in dark buildings, with no light or weapons to utilize. I am, in essence, screwed.

Creak. Crack.

Not wanting to wait and see if it would come out, I turn around and head back towards the door but realize I couldn't leave.

The dark figure is outside.

Frantically, I run into a room and look out from the weathered glass. Sure enough, I see a tall person, shrouded in darkness, standing near the tree line, not moving.

"Shit…"

There is no way I can go out yet. Not without risking my life. I spin and examine the room. Nowhere to hide here. But I do spot the staircase across the hallway, in the other room. Upstairs. Do I go upstairs? As I frantically mull over what to do, I hear the telltale sound of heavy shoes on wood. *Someone is here.*

I run.

Hitting the stairs two at a time, I jet up until I hit the landing at the top. I can hear heavy shoes, maybe boots, running below. Whoever it is, they will catch me in no time. I need to hide. And now. My eyes spot rooms with doors halfway open so I quickly run to each and peer in.

A desk, a filing cabinet, a chair. Nothing I can hide under or behind. Frantic doesn't even begin to describe how I feel. I am sweating and my heart feels like it will explode.

Hide! Now!

The boots begin to hit the stairs. I have seconds to find a place to hide. I spot something on the wall at the end of the hallway; it looks like a hidden closet. There is no handle on it. I run and with shaky fingers, feel along the seam. It pops open. With seconds to spare, I climb into the dark hole and close the wall behind me, until only a sliver of light is left. And I wait.

My breathing is labored but silent. I hear heavy footsteps on the ground in the hallway. The person made it upstairs. Whoever it is, it was waiting for me. But why?

Can ghosts sound as loud as this?

Kate's words echo in my mind. Ghosts can do a lot, and they can even move objects, which makes my blood feel like ice flowing through my veins. What does a ghost want from me? The footsteps pause every so many seconds. I picture it looking into each room. Looking for me.

In the closet where I am hiding, it is cold and dirty. My hands are touching dirt and dust as I crouch. At some point I need to get out of here. The footsteps continue to get closer, and I find myself holding my breath.

Please God, don't let him find me.

Boots stop right next to the wall, and I can hear heavy breathing.

The heavy breathing again. There is more than one of them.

I whimper and pray silently. Clothing rustles, almost as if the person is shifting their weight. The sounds of a hand dragging along the paint on the wall fill my ears. I squeeze my eyes shut and listen to the hammering of my heart. This is a literal nightmare. If only Kate hadn't needed the document sleeves, I'd be safe with my coworkers.

Thump.

A sound downstairs startles whatever is on the other side of the wall. Boots rapidly leave and I hear them thumping down the stairs, quickly. Then silence fills the building again. I exhale shakily and shift my weight, feeling faint suddenly. I need to stop squatting. Sitting on my butt in the dirt, I try to regulate my breathing. The last thing I need to do is pass out. Maybe the other figure is trying to get into the building. It can join the ghost or man or whoever is stalking me.

I hear the front door open and shut. Then silence again.

Did he leave?

213

I wait and wait, at least ten minutes, then I realize he, it, must have left. Getting back up into a crouch, I slowly climb out of my hiding place. Dirt falls on the carpet runner along with my legs and shoes. I don't even bother to brush it off. I am too focused on listening for any sounds. The man, thing, might still be here, I just don't know.

The stairs look so far away but I slowly make my way to them, one step at a time. The building is still absolutely quiet. No sound at all, only my feet and my heart thundering loudly that only I can hear. I creep down each step until I make it through the darkness and into the soft light of the room by the front door. I feel so much anxiety I might pass out.

Is the man thing gone?

I move as quietly as I can and peer out of the room and into the main hallway. I see no one. The urge to bolt takes over. I have to leave. I spot the document sleeves leaning up against the wall near the door, so I grab them hastily and fling the front door open. Half expecting to be met by the other figure, I am surprised that I am not. Nothing but cold air, sprinkles from rain and wet everything greets me.

Time to run.

I run and run, darting along the gravel path connecting the buildings until I reach the one we are working in. Relief doesn't hit until I have made it through the building and down the rickety stairs to my coworkers.

"Oh my God, Lil! You are so dirty, are you okay?"

Brian lowers his mask, "You look like you've seen a ghost!"

Tears fill my eyes then spill down my cheeks.

All I can do is nod my head.

CHAPTER THIRTY-EIGHT

"Here, you are shaking." Kate puts a heavy wool blanket around my shoulders as wind from the ferry hits our faces. It's cold outside, almost winter temps this afternoon. My coworkers were understandably scared when I told them about the figure, and I left out the part about being chased by a man in the building with the folders. I will tell Kate later. Brian sounded the alarm, and we got told the ferry would take us to our cabins.

The Navy is taking it pretty seriously, that a man chased us in the woods. They made all of us evacuate actually. The other contracted workers too. Men mill about in construction hats, hands in their jackets on the ferry deck nearby. I wonder if they believed a strange man was loose or not. Only I saw it.

"So, are you going to tell me why you are covered in dirt? It's not from outside. I can tell."

I turn to Kate, her face inquiring.

Shaking my head, I look out over the water. It's choppy and dark. Just like my mind right now. I should probably tell her. We are so close to being done with this job, it doesn't matter if there is a ghost or whoever was in that building with me. In a matter of days, I will be gone.

"Lil..."

"The building the document sleeves were in, there was someone in there with me. It chased me. I think it was a man. A ghost. I don't know."

"Holy crap! What do you mean, was it the one from outside? When you went in, you saw it?"

"No. Something chased me outside. I ran to the door and locked it from inside to make sure the figure wasn't following me. When I noticed it was still there, I heard some sounds in the building. Like a person was walking or moving."

"Shit. Lil. What happened then?"

"I ran and found the second story, then the sounds, they were boots or some sort of heavy shoes. They followed me. Thank God I found a secret wall closet to hide in. It was just enough space to crouch. Dirty as fuck, though. That's how I got so filthy."

"Then you ran out?"

"I did, after I heard the footsteps go outside. He didn't return. Then I took my break and got away. Ran back," I say, choking as tears fill my eyes. "I never saw who it was. Or what it was. Kate, I can't take this though...I don't know what to do."

"I know what to do. We are going to get you cleaned up, you will call Levi. And we are going to talk about what your married life will be like, far away from here."

I can't argue with her; I have zero energy. Instead, I grip the blanket and pull it tighter, watching the ferry bow cut through the waves. The water is choppy, like there is an impending storm. There is no rain at the moment, only chill in the air and gusts of wind. Any whales that might still be in the Sound migrating are deep below the surface. I wonder if the giants that overturned me are still in the area.

Conversation floats over to us. The men are talking about the man that I saw outside, the one who chased me. They think the island is cursed. I am beginning to think so, too. Brian and Peter stand with them.

"If Levi can't come tonight, I think I should sleep on your couch. Is that okay?" Kate asks.

I nod.

"Yeah, thank you."

I feel weak. More than exhausted. Mentally, this has reached a point that I can't navigate by myself anymore. I need Levi.

An eagle chirps in nearby trees. Glancing up, I look for it but, of course, I can't see it. Then another chirps in the distance. They are fascinating animals, hunt solo or in pairs but seem to always communicate with each other, kind of like Kate and I on this job assignment. I glance down; the water is darker than normal. Probably because of the lack of sunlight.

Crack.

Lighting strikes in the distance followed by the rumble of thunder. It scares me and I jump on the cold wooden bench.

"Great, another storm. Looks like a big one is blowing in, too. I'll make us some comfort food tonight," Kate says.

The boat pitches more than normal, tossing us up, then down as it speeds through the water towards our island, the captain keeps us on a steady course. Since the other ferry sunk, the crew has been meticulous about keeping this new one maintained. I watch the tree lined shores pass by from further off islands. But then the image of the tall man comes to mind. His sneer and grin, the lanky body he has. The way he is always lurking in the shadows of various places. Plus, the tall dark figure outside. Was it the same man?

Squeezing my eyes shut, I exhale. I don't want to see him. I only want to go back to normal. With Levi and my job. The boring old life I had before coming to this location. It was good, and I feel like I took it for granted in a way.

The island appears in the distance, and I can see our cabins close to the shore. They look like a movie set, as if Hollywood was going to film a thriller or horror flick. Another crack of lighting hits and I flinch. Why does it need to storm *now*? The ferry captain navigates up to the dock and idles the boat. Time to get off. I shrug out of the wool blanket and Kate hands it back to the crew as we disembark.

"Storm is coming, stay inside your cabins tonight. The weather is supposed to get wild."

"Thanks!" Kate shouts over her shoulder, as the wind begins to whip, and rain drops start to fall.

We say our goodnights to the men and run to my cabin as rain pelts harder. The captain wasn't lying. It feels like the storm is already here. I almost slip on the front porch steps but grab the railing. Fumbling for my key from my bag, I shiver.

"First thing's first. I'll get a fire going," Kate promises.

I won't argue with that.

Finally, I get the door unlocked and we step into the living room. I had left the only baseboard heater on this morning, so it sort of made the cabin warm but only slightly. We drop our coats and take off our shoes.

"You should go shower, Lil. You will feel better, and you are filthy."

"You're right, I am. Be back in a minute."

She waves me off to the bedroom as she readies a new stack of wood for the fireplace. As quicky as I can, I shed my dirty clothes in the bedroom once the door is shut and get into the shower. Hot water immediately soothes my senses. I close my eyes as I stand under the stream.

What a day.

I need to text Levi, and I will as soon as I am clean. Hopefully, he is able to respond. Usually, I don't want to worry him but now, I am scared. The man chasing me in the building was the last straw. He will definitely know what to do, like Kate said. I finish rinsing the soap off and conditioner from my hair, and I step out of the shower, wrapping a large towel around myself. Pajamas next. I left mine on the bottom of my bed, folded next to my laptop.

Going to retrieve them, I can hear Kate in the other room. She is moving around in the kitchen as the sound of logs crackling and popping fills my ears. Soothing as it is, I am still on edge. Having her sleep over will certainly help and Levi would recommend that first thing too. It's safer this way.

"Lil…. Lil.."

Kate calls me suddenly as I slip on my pajama set and slippers.

"Yeah?"

"Did you search for this on your laptop?"

My laptop?

Glancing at the bed, I see my laptop isn't here. A pit immediately forms in my stomach. I *know* I left it on the bed. How had it moved? I search the room for it, looking under the bed, the dressers and nightstand and the floor. It's not here.

"Lil?"

Kate is standing by my laptop on the counter in the kitchen next to a barstool when I exit my bedroom. Her eyes meet mine as I glance at the computer screen.

"I wanted to search for any videos on the weather, and this was already pulled up.."

'Gold Mountain, Naval Secrets' pops off the screen.

"I didn't move my laptop, Kate…"

"What do you mean?"

"I left it in my bedroom, next to my folded pajamas. Was it here? Out on the counter like this?"

Her face briefly flashes with fear.

"Yes. Just like this. The screen was blank but then I moved my finger on the keypad, and this popped up…"

Glancing down, I notice something I had seen before on my porch.

Sand.

"Kate.."

She glances down as well then sucks in her breath.

"Lil. Someone was in here."

"The door was locked," I reply in a trance, unable to stop looking at the sand.

"I know."

The fire cracks in the background as my heart begins to race.

"Lil, I am going to call Levi. Where is your phone?"

CHAPTER THIRTY-NINE

Lights flicker in the cabin.

Outside the wind batters against the wood and windowpanes as rain hits the roof like a snare drum. The storm has hit and unleashes all its fury on the island.

"The power may go out. Where are the flashlights? Mine were under the kitchen sink, but yours are missing.."

Shrugging, I help Kate search. We check the bathroom and then find two large flashlights.

The lights flicker again as the wind howls so loudly we can hear it inside. We move back to my living room and stand in the middle of the floor, waiting to see if the lights will go out. And then, they do. The fire, the only light source now in the room, besides the flashlights, dances with the updraft coming from the chimney.

"Okay, so a man was ready and waiting for you. He might have been lurking around for any one of us and you going into the building to get the folders might have been a coincidence, but still. We know this is a fact."

"Thank God for flashlights."

"Yeah, no kidding," Kate says.

We click them on and sweep the room with swathes of bright light. The fireplace shoots out an orange glow of flames and shadows that dance on the floors and walls. It's comforting to have a fire but also a bit creepy. My laptop has a black screen as it does when you walk away from it for a few minutes. I'm going to check it again. I want to see what the article says that whoever broke in was looking at.

'Gold mountain' says the title on the webpage. It talks about hidden secrets that the Navy has for the area surrounding the mountain. Why would this be open? What for?

"Whoever did this was trying to tell you something, Lily. There is no other reason for it."

I scroll down and skim.

"Kate, look at this.."

She stands next to me as we stare at the blue glowing screen. It's a website that is run by former anonymous Naval employees, and they give individual stories of having to go to Gold Mountain for Top-Secret projects. They don't detail what is happening there but the story I am looking at talks about train cars coming from Whidbey air base. And people being inside of them. People like I saw.

"Shit, Lil. That is something you saw…it had to have been real."

"I know."

"Levi. Call Levi. Have you tried yet?"

"No, right. I need to call him. If my cell works in this storm."

Stepping away from the computer, I take my phone and dial my fiancé. Ony the phone won't go through. The call drops immediately, no matter how many times I try.

"Not going through?"

"Ugh, no," I sigh. "The storm is messing up cell towers."

"Well, we *are* in the boonies out here. It's kind of scary to think about, in all honesty. You can't get on the island unless you come by boat. So how did the person who broke in get here?"

"That's if it's an actual person. I mean Kate, could it be a ghost?"

"I don't know Lil. I guess but…"

Suddenly, a loud sound emits from outside. A loud screech, almost like a person who was in pain. My pulse races at the sound and my blood runs cold. It's *not* from an animal. I jog to the front window and peer out. I can see nothing. It's pitch-black outside, and I only see darkness and the blur of white caps from the Sound in the distance. Rain is pelting so hard, even the water is almost unrecognizable. Another screech rings out. A shiver runs down my back. Not from the cold, either.

"What was that?" Kate yelps.

"I don't see anything!"

We hear a loud scraping sound along the walls, almost as if something is tearing the cabin apart. It's intense and beyond anything I have heard in a storm before.

"We need to go on the porch and check that out!"

Before I can protest, Kate has the front door unlocked and steps out with her flashlight. I groan. The last thing I think we should do is go outside, with the storm and the shrieking, but I need to find Kate. Wind hits me full force as I shrug into my jacket and step out onto the dark porch. I can't see her anymore. She has disappeared. My heart sinks. Walking slowly, I can't help but think about someone or something getting into my cabin. And where did the screeching come from? Was it a ghost? My thoughts are now racing.

How could whoever have gotten into my cabin have locked the door without a key?

The immediate thought frightens me. It points to a ghost, as I keep thinking.

"Kate!" I shout into the relentless darkness.

There is no answer above the roar of the wind and rain. She is not on the porch; I shine the flashlight in all directions but can't see her. Pulling the jacket hood on, I brave the rain and step slowly off the porch. Sweeping the flashlight beam around the front yard, I call for her again.

"Kate! Kate!"

The wind sounds like a train, roaring through the island. There is no way that she can hear me. I need to find her. The grass squishes under my boots as I decide to round the corner of the cabin. Seeing nothing but large tree branches, I keep going.

The light from my flashlight is weaker here.

Rain dumps on top of me, and I know I am completely soaked. I yell again, as loud as I can this time.

"*Kate!*"

She isn't around the back, but I can vaguely see the side of her cabin, a bit of a ways off alongside mine. All the lights are out still. Then my flashlight beam captures something that I can barely believe. Three Asian women are standing behind Kate, pale as ghosts. I drop the flashlight.

"Lil!" Kate shouts.

I gasp, rain pelting my face.

The women! The Asian women from the day in the kayaks!

Bending down, I reach for the flashlight. My fingers dig in the soaked grass until I find the light and bring it back up. I shine the light on Kate then directly behind her. The women are gone.

"Lily, a branch rolled on my foot! Help me get it off!"

Sure enough, Kate's foot is stuck under a section of a tree branch. Running to her, I can see she is stuck as she said.

"I can't get it off!" Kate yells.

Shit!

My heart races.

Sure enough, the tree section is heavy. Dropping the flashlight, I huff and puff and try to shove it off. It's barely moving.

"Kate, I'm trying! How did this roll onto you?"

We struggle to move the tree section. Kate is pushing as well, as best she can.

"I heard the screeching again and it sounded like a hurt woman, so I ran over here, then the tree section rolled onto me!"

"It's not budging!"

I huff and puff more, pushing as my legs dig in and my feet slide in the muddy grass. At this rate, we won't free her. We need to get leverage to pop it up, so we can slide her foot out.

But with what? I look around frantically for something, anything, but it's too dark.

"Here!" A man's voice yells. "Put this under the base!"

Miraculously, Brian appears with a heavy-duty iron bar, like a large tire iron, but sized for a monster truck. He thrusts it in my hands and points, telling me where to brace it. I comply, getting on my knees and shoving the bar under the branch.

"Stand back!" He shouts.

Standing on the metal bar, he rocks up and down until the tree section moves upwards off of Kate. Physics at work.

"Lil, pull her out!"

I tug and pull Kate out. Lightning cracks very close and thunder resounds. Another screech emits from the wood line, but Kate and Brian are too preoccupied to notice.

"We need to go!" Brian yells. "The lightning!"

Kate hobbles, with Brain's assistance, towards our cabin.

"We are going back inside!" Kate shouts over her shoulder.

I pick up the flashlight as another screech emits from behind me. Kate and Brian disappear in the darkness around the other side of the house. Swallowing a lump in my throat, I pivot and shine the light towards the trees. The wind is howling now and the branches whip violently. The flashlight beam is weak, barely cutting through the rain as it blows sideways.

Then I see something. A dark shadow. It moves, or darts, out of the trees then back again. I blink and hesitate.

Should I follow?

Usually when I pause like this, my intuition is telling me something. But I decide to go against it. I need to know what is there, what is actually going on. Slowly I move through the rain, sweeping my flashlight towards the woods as I do. A loud screech sounds again but accompanied by a heavy groan afterwards.

"Who is there?" I shout.

There's no reply.

224

No one can most likely hear me. The rain is battering too loudly for my voice to carry. Before I get too close to the trees I hear someone whisper my name behind me. I drop the flashlight and run.

CHAPTER FORTY

I lay on the couch as Kate is curled up in the large leather chair by the fire. We both fell asleep in the living room, and the power is still out. The storm rages outside, though not as strong as earlier. I can hear thunder in the distance, the kind that indicates how far way it actually is.

I need to talk to Levi.

Fire popping, I pick up my phone and try dialing him again, to no avail. The call still won't go through. I sigh and pull the blanket that I have been cuddling up to my chin t. Hopefully the storm will pass soon and then I can talk to him. I *need* to talk to him. Imagining him out in the weather also scares me. Is he safe? Mind wandering all over the place, I eventually drift off again.

I am in a room in Fort Warren.

It's dark and I can hear voices around me but can't see anyone. This is obviously a dream, and I am aware of it. Usually while dreaming, you don't realize that you are, though. So, that's weird.

"She must go.."

"She needs to be eliminated…"

"She knows too much now.."

"They are trying to contact her."

"I know they are, but she doesn't know it yet."

The voices go on and on about a 'she'. I feel sick to my stomach and scared. I don't want to be in the dark anymore and try walking around the room slowly, but I keep bumping into things. Reaching my arms down, I touch something warm. Then I hear something moan. It sounds like a person.

"Who is that?" I ask, recoiling my hand.

Only, no one answers back. Just more moaning. I move backwards and bump into something else and touch another warm object.

People. I am touching people.

Bang! Bang! Bang!

A loud noise wakes me suddenly. Someone is at my cabin door..

"God!" Kate exclaims, bolting upright.

I get up and drop the blanket, flashlight in hand. It's still dark out, and it will be impossible to see who is outside.

"Brian?" I call out.

The wind is still too loud, and I doubt he can hear me. He is probably coming by to check on Kate. Or it could be Peter checking, I've no idea except one that I don't want to think about. Grinning men with the bluest eyes in a black hoodie. Asian women. Skeletal people from the train cars.

I unlock the door and open it as the wind catches and flings it back, making me gasp.

"Lil!"

Levi's face greets me, standing out under the hood of his dark rain jacket. He is soaked and looks cold.

"Levi!" I exclaim, rushing into his arms.

Wet drops pepper on my face as he bends his head down to kiss me. He still smells like him. Like my home. Relief washes over me, and I feel like crying but I hold back.

"Come inside! Get out of your wet stuff."

Kate busies herself with Levi's coat as he takes off his boots.

"How did you get here?" she asks.

"I took a small craft. I'm alone. The rest of the team are off with their families. I had to get to mine."

My heart swells at the words.

I am his home.

"There is a huge branch on the ground outside…it hit your cabin," he says to me.

"I know. Kate's foot was stuck under it…"

"Her foot?"

"We heard screeching sounds, and it was loud, like a woman was in pain. Kate ran out and somehow the tree section rolled onto her foot." I explain, hesitant to say more in front of Kate.

Levi takes my hand in his and walks to the couch. His pants are remarkably dry I notice. He is a master at his job, and this is just another sign.

"Instinct is real. You have to listen to it when you feel a certain warning, but I wouldn't run out into potential danger," he says.

No mention of the screeching, which I find odd. My stomach turns a bit as I remember the sound outside, and the dark figure I saw in the woods.

"Yes. I think I am gonna run over to Brian's, check on them and give you two a moment to yourselves." Kate interrupts.

"Ok, be careful, it's still storming." I say.

"I will.."

She puts on her boots and jacket and exits out the door of the cabin, leaving Levi and I alone in the dark with the fire crackling. The room is still dancing with orange and shadows of flames. It's oddly soothing now. Now he is here. Like I can exhale finally.

"Babe, what sounds did you exactly hear?"

I sigh. I have to tell him.

"We heard a loud screeching. It was like nothing I have ever heard before. Like a wounded person. It wasn't an animal; it was human, Levi."

Levi stiffens.

"The storm was bad, Lil. It was almost hurricane winds. It's possible you heard storm sounds; how could an injured woman be on the island?"

"I heard it, Levi." I say, firmly.

Turning to the fire, I shift on the couch. Something doesn't feel right. It just doesn't.

"I know you thought you did, babe," Levi sighs. "But in

228

moments of stress, of *high* stress, things can happen. I have been there before on missions. I know."

I look up at Levi's face. It is illuminated by the fire.

"I saw a dark figure in the woods."

I decide to blurt it out. I need to get it off my chest.

"You saw a what?"

He stares back at me, his eyes changing color in the dimly lit living room. My stomach churns again.

"In the wood line. Brian was busy helping Kate back to my cabin when I turned and saw this figure. It was darting in between the trees. I saw it, Levi, I know what I saw."

I see him swallow; his Adams apple bobs as he does.

"Lily, I think it's time you seriously think about quitting your job. The stress of everything is proving too much for you. I told you I would take care of you..."

"No, I can't quit. Not yet, I have to finish the job here, Levi. I..."

"I'm worried about you, babe. I can't help it."

He interrupts me, reaching out to take my hand in his. Silence fills the room as I can't think straight to argue. Why doesn't he believe me? He always used to. I remain silent. Something is wrong, but I can't place what. Beyond the things I have been seeing, the ghosts, the coins, the ferry capsizing the Asian women in the water. Feeling a sudden urge to explain I try one more time.

"I also saw one yesterday on the fort. It chased me immediately. I ran into a building, the one that I was walking to in the first place to get folders for Kate and then someone was in the building. I never saw him, only heard the loud sounds of heavy boots or shoes on the ground."

"Wait, you saw another figure yesterday on the fort then went into a building and a person was in there? Who was it?"

"Yes. And I had to hide in a hidden closet in the wall. So no, I didn't get a look at him. Then he left and didn't come back so I ran back to the building with the others and after that, we got evacuated off the island by the Navy because of what I saw. We came back here and then the storm hit."

Levi stares silently at me as the fire cracks in the background. I know he is deep in thought.

"Lil, I just..." he begins, "I just don't..."

A loud sound comes from my bedroom. Like something heavy was dropped on the floor. Levi immediately stands up and puts his hand out to tell me to stay put. Without a word, he slinks off in silence. I feel my heart race again, thumping silent this time, but hard in my chest. Could someone be here with us? Frozen to my spot, I grip the flashlight. I don't have the firearm on me; it's in the kitchen drawer.

Holding my breath I wait. I hear nothing. Then I see Levi return from the darkness, holding his firearm. He has a serious look on his face and only briefly glances at me. He walks around in silence, checking behind the couch, in the kitchen and then opens the front door to go out onto the porch.

As he does, a tall figure walks out of my bedroom.

Oh my God... what is going on?

I stop breathing as the figure turns into a man. A tall man. He comes into the light form the fireplace and I see him as clearly as I can without the power being on.

The creepy grin. The bluest eyes. It's him!

The cabin door opens and Levi steps back inside.

"Instinct *is* real, Levi. You are right."

Levi goes pale and utters one word, "Robert."

CHAPTER FORTY-ONE

Time stands still as the two men stare at each other.

I exhale and inhale with sharp breaths. Levi knows this man. But how? Neither say a word. Reaching behind him, Levi shuts the door. The fire continues to crackle, oblivious to the drama unfolding in front of it. I stare at the tall man. He is real. *Real.* Flesh and blood and standing in front of me.

My mind races back to the first time I saw someone watching me. I was swimming, the water was cold, but I loved it. Never had I felt scared to swim anywhere until that morning. Thinking back to how terrified I was and how I was chased, it makes me wonder if this man was the one I saw in the bowels of the woods. Could it be him?

"Been so long, Levi," he says, his voice cracking.

Then I recalled being in the bathroom when the lights went out. I was alone, just like when I was swimming. Remembering my heart racing and the fear that shot through me as I heard noises, it renders goosebumps to form on my arms. I hit my head with Kate the second time and then I saw a dark figure of a man in the corner. Again. What if what I saw was real? If it was this man?

"You think I am a ghost, don't you?" he says to Levi.

The ferry sunk shortly after. I could have drowned, if not for the captain and crew making sure we had life jackets when it began to take on water. What if they hadn't had time to help us? Kate and I bobbed in Puget Sound among predators. Sharks and whales circled deep below us. Close by, actually, as Levi had said after our rescue. That wasn't a coincidence.

"Don't be scared now..."

Levi's eyes are wide, as if he is stuck in a trance. His face looks pale in the flickering light. My pulse pounds over and over. So many pieces are missing. As if a puzzle was overturned off a

.

table and the pieces are scattered all over the floor. He continues to stare.

"Why are you here?" Levi finally asks.

Confusion fills my mind. He isn't afraid, not like I thought he was. He is *surprised*.

"I am here to keep you from doing things..."

Suddenly, Levi draws out his gun, sending the man's hands up in the air and a loud gasp from me.

What is he doing?

"If I wanted to harm her I would have already Levi, and you know it."

Levi stays silent. Everything inside of me is screaming for him to respond. To put his firearm back where he drew it from. But he doesn't. The air is thick with anticipation, and the fire keeps popping, adding an extra layer to the tension. In Levi's left hand is his sidearm. I stare at it, and wonder would he use it if the man advanced on me, or on him. I've never seen him shoot anyone. And I don't want to either.

"Did you figure out Deception Pass, Lily?"

The man addresses me. *Me.* It both surprises and scares. I look at the man's face as he turns towards my direction.

"Don't speak to her," Levi finally says, his voice low and steady.

The man laughs, his grin appearing in a ghoulish manner with orange firelight illuminating his features. A shiver rushes up my back and legs.

"She is smart, though. I know she probably figured it out by now."

Figured what out?

Levi clenches his jawline in anger. Who is this man to Levi and what have I figured out?

"Deception Pass is important. It's everything."

The man walks past me towards the fireplace, and I notice Levi moves his index finger towards the trigger of his Glock.

232

I sit frozen as I watch the man stand and observe the fire.

"If you noticed, I left clues. You guys, your job is pretty interesting. Going through old documents. Wild, isn't it, the absolute *waste* the Navy produces?" He sneers and laughs, a high pitch laugh before turning to face Levi. "And I also left clues in various other spots. Like the bunker."

The bunker.

My blood runs cold. I can feel the darkness and chill, the damp dank smells and the ghost. I became delirious as I waited like a fish out of water for my rescue. There was no hope, only my mind and what Levi taught me to cling to in emergency situations. This man had something to do with it. 'Deception Pass' was scratched on the wall. Why? I decided to ask, blurting out the obvious question.

"Why?"

Levi looks at me angrily and shakes his head, 'No'. The man ignores me, and addresses Levi instead.

"It's still very active, isn't it, Levi? The missions. What you all are doing. It didn't stop. Not even for a few weeks. Nothing stopped, did it?"

What has been going on?

Confusion hits again.

Raking his hands through his hair, the man scoffs. He is angry, and his agitation only grows with whatever he is bringing up to Levi. I try to decipher their words but can't. Finally shifting my weight so I am perched on the edge of the couch, I grip the fabric tightly, using it for support.

"Robert, you..." Levi begins.

He looks angry now and my confusion grows even more.

"Is it just Lily or did you find more?"

"Robert..." Levi warns, his hand still steady on his firearm.

"No. You can say it was okay, but it wasn't. Nothing about it was 'okay'. I saw you were involving her, and I just couldn't... watch." He considers his words carefully.

The man Levi called Robert begins to pace in front of me. He walks from the fireplace to the kitchen and back. I get a better look at his clothing as he does, realizing that he isn't as clean as he appears. In fact, he smells, and it is familiar. My brain wracks itself trying to place from where. The ends of his black cargo pants are frayed, and clumps of sand are coating the strings.

Sand.

Just like what I saw on the ground in here, next to my open laptop. He had to be the one that broke in. But how did he do it without a key to lock it back? Who is this man? Then it hits me! The odor.

He is the man from the building. The one who chased me and had me trapped in the hidden compartment in the wall.

"You heard her, too; she knows about the ghosts!"

"Robert…" Levi cries out, his voice cracking.

"No!" The man shouts, silencing my boyfriend.

"No," he whispers again.

He continues to keep pace, and I realize that his mental state may seem in control, but he isn't. He has a heavy burden that he is carrying.

"This place is haunted. It always was and always will be. Lily figured it out, and I tried to warn her."

"Robert, stop right there!" Levi warns again.

"That's not the worse part. You didn't tell her. I wasn't told either, remember? Remember at the beginning? I was recruited first. I even thought it was good work, for a bit."

"You were injured, Robert and it was the best job at the time, you and I both know it.."

"I could have just been retired, Levi. Like the other SEALs."

A lump forms in my throat. He is a former SEAL! A former team member of Levi's. And something happened to him. Something bad, but how does it play into the ghosts here?

"I didn't know the ghosts were so active. Nothing like when

234

I was active on the team. How could you drag this innocent woman into it?"

He pauses and looks at me.

"I can say this in front of you, Lily. Only because you already found out some of all this, didn't you?"

A chill runs down my spine. Emotion wells up inside of me for some reason. A tear slips out of my eye, and I blink it away. This man, this scary man, who I saw over and over, he could have killed me but didn't. He had all the opportunities to. And he has the skill set to as a former SEAL, but he is speaking as if he *protected* me.

"This place *is* haunted, Fort Warren. It's just the tip of the iceberg…"

More tears spill from my eyes. I can't make sense of what is happening.

"You feel sad? See, Levi, this is why I picked her. Look at her! She is fucking prefect. A wonderful woman."

"Don't talk about Lily…" Levi snaps, finally making a move away from the door. "She has *nothing* to do with this."

"Yes, she does. Is anything ever really over? Not until you step away, old friend. Like I was forced to do."

Levi takes steps forward slowly, so he is closer to his former colleague.

"I'm not going to tell you again. Shut your mouth!"

"That's fine, do what you must. But Lily deserves to know, and she deserves to leave this God- forsaken place. She has more friends here than she knows."

More friends than I know?

"The ghosts have been *very* active. Unchecked."

"Not asking you again!" Levi loudly says, aiming at his friend.

The man pulls something out from his pocket, and I see a flash of metal.

"You are part of it," his last words to Levi tumble out.

A shot rings loudly.

235

The man, the tall man that has haunted me for weeks, falls on the ground. My ears ring with a high-pitched whine. Time stands still. There is movement around me and I know it's from Levi. But I am frozen to my spot on the couch. I can't hear anything Levi is shouting; all I can do is stare at the bullet holes in the man's forehead and then I realize one last thing. It makes perfect sense now what he wanted to let me know.

He was the key to Deception after all.

And now I need to piece it together.

EPILOGUE

Levi stands by the mountainside.

The wind blows as I pull up the collar on my ski jacket. Snow falls softly, little specs of white dancing about in the air. He mutters words that I can't hear and honestly, I don't want to. It's his moment with his friend. His colleague. He needs to do this alone.

I think back to this last assignment and to Kate. She was more than a coworker; she was my friend as well. We got through that time together and I definitely couldn't have done that by myself. Working with the Navy showed me what I already knew but hadn't absorbed enough. The military can only function on teamwork.

And now, months later, I still don't know what the government is doing with sick or injured service members. I won't know either. Levi can't and won't discuss it and my days of snooping around are over. Knowing what happened is enough. Levi opens the small box that contains the ashes of his former SEAL friend and tosses them out into the ravine. We hiked for a few hours to get to this spot. He said they loved this place, once, long ago.

Far from Deception Pass and the secrets it keeps.

He stands for a few extra minutes then turns to join me. We have a hike ahead of us, back down to my Jeep, and the temperature is dropping fast, as is the daylight. I take his gloved hand in mine, and we begin walking down the trail. But before we reach a bend that takes us out of view from the area, I hear a soft crack behind me. I glance up at Levi, but he is deep in thought, so I turn and look over my shoulder.

A tall dark figure stands in the trees, staring back at me. Then a few more shadows can be seen next to it.

Robert's words echo in my mind.

"Deception Pass is important. It's everything."

The car is warm and threatens to lull me to sleep, but I fight to stay awake. The figure of a man, and more near him in the woods, is seared in my brain. I don't know if it was real, and I don't dare bring it up to my boyfriend. Not after everything that has happened and not today of all days. Levi drives us down the mountainside, the road winding past sheer drop off sections. It is gorgeous and terrifying at the same time.

"I'm going to stop at the first gas station; we are low on fuel."

I know Levi and he hates it when the dial shows that the fuel tank is almost empty. Always prepared and never caught off guard describes his way of living. The road straightens suddenly, and we exit out of the National Park. The gas station shines like a warm beacon up ahead as light is fading for the day. Pulling up to an open pump, Levi looks at me.

"Want anything from inside babe? I'm going to get a cup of coffee."

"Sure, I'll have one, too." I say. "I want to call Kate once I get reception."

"Kate?"

"Yeah, I need to check on her, we promised to stay in touch."

"Who is Kate?"

My pulse quickens and a familiar feeling washes over me. Confusion.

"My coworker. Kate. And Brian and Peter. Though I am not staying in touch with them."

"Lil. You don't have coworkers. You were here alone, remember?"

"I wasn't alone! You saw Kate! You met Brian and Peter!" I exclaim frantically.

"You *have* been alone, Lil. I can promise you that. Except for the figures or ghosts you said you've seen," he says, carefully. "I'll be back."

He leans over to kiss my cheek and smiles, exiting the car. I try to answer but no words come, only a soft moan of confusion.

Why is he saying I don't have coworkers? Does that mean...

Fear begins to travel up my spine. Had I seen more ghosts than I thought? Readjusting myself in the leather sports seat, my boots kick something that sound like glass. Frowning, I glace down. I can't see anything, but I shuffle my feet and hear it again. With a groan, I bend forward and reach with my fingers. I touch something smooth and pull it up. It's a tiny vial. Turning the bottle so I can see the words imprinted on the label, I almost faint. My blood runs cold, and time suspends. The words leap out at me.

Lily Morgan. Project Deception Pass.

And under my name is the only one I didn't want to see.

Chief Petty Officer O'Neill. Program supervisor.

A familiar voice from the backseat makes my heart stop. I drop the vial.

Kate's voice.

"Figure it out yet, Lily?"

Then it clicks.

I was the next one. The next victim in the experiments.

The real key to Deception laid at my feet.

AFTERWORD

Deception Pass is real. It's a strait which separates Whidbey Island from Fidalgo Island in the northwest part of Washington, US. Human smuggling did take place there, but any reference to naval involvement in smuggling or human experimentation is entirely fictional, although the US Navy has conducted training and experiments in the Deception Pass area, particularly around the Naval Air Station, Whidbey Island. Although there have been some rumors of a 'Philadelphia Experiment' being carried out there, this has been refuted by the US Navy and there is no evidence to support any such claims.

ABOUT THE AUTHOR

Writing began as a hobby and morphed into a passion for KE Jennings. She loves crafting stories and characters that make you think, as well as showcasing the gritty side of life. The more realness, the better. Her favorite genre to write are thrillers that have a heart pounding flair.

She spent half of her childhood in the deserts of West Texas and the other in the mountains of Washington state. Quite the landscape difference, she learned to appreciate aspects of both, to include developing a lifelong love of the sea. KE learned to surf in the frigid waters of the Pacific Ocean, where she often longboarded and thankfully, never once saw a shark.

She served in the United States Army as an active-duty NCO for eight years as a Chaplain Assistant and was deployed for fifteen months to Iraq with a combat engineer battalion. While in the service, she lived in various locations to include Germany, Hawaii, and South Carolina. Her love of travel wasn't limited to her service though. She has taken trips to Australia, Austria, Mexico, Jamacia, St. Lucia, Canada, and all over the continental United States, her favorite being Australia, because where else can you see kangaroos running wild?

After the Army, she obtained various college degrees in the healthcare field to include a Master's in Hospital Administration (MHA) and a Master's in Health Systems Management (M-HSM), as well as spending time volunteering at hospitals. Her other volunteer experience includes community outreach with local schools and with homeless programs run through her church.

In addition to writing, she is a self-professed outdoor fanatic and loves to fish, though worms make her squeamish. She loves hiking as well, preferring longer hikes that start after daybreak so the spider webs are already cleared off the trail by someone else's face. Avoiding bears and cougars the best she can, she likes the trails in the Cascade mountains as well as Mt. Rainier and surrounding areas. She also has a penchant for tacos and sunny weather, being Texas born.

You can find her at home with her family, out on a run, or cruising on her skateboard on a beachside trail. At the moment, she is working on various writing projects. Key to Deception is her third novel for Provoco, her debut, The Only Ones Left, achieved much acclaim and was Provoco's best-selling novel of 2024. Her second novel, Bodies of Evidence is also available.

All net royalties from Katie's current books are being donated to UK Veteran's charity Combat Stress.

BODIES OF EVIDENCE

Stars are supposed to shine in the desert.

People will come from miles away, sometimes from other countries, to get a glimpse at the vast star fields that take up residence in our desert skies late at night. Starwatchers, we call them in my town. They descend from cities far away, hoping to experience what we take for granted. It can change your life to gaze upon the stars, like it did for me years ago.

My head whips to the left as I remember why I loved this place so much. Inertia pulls at my body as I grip the steering wheel.

The stars aren't shining right now.

"*Crap!*" I scream, but it sounds far away, distant almost.

The hearse jerks violently on the roadway, tires skidding with pressure from the brakes. Of course, this would happen to me. I felt an awful omen when I left the graveside. It stuck like super glue, adhering to every part of my mind. The car now begins to spin, whipping my hair around, hitting my face violently.

I think I hear myself screaming again, but I am not sure. Hoping the hearse will stay upright, I let up on the brakes. It must have worked because I can feel the sedan hitting gravel beyond the blacktop. Bouncing harshly, I brace for the car to go airborne.

"Shit!" I mutter.

My head hits the low ceiling, hard. Bruises will undoubtably manifest after this. With a resounding thud, the hearse comes to a stop, the contents that were nicely placed in the back now resting haphazardly where a casket had just been. My breathing is labored. I try to slow it down as my skin tingles and begins to slowly go numb.

"I almost crashed."

Speaking out loud to myself, as I tend to often do, I know I won't get a reply.

Somewhere outside of the sedan is something or *someone* that I hit. I blame it on the lack of stars out tonight. It is unusually dark. Clouds had rolled in mid-funeral and with them, a type of weather we desert folks' dislike. Thunderstorms. As if on cue, a loud *crack* fills the air. I see a flash of light way off in the distance. Just lovely. I might have killed someone *and* it's going to rain soon.

My heart rate has slowed enough for my brain to begin functioning again, so I reach for my seatbelt. Undoing it easily enough, I hesitate before opening the door. What if I *did* kill someone? Whatever I hit felt large, and I didn't see it. I had just glanced down to grab my coffee cup when the impact happened.

Dealing with dead bodies all day long means this body shouldn't get me into such a state. It should be normal. Except, they are already dead when they come to us.

"Please be alive," I say to the darkness, beyond the windshield.

Letting out a deep sigh and with an unsteady hand, I grab my cellphone from the center console. It had been wedged in nicely, so it held during the spinout. My fingers shake ever so softly, I wrap them around the phone. My body is going to react, no matter what my brain tells it to do. If I find I *have* actually hit a person, I will simply call the sheriff.

"It's going to be okay. It was an accident."

Finally ready to face the aftermath, I open the car door.

Night air fills my nostrils as feet touch the ground. The sedan lets out a soft dinging sound, but it fades away as my heartbeat takes its place. Each beat grows louder as my eyes adjust to the darkness. The hearse's headlights are facing outwards, up towards the road. They do little in the way of helping at the moment, though. Nothing is in their path. I slowly scan to the left.

It is quiet outside. No chirps from crickets. No other sounds at all, except for the engine in the sedan. I've never actually heard the desert be this quiet, this still. A soft breeze hits my legs, causing goosebumps to form. The air is cold, colder than normal. I look to the right but only see the sedan. Something rustles in the darkness. I can hear a faint noise. There is scrub brush sporadically growing on the side of the road, extending far into the desert. Something must be moving a clump of it.

"What's there?" I call out, weakly.

The noise only intensifies, rustling louder now. Fear begins to overtake my mind, and I move quickly to stand in a beam of the headlights. The air whips at my body, a sinister chill that shouldn't accompany a thunderstorm. Usually, the air would get *warmer* during a storm. I shiver and look in all directions. The sound is loud and is getting closer to me.

"Who is there?" I shout.

Then it stops. The air, the sound. All of it. Quiet settles back over the desert. My heart thumps rhythmically, just like the hearse's engine is ticking over as it sits idle. I see something from the corner of my eyes and turn just in time to spot a dark brown animal running to the side of the sedan.

A coyote.

As quickly as it appeared, it takes off. Far into the desert.

"For God's sake," I mutter.

Just to be sure, I walk outwards, scanning the road within the limited light that I have from the hearse. I can't see anything but worn pavement. No bodies, no blood, nothing. The thud must have been the animal I just saw. Maybe I stunned it?

Lightning flashes again, closer this time. I can't stay out here much longer. It isn't smart to do that in a storm. That is how you get fired. Like my boss had when he was a kid. I'm convinced that's why he is the way he is now. Too many brain cells were damaged all to hell. Good thing dead bodies can't talk, they don't care who works on them.

Wind lightly moves my hair again, and this time the air is much warmer. I walk back to the opened car door and slide in, shutting myself into the interior.

"I hope it was the coyote."

Putting the hearse back into drive, I carefully ease back onto the highway, heading towards town.

Killom, Arizona, isn't on the map.

In fact, I don't think many people outside of my town even know it exists. With a population of roughly six hundred, we are pretty much self-contained. There is everything you could need, minus the big box stores. Online shopping then takes care of the rest.

I love the town and chose to call it my home about a decade ago. Found an advertisement online for a job I thought was interesting and moved without looking back. Los Angeles wasn't good to me anyways. Here, I can thrive.

The dark stretch of desolate highway runs straight into Killom after about a half hour of driving. I see the tiny lights twinkling in the distance. Though not large, we do have a working city, complete with a main drag in the middle and a town hall. My office is next door to the police substation and jail.

Driving through a band of heavy rain after almost wrecking makes the trip back laborious. But now, the storm has passed, and the town is soaked in the newly fallen precipitation. The only streetlights are in the middle of the town, and are currently flashing red. The storm must have knocked them out temporarily. Someone from the city maintenance crew will have to fix them once daylight hits.

A yawn overtakes my mouth as I slow down, easing into a much slower speed. The hearse slows at my application of the brakes. I see most of the homes have their porch lights on, but their window shades are down. It is late, almost midnight. Most people here choose to have evening funerals. There isn't a discernable reason why, it's just what is done in Killorn, and the surrounding cities, for that matter. Tonight's job had been a car accident victim from a town an hour over. We are the only morgue for the county, and the county is huge.

Another yawn overtakes me.

"Ugh," I groan.

I really need to wake up more. The night isn't done yet.

Turning down a side street, I make my way to the back of the mortuary. We always have to park back here, according to my boss's orders. It scares the kids less this way, he says. Being our location is a block away from the only school in town. A few stray pieces of loose garbage tumble down the alley as I drive carefully through. I am always worried I'll scrape the sides of this thing in such narrow roadways.

Finally reaching our building, I hit the garage door opener and wait as the large bay door shifts itself upwards. Ernest must have left the interior light on as warm brightness floods the alley. That was mighty nice of him. Usually, he forgets. Carefully, I do a ten-point turn to get the hearse backed into the bay. The tires squeal on the polished concrete, causing my focus to waver. I really hate that sound.

Finally, I maneuver the hearse all the way and its in.

Pushing the button to close the garage door, I turn off the sedan and get out. What a night this has been. Too many things have happened, ending with the near wreck. It is more than enough to make one want to hide in bed all night and the entirety of the next day.

But my chores aren't done yet. I have to offload the casket carrier and the various other items that we bring to a funeral. It's of no consequence, but I find this part of the day to be the best. Being alone in the funeral parlor should be freaky, and probably is to most people, but I find it cathartic. I can be alone with my thoughts.

Busying myself with putting everything away, I make sure to set the alarm when I am done. Ernest will kill me if he comes in the morning and finds it unsecured. This place is his baby.

"Finally. I can go home," I say aloud, locking the side door behind me.

The night air is chilly now, and the wind has begun to pick up. The cold breeze that had overtaken me in the desert comes back to mind. It was odd, there were no doubts about it. But I don't want to scare myself further tonight. And especially not with things out of my control.

I reach the rusty frame of my old beater and use a key to unlock the door. My car is on the verge of falling apart. There's nothing fancy about it, being over twenty years old. The paint is peeling beyond repair, and it has all sorts of dings from past owners. It's certainly not a car to brag about. Simply a tool to get from point a to point b. Possessions mean nothing in the grand scheme of things anyway.

The engine turns over as I turn the key. Time to go home. I will only get a few hours' sleep before my alarm is set to go off. Funeral days are long ones.

Motoring out of town, I pass by each of the buildings on the main street. They are fast asleep with lights off and 'closed' signs up. The darkness makes them feel alive for some reason. This time of the night always brings an air of creepiness to it. The bewitching hour they call it, or the time when Puca come out. Puca are goblins in Irish lore, and our towns founders were Irish.

But I don't believe in such things. Besides, the tribes nearby have their own lore, which many in our town *do* believe in. The only things that scare me now are what I can see, touch, or feel. Not simply conjure up in my mind. It's served me well working in this profession.

"I hope the coyote is okay," I mutter.

The poor thing. It didn't appear to be hurt though, merely wanting to get away from me.

As the thoughts from earlier fill my head, the city passes, and I head back into the darkness. My modest home is on the outskirts of town. Just a little bit further to go. I feel myself getting sleepy, so I roll down the driver's side window using the plastic hand crank on the side of the door. Cool air blasts my face once it is down to a sufficient degree. I inhale. Then, it happens.

"Holy crap!"

I yelp as my car passes by two figures walking in the road. Two tribal youths, both girls with long black hair. The headlights had captured their faces right as I drove by. Now I have another vision in my mind.

That of spirits long past.